John Dryden

The select dramatic works of John Dryden

John Dryden

The select dramatic works of John Dryden

ISBN/EAN: 9783337278878

Printed in Europe, USA, Canada, Australia, Japan

Cover: Foto ©Andreas Hilbeck / pixelio.de

More available books at **www.hansebooks.com**

THE SELECT

DRAMATIC WORKS

OF

JOHN DRYDEN.

EDITED BY

JAMES LOCKWOOD SETON.

LONDON: HAMILTON, ADAMS, & CO.
GLASGOW: THOMAS D. MORISON.
1877.

EDITORIAL PREFACE.

THERE not having been an issue of Dryden's Plays since 1821, when Sir Walter Scott brought out an edition of the poet's whole works in eighteen volumes, an apology for the present publication is scarcely necessary, except indeed, on the score of the limited character of the selection. Our intention was to give a considerable number of the Plays, but, on after consideration, the others were dropped from the list, as probably unsuitable to the tastes of the present time, thus confining selection to two—the two best in various respects. Indeed, as regards the comparative merits and purity of the various Plays, there seems to be but one opinion among Dryden's numerous biographers and critics—all appear to agree in giving the two in question the first place.

In judging of Dryden's dramatic writings, as compared with his other works, it might be well to bear in mind that neither the object for which they were composed—in great part a pecuniary one—nor the tastes of the period, were calculated to prove strikingly elevating or inspiring in their influences. In the course of two hundred years, society has made great advances in many respects, and probably in no section is this more marked than in that of the theatre and its relationships. It may be interesting to admirers of Dryden to have a specimen of his dramatic writings; even although these writings have never attained a position approaching that of what may be more strictly designated his poetical works, they nevertheless bear all the marks of an extraordinary mind, and have been greatly admired by many prominent literary men.

During the last and preceding centuries various editions of the Plays were published, but these are now rarely to be seen, and command high prices. Of late years, through the system of reprints, now so common, many dramatic writers of less note have been brought within the reach of all interested in this department of literature; but as yet Dryden has not been included in any of the series of the old dramatists at present before the public, partly, perhaps, on account of his dramatic writings being so voluminous, and many of the respective Plays likewise being of very considerable length.

CONTENTS.

———

ALL FOR LOVE:

OR,

THE WORLD WELL LOST.

DRAMATIS PERSONÆ.

MARC ANTONY.

VENTIDIUS, *his General.*

DOLABELLA, *his Friend.*

ALEXAS, *the Queen's Eunuch.*

SERAPION, *Priest of Isis.*

Another Priest.

Servants to ANTONY.

CLEOPATRA, *Queen of Egypt.*

OCTAVIA, ANTONY'S *Wife.*

CHARMION, } CLEOPATRA'S *Maids.*
IRAS, }

ANTONY'S *two little Daughters.*

"A tragedy founded upon the story of Antony and Cleopatra, Dryden tells us, is the only play which he wrote for himself, the rest were given to the people. It is by universal consent accounted the work in which he has admitted the fewest improprieties of style or character."—JOHNSON, *Lives of the Poets.*

"Incomparably the best of Dryden's plays."—BELL, *English Poets.*

"Universally considered the best of Dryden's plays—was produced at the King's Theatre in the beginning of 1678."—CHRISTIE, Editor of *Dryden's Poems,* Globe Edition.

ALL FOR LOVE:

or,

THE WORLD WELL LOST.

PROLOGUE.

WHAT flocks of critics hover here to-day,
As vultures wait on armies for their prey,
All gaping for the carcase of a play!
With croaking notes, they bode some dire event,
And follow dying poets by the scent.
Ours gives himself for gone; you've watched your time!
He fights this day unarm'd—without his rhyme.
And brings a tale, which often has been told,
As sad as Dido's, and almost as old.
His hero, whom you wits his bully call,
Bates of his mettle, and scarce rants at all:
He's somewhat lewd, but a well meaning mind;
Weeps much; fights little; but is wondrous kind.
In short, a pattern, and companion fit
For all the keeping tonies of the pit.
I could name more: a wife and mistress, too;
Both (to be plain) too good for most of you:
The wife well-natured, and the mistress true.
  Now, poets, if your fame has been his care,
Allow him all the candour you can spare.
A brave man scorns to quarrel once a day,
Like Hectors, in at every petty fray.
Let those find fault whose wit's so very small,
They've need to show that they can think at all:
Errors, like straws, upon the surface flow;
He who would search for pearls must dive below.
Fops may have leave to level all they can,
As pigmies would be glad to lop a man.

Half-wits are fleas; so little and so light,
We scarce could know they live, but that they bite.
But, as the rich, when tired with daily feasts,
For change, become their next poor tenant's guests;
Drink hearty draughts of ale from plain brown bowls,
And snatch the homely rasher from the coals:
So you, retiring from much better cheer,
For once, may venture to do penance here.
And since that plenteous Autumn now is past,
Whose grapes and peaches have indulged your taste,
Take in good part, from our poor poet's board,
Such rivelled fruits as Winter can afford.

ACT I.

Scene I.--*The Temple of Isis.*

Enter Serapion, Myris, *and Priests of Isis.*

Serap. Portents and prodigies are grown so frequent,
That they have lost their name. Our fruitful Nile
Flowed ere the wonted season, with a torrent
So unexpected, and so wondrous fierce,
That the wild deluge overtook the haste
Even of the hinds that watched it: men and beasts
Were born above the tops of trees, that grew
On the utmost margin of the water-mark.
Then, with so swift an ebb the flood drove backward,
It slipt from underneath the scaly herd:
Here monstrous phocæ panted on the shore;
Forsaken dolphins there, with their broad tails,
Lay lashing the departing waves: hard by them,
Sea-horses floundering in the slimy mud,
Toss'd up their heads, and dashed the ooze about them.

Enter Alexas *behind them.*

Myr. Avert these omens, heaven!
Serap. Last night, between the hours of twelve and one,
In a lone aisle o' th' Temple while I walked,
A whirlwind rose, that, with a violent blast,
Shook all the dome: the doors around me clapt;
The iron wicket that defends the vault

Where the long race of Ptolemies is laid
Burst open, and disclosed the mighty dead.
From out each monument, in order placed,
An armed ghost starts up: the boy-king last
Reared his inglorious head. A peal of groans
Then followed, and a lamentable voice
Cried, Egypt is no more. My blood ran back,
My shaking knees against each other knocked;
On the cold pavement down I fell entranced,
And so unfinished left the horrid scene.

    Alex. And dream'd you this? or did invent the story,
                                       [*Showing himself.*
To frighten our Egyptian boys withal,
And train them up betimes in fear of priesthood?

    Serap. My lord, I saw you not,
Nor meant my words should reach your ears; but what
I uttered was most true.

    Alex. A foolish dream,
Bred from the fumes of indigested feasts,
And holy luxury.

    Serap. I know my duty:
This goes no farther.

    Alex. 'Tis not fit it should.
Nor would the times now bear it, were it true.
All southern, from yon hills, the Roman camp
Hangs o'er us, black and threatening, like a storm
Just breaking on our heads.

    Serap. Our faint Egyptians pray for Antony;
But in their servile hearts they own Octavius.

    Myr. Why then does Antony dream out his hours,
And tempts not fortune for a noble day,
Which might redeem what Actium lost?

    Alex. He thinks 'tis past recovery.

    Serap. Yet the foe
Seems not to press the siege.

    Alex. O, there's the wonder.
Mecænas and Agrippa, who can most
With Cæsar, are his foes. His wife Octavia,
Driven from his house, solicits her revenge;
And Dolabella, who was once his friend,
Upon some private grudge, now seeks his ruin:
Yet still war seems on either side to sleep.

Serap. 'Tis strange that Antony, for some days past,
Has not beheld the face of Cleopatra :
But here, in Isis' Temple, lives retired,
And makes his heart a prey to black despair.

Alex. 'Tis true; and we much fear he hopes by absence
To cure his mind of love.

Serap. If he be vanquished,
Or make his peace, Egypt is doomed to be
A Roman province ; and our plenteous harvests
Must then redeem the scarceness of their soil.
While Antony stood firm, our Alexandria
Rivalled proud Rome (dominion's other seat) ;
And Fortune, striding like a vast Colossus,
Could fix an equal foot of empire here.

Alex. Had I my wish, these tyrants of all nature,
Who lord it o'er mankind, should perish, perish,
Each by the other's sword ; but, since our will
Is lamely followed by our power, we must
Depend on one ; with him to rise or fall.

Serap. How stands the Queen affected ?

Alex. O, she dotes,
She dotes, Serapian, on this vanquished man,
And winds herself about his mighty ruins ;
Whom would she yet forsake, yet yield him up,
This hunted prey, to his pursuer's hands,
She might preserve us all : but 'tis in vain.
This changes my designs, this blasts my counsels
And makes me use all means to keep him here,
Whom I could wish divided from her arms
Far as the earth's deep centre.   Well, you know
The state of things : no more of your ill omens
And black prognostics ; labour to confirm
The people's hearts.

Enter VENTIDIUS,
talking aside with a gentleman of ANTONY's.

Serap. These Romans will o'erhear us.
But who's that stranger ?   By his warlike port,
His fierce demeanour, and erected look,
He's of no vulgar note.

Alex. O, 'tis Ventidius,
Our Emperor's great lieutenant in the East,
Who first showed Rome that Parthia could be conquered.

When Antony returned from Syria last,
He left this man to guard the Roman frontiers.
  Serap. You seem to know him well.
  Alex. Too well. I saw him in Cilicia first,
When Cleopatra there met Antony:
A mortal foe he was to us and Egypt.
But let me witness to the worth I hate:
A braver Roman never drew a sword.
Firm to his Prince; but as a friend, not slave.
He ne'er was of his pleasures; but presides
O'er all his cooler hours, and morning counsels:
In short, the plainness, fierceness, rugged virtue
Of an old true-stampt Roman lives in him.
His coming bodes I know not what of ill
To our affairs. Withdraw, to mark him better;
And I'll acquaint you why I sought you here,
And what's our present work.
       [*They withdraw to a corner of the stage, and* VEN-
         TIDIUS, *with the other, comes forward to the front.*
  Vent. Not see him, say you?
I say, I must, and will.
  Gent. He has commanded,
On pain of death, none should approach his presence.
  Vent. I bring him news will raise his drooping spirits,
Give him new life.
  Gent. He sees not Cleopatra.
  Vent. Would he had never seen her.
  Gent. He eats not, drinks not, sleeps not, has no use
Of anything, but thought; or, if he talks,
'Tis to himself, and then 'tis perfect raving;
Then he defies the world, and bids it pass;
Sometimes he gnaws his lip, and curses loud
The boy Octavius; then he draws his mouth
Into a scornful smile and cries, Take all,
The world's not worth my care.
  Vent. Just, just his nature.
Virtue's his path; but sometimes 'tis too narrow
For his vast soul; and then he starts out wide,
And bounds into a vice that bears him far
From his first course and plunges him in ills:
But, when his danger makes him find his fault,
Quick to observe, and full of sharp remorse,

He censures eagerly his own misdeeds,
Judging himself with malice to himself,
And not forgiving what as man he did,
Because his other parts are more than man.
He must not thus be lost.

           [ALEXAS *and the Priests come forward.*

  Alex. You have your full instructions, now advance;
Proclaim your orders loudly.

  Serap. Romans, Egyptians, hear the Queen's command.
Thus Cleopatra bids, Let labour cease,
To pomp and triumph give this happy day,
That gave the world a lord: 'Tis Antony's.
Live, Antony; and Cleopatra live.
Be this the general voice sent up to heaven,
And every public place repeat this echo.

  Vent. Fine pageantry!   [*Aside.*

  Serap. Set out before your doors
The images of all your sleeping fathers,
With laurels crowned; with laurels wreathe your posts;
And strew with flowers the pavement; let the priests
Do present sacrifice; pour out the wine,
And call the gods to join with you in gladness.

  Vent. Curse on the tongue that bids this general joy.
Can they be friends of Antony, who revel
When Antony's in danger? Hide, for shame,
You Romans, your great grandsires' images,
For fear their souls should animate their marbles,
To blush at their degenerate progeny.

  Alex. A love which knows no bounds to Antony
Would mark the day with honours; when all heaven
Laboured for him, when each propitious star
Stood wakeful in his orb, to watch that hour,
And shed his better influence. Her own birth-day
Our Queen neglected, like a vulgar fate,
That passed obscurely by.

  Vent. Would it had slept,
Divided far from his—till some remote
And future age had called it out, to ruin
Some other prince, not him.

  Alex. Your Emperor,
Tho' grown unkind, would be more gentle than
T' upbraid my Queen for loving him too well.

Vent. Does the mute sacrifice upbraid the priest?
He knows him not his executioner.
O, she has deck'd his ruin with her love,
Led him in golden bands to gaudy slaughter,
And made perdition pleasing: she has left him
The blank of what he was;
I tell thee, eunuch, she has quite unman'd him:
Can any Roman see and know him now,
Thus altered from the lord of half mankind,
Unbent, unsinewed, made a woman's toy,
Shrunk from the vast extent of all his honours,
And cramped within a corner of the world?
O, Antony,
Thou bravest soldier, and thou best of friends!
Bounteous as nature, next to nature's God!
Could'st thou but make new worlds, so would'st thou give
As bounty were thy being.   Rough in battle,   [them,
As the first Romans, when they went to war;
Yet, after victory, more pitiful
Than all their praying virgins left at home!
    Alex. Would you could add to those more shining
His truth to her who loves him.   ,   [virtues
    Vent. Would I could not.
But wherefore waste I precious hours with thee?
Thou art her darling mischief, her chief engine,
Antony's other fate.   Go, tell thy Queen,
Ventidius is arrived, to end her charms.
Let your Egyptian timbrels play alone;
Nor mix effeminate sounds with Roman trumpets.
You dare not fight for Antony; go pray,
And keep your cowards holy-days in temples.
                    [*Exeunt* ALEX. *and* SERAP.

            Re-enter the Gentleman of ANTONY'S.

    2 Gent. The Emperor approaches, and commands,
On pain of death, that none presume to stay.
    1 Gent. I dare not disobey him.   [*Going out with the*
    Vent. Well, I dare.   [*other.*
But I'll observe him first unseen, and find
Which way his humour drives: the rest I'll venture.
                    [*Withdraws.*

Enter ANTONY,
walking with a disturbed motion before he speaks.

Ant. They tell me, 'tis my birth-day, and I'll keep it
With double pomp of sadness.
'Tis what the day deserves which gave me breath.
Why was I raised the meteor of the world,
Hung in the skies, and blazing as I travelled,
Till all my fires were spent; and then cast downward
To be trod out by Cæsar?
    Vent. On my soul,   [*Aside.*
'Tis mournful, wondrous mournful!
    Ant. Count thy gains.
Now, Antony, would'st thou be born for this?
Glutton of fortune, thy devouring youth
Has starved thy wanting age.
    Vent. How sorrow shakes him!   [*Aside.*
So, now the tempest tears him up by the roots,
And on the ground extends the noble ruin.
    Ant. [*Having thrown himself down.*] Lie there, the
          shadow of an Emperor;
The place thou pressest on thy mother earth
Is all thy empire now: now it contains thee;
Some few days hence, and then 'twill be too large,
When thou'rt contracted in thy narrow urn,
Shrunk to a few cold ashes; then Octavia
(For Cleopatra will not live to see it),
Octavia then will have thee all her own,
And bear thee in her widowed hand to Cæsar;
Cæsar will weep, the crocodile will weep
To see his rival of the universe
Lie still and peaceful there. I'll think no more on't.
Give me some music; look that it be sad:
I'll soothe my melancholy till I swell,
And burst myself with sighing——   [*Soft music.*
'Tis somewhat to my humour: stay, I fancy
I'm now turned wild, a commoner of nature;
Of all forsaken, and forsaking all;
Live in a shady forest's sylvan scene,
Stretched at my length beneath some blasted oak,
I lean my head upon the mossy bark,
And look just of a piece, as I grew from it:
My uncombed locks, matted like mistletoe,

Hang o'er my hoary face; a murmuring brook
Runs at my foot.

Vent. Methinks I fancy
Myself there, too.

Ant. The herd come jumping by me,
And fearless quench their thirst, while I look on,
And take me for their fellow-citizen.
More of this image, more; it lulls my thoughts.

[*Soft music again.*

Vent. I must disturb him; I can hold no longer.

[*Stands before him.*

Ant. [*Starting up.*] Art thou Ventidius?

Vent. Are you Antony?
I'm liker what 1 was than you to him
I left you last.

Ant. I am angry.

Vent. So am I.

Ant. I would be private: leave me.

Vent. Sir, 1 love you,
And therefore will not leave you.

Ant. Will not leave me?
Where have you learnt that answer? Who am I?

Vent. My Emperor; the man I love next Heaven!
If I said more, I think 'twere scarce a sin:
You're all that's good, and god-like.

Ant. All that's wretched.
You will not leave me then?

Vent. 'Twas too presuming
To say I would not; but I dare not leave you:
And, 'tis unkind in you to chide me hence
So soon, when I so far have come to see you.

Ant. Now thou hast seen me, art thou satisfied?
For, if a friend, thou hast beheld enough;
And, if a foe, too much.

Vent. Look, Emperor, this is no common dew;

[*Weeping.*

I have not wept this forty years; but now
My mother comes afresh into my eyes:
I cannot help her softness.

Ant. By Heaven, he weeps, poor, good old man he
The big round drops course one another down   [weeps!
The furrows of his cheeks. Stop them, Ventidius,

Or I shall blush to death; they set my shame,
That caused them, full before me.
    Vent. I'll do my best.
    Ant. Sure there's contagion in the tears of friends;
See, I have caught it too. Believe me, 'tis not
For my own griefs, but thine——Nay, father.
    Vent. Emperor.
    Ant. Emperor! Why, that's the style of victory.
The conquering soldier, red with unfelt wounds,
Salutes his general so; but never more
Shall that sound reach my ears.
    Vent. I warrant you.
    Ant. Actium, Actium! Oh——
    Vent. It fits too near you.
    Ant. Here, here it lies; a lump of lead by day,
And, in my short, distracted, nightly slumbers,
The hag that rides my dreams——
    Vent. Out with it; give it vent.
    Ant. Urge not my shame.
I lost a battle.
    Vent. So has Julius done.
    Ant. Thou favour'st me, and speak'st not half thou
For Julius fought it out, and lost it fairly;   [think'st;
But Antony——
    Vent. Nay, stop not.
    Ant. Antony—
(Well, thou wilt have it) like a coward, fled,
Fled while his soldiers fought; fled first, Ventidius.
Thou long'st to curse me, and I give thee leave.
I know thou cam'st prepared to rail.
    Vent. I did.
    Ant. I'll help thee—I have been a man, Ventidius.
    Vent. Yes, and a brave one; but——
    Ant. I know thy meaning.
But, I have lost my reason, have disgraced
The name of soldier, with inglorious ease.
In the full vintage of my flowing honours,
Sat still, and saw it press'd by other hands.
Fortune came smiling to my youth, and woo'd it,
And purple greatness met my ripened years.
When first I came to empire, I was borne
On tides of people, crowding to my triumphs;

The wish of nations, and the willing world
Received me as its pledge of future peace;
I was so great, so happy, so beloved,
Fate could not ruin me; till I took pains
And worked against my fortune, chid her from me,
And turned her loose; yet still she came again,
My careless days, and my luxurious nights,
At length have wearied her, and now she's gone,
Gone, gone, divorced for ever.   Help me, soldier,
To curse this madman, this industrious fool,
Who laboured to be wretched: prithee curse me.

   Vent. No.

   Ant. Why?

   Vent. You are too sensible already
Of what you've done, too conscious of your failings,
And, like a scorpion, whipped by others first
To fury, sting yourself in mad revenge.
I would bring balm, and pour it in your wounds,
Cure your distempered mind. and heal your fortunes.

   Ant. I know thou would'st.

   Vent. I will.

   Ant. Ha, ha, ha, ha.

   Vent. You laugh.

   Ant. I do, to see officious love
Give cordials to the dead.

   Vent. You would be lost then?

   Ant. I am.

   Vent. I say you are not.   Try your fortune.   [perate,

   Ant. I have, to the utmost.   Dost thou think me des-
Without just cause?   No, when I found all lost
Beyond repair, I hid me from the world,
And learnt to scorn it here; which now I do
So heartily, I think it is not worth
The cost of keeping.

   Vent. Cæsar thinks not so:
He'll thank you for the gift he could not take.
You would be killed, like Tully, would you? do
Hold out your throat to Cæsar, and die tamely.

   Ant. No, I can kill myself; and so resolve.

   Vent. I can die with you too, when time shall serve:
But Fortune calls upon us now to live,
To fight, to conquer.

Ant. Sure thou dreamest, Ventidius.

Vent. No; 'tis you dream; you sleep away your hours
In desperate sloth, miscalled philosophy.
Up, up, for honour's sake; twelve legions wait you,
And long to call you chief.   By painful journeys
I led them, patient, both of heat and hunger,
Down from the Parthian marches to the Nile.
'Twill do you good to see their sunburnt faces,
Their scarr'd cheeks, and chopt hands: there's virtue in
They'll sell those mangled limbs at dearer rates   [them.
Than yon trim bands can buy.

Ant. Where left you them?

Vent. I said, in lower Syria.

Ant. Bring them hither;
There may be life in these.

Vent. They will not come.

Ant. Why did'st thou mock my hopes with promised
To double my despair?   They're mutinous.   [aids,

Vent. Most firm and loyal.

Ant. Yet they will not march
To succour me.   O trifler!

Vent. They petition
You would make haste to head them.

Ant. I'm besieged.

Vent. There's but one way shut up: how came I hither?

Ant. I will not stir.

Vent. They would perhaps desire
A better reason.

Ant. I have never used
My soldiers to demand a reason of
My actions.   Why did they refuse to march?

Vent. They said they would not fight for Cleopatra.

Ant. What was't they said?

Vent. They said they would not fight for Cleopatra.
Why should they fight, indeed, to make her conquer,
And make you more a slave? to gain you kingdoms,
Which, for a kiss, at your next midnight feast,
You'll sell to her? then she new-names her jewels,
And calls this diamond such or such a tax,
Each pendant in her ear shall be a province.

Ant. Ventidius, I allow your tongue free licence
On all my other faults; but, on your life,

No word of Cleopatra: she deserves
More worlds than I can lose.
    Vent. Behold, you powers,
To whom you have intrusted humankind;
See Europe, Afric, Asia put in balance,
And all weighed down by one light, worthless woman!
I think the gods are Antonies, and give,
Like prodigals, this nether world away
To none but wasteful hands.
    Ant. You grow presumptuous.
    Vent. I take the privilege of plain love to speak.
    Ant. Plain love! plain arrogance, plain insolence!
Thy men are cowards; thou, an envious traitor;
Who, under seeming honesty, hath vented
The burden of thy rank o'erflowing gall.
O that thou wert my equal; great in arms
As the first Cæsar was, that I might kill thee
Without a stain to honour!
    Vent. You may kill me;
You have done more already, called me traitor.
    Ant. Art thou not one?
    Vent. For showing you yourself.
Which none else durst have done; but had I been
That name, which I disdain to speak again,
I needed not have sought your abject fortunes,
Come to partake your fate, to die with you.
What hindered me to have led my conquering eagles
To fill Octavius' bands? I could have been
A traitor then, a glorious happy traitor,
And not have been so called.
    Ant. Forgive me, soldier:
I've been too passionate.
    Vent. You thought me false;
Thought my old age betrayed you: kill me, sir;
Pray kill me; yet you need not, your unkindness
Has left your sword no work.
    Ant. I did not think so;
I said it in my rage: prithee forgive me:
Why did'st thou tempt my anger, by discovery
Of what I would not hear?
    Vent. No prince but you
Could merit that sincerity I used,

Nor durst another man have ventured it;
But you, ere love misled your wandering eye
Were sure the chief and best of human race,
Framed in the very pride and boast of nature;
So perfect, that the gods who formed you wondered
At their own skill, and cried, A lucky hit
Has mended our design.   Their envy hindered,
Else you had been immortal, and a pattern,
When heaven would work for ostentation sake,
To copy out again.

 Ant. But Cleopatra——
Go on; for I can bear it now.

 Vent. No more.

 Ant. Thou dar'st not trust my passion; but thou may'st:
Thou only lov'st; the rest have flattered me.

 Vent. Heaven's blessing on your heart for that kind
May I believe you love me? Speak again. [word.

 Ant. Indeed I do.   Speak this, and this, and this.
            [*Hugging him.*
Thy praises were unjust; but Ill deserve them,
And yet mend all.   Do with me what thou wilt:
Lead me to victory—thou know'st the way.

 Vent. And, will you leave this——

 Ant. Prithee do not curse her,
And I will leave her; though heaven knows, I love
Beyond life, conquest, empire; all but honour:
But I will leave her.

 Vent. That's my royal master.
And shall we fight?

 Ant. I warrant thee, old soldier.
Thou shalt behold me once again in iron,
And, at the head of our old troops, that beat
The Parthians, cry aloud, Come, follow me!

 Vent. O, now I hear my Emperor! in that word
Octavius fell.   Gods, let me see that day,
And, if I have ten years behind, take all;
I'll thank you for th' exchange.

 Ant. Oh, Cleopatra!

 Vent. Again?

 Ant. I've done: in that last sigh, she went.
Cæsar shall know what 'tis to force a lover
From all he holds most dear.

Vent. Methinks you breathe
Another soul: your looks are more divine;
You speak a hero, and you move a god.
  Ant. O, thou hast fired me; my soul is up in arms,
And mans each part about me: once again,
That noble eagerness of fight has seized me;
That eagerness, with which I darted upward
To Cassius' camp: in vain the steepy hill
Opposed my way; in vain a war of spears
Sung round my head, and planted on my shield;
I won the trenches, while my foremost men
Lagged on the plain below.
  Vent. Ye gods, ye gods,
For such another hour!
  Ant. Come on, my soldier!
Our hearts and arms are still the same: I long
Once more to' meet our foes; that thou and I,
Like Time and Death, marching before our troops,
May taste fate to them; mow them out a passage,
And, entering where the foremost squadrons yield,
Begin the noble harvest of the field.   [*Exeunt.*

ACT II.   SCENE I.

Enter CLEOPATRA, IRAS, *and* ALEXAS.

  Cleo. What shall I do, or whither shall I turn?
Ventidius has o'ercome, and he will go.
  Alex. He goes to fight for you.
  Cleo. Then he would see me, ere he went to fight:
Flatter me not: if once he goes, he's lost;
And all my hopes destroyed.
  Alex. Does this weak passion
Become a mighty queen?
  Cleo. I am no queen;
Is this to be a queen, to be besieged
By yon insulting Roman; and to wait
Each hour the victor's chain? These ills are small;
For Antony is lost, and I can mourn
For nothing else but him.   Now come, Octavius,
I have no more to lose; prepare thy bands
                    C

I'm fit to be a captive: Antony
Has taught my mind the fortune of a slave.
   Iras. Call reason to assist you.
   Cleo. I have none,
And none would have: my love's a noble madness,
Which showed the cause deserved it.   Moderate sorrow
Fits vulgar love; and for a vulgar man:
But I have loved with such transcendent passion,
I soared, at first, quite out of reason's view,
And now am lost above it.——No, I'm proud
'Tis thus: would Antony could see me now
Think you he would not sigh? though he must leave me,
Sure he would sigh; for he is noble-natured,
And bears a tender heart: I know him well.
Ah, no, I know him not; I knew him once,
But now 'tis past.
   Iras. Let it be past with you:
Forget him, madam.
   Cleo. Never, never, Iras.
He once was mine; and once, though now 'tis gone,
Leaves a faint image of possession still.
   Alex. Think him unconstant, cruel, and ungrateful.
   Cleo. I cannot: if I could, those thoughts were vain;
Faithless, ungrateful, cruel, though he be,
I still must love him.

       Enter CHARMION.

Now, what news, my Charmion?
Will he be kind? and, will he not forsake me?
Am I to live or die? nay, do I live?
Or am I dead? for when he gave his answer,
Fate took the word, and then I lived or died.
   Char. I found him, madam——
   Cleo. A long speech preparing?
If thou bring'st comfort, haste, and give it me;
For never was more need.
   Iras. I know he loves you.
   Cleo. Had he been kind, her eyes had told me so,
Before her tongue could speak it: now she studies
To soften what he said; but give me death,
Just as he sent it, Charmion, undisguised,
And in the words he spoke.

Char. I found him then
Encompass'd round, I think, with iron statues,
So mute, so motionless his soldiers stood,
While awfully he cast his eyes about,
And every leader's hopes and fears surveyed:
Methought he looked resolved, and yet not pleased.
When he beheld me struggling in the crowd,
He blushed, and bade make way.

    Alex. There's comfort yet.

    Char. Ventidius fixed his eyes upon my passage
Severely, as he meant to frown me back,
And sullenly gave place. I told my message,
Just as you gave it, broken and disordered;
I numbered in it all your sighs and tears,
And while I moved your pitiful request
That you but only begged a last farewell,
He fetched an inward groan, and every time
I named you, sighed as if his heart were breaking,
But shunn'd my eyes, and guiltily looked down;
He seemed not now that awful Antony
Who shook an arm'd assembly with his nod,
But, making show as he would rub his eyes,
Disguised and blotted out a falling tear.

    Cleo. Did he then weep? And was I worth a tear?
If what thou hast to say be not as pleasing,
Tell me no more, but let me die contented.

    Char. He bid me say, he knew himself so well,
He could deny you nothing if he saw you;
And therefore——

    Cleo. Thou would'st say he would not see me?

    Char. And therefore begged you not to use a power
Which he could ill resist; yet he should ever
Respect you as he ought.

    Cleo. Is that a word
For Antony to use to Cleopatra?
Oh that faint word, respect! how I disdain it!
Disdain myself, for loving after it!
He should have kept that word for cold Octavia.
Respect is for a wife: Am I that thing,
That dull insipid lump, without desires,
And without power to give them.

    Alex. You misjudge:

You see through love, and that deludes your sight, –
As what is straight seems crooked through the water;
But I, who bear my reason undisturbed,
Can see this Antony, this dreaded man,
A fearful slave, who fain would run away,
And shuns his master's eyes; if you pursue him,
My life on't, he still drags a chain along,
That needs must clog his flight.
 Cleo. Could I believe thee?
 Alex. By every circumstance I know he loves.
True, he's hard press'd, by interest and by honour :
Yet he but doubts, and parleys, and casts out
Many a long look for succour.
 Cleo. He sends word
He fears to see my face.
 Alex. And would you more?
He shows his weakness who declines the combat;
And you must urge your fortune. Could he speak
More plainly? To my ears the message sounds,
Come to my rescue, Cleopatra, come;
Come, free me from Ventidius—from my tyrant :
See me, and give me a pretence to leave him.
I hear his trumpets. This way he must pass.
Please you, retire awhile; I'll work him first,
That he may bend more easy.
 Cleo. You shall rule me :
But all, I fear, in vain. [*Ex. with* CHAR. *and* IRAS.
 Alex. I fear so, too;
Though I concealed my thoughts, to make her bold—
But 'tis our utmost means, and fate befriend it.
         [*Withdraws.*

*Enter Lictors with Fasces, one bearing the Eagle: Then
 enter* ANTONY *with* VENTIDIUS, *followed by other
 Commanders.*

 Ant. Octavius is the minion of blind chance,
But holds from virtue nothing.
 Vent. Has he courage?
 Ant. But just enough to season him from coward;
O, 'tis the coldest youth upon a charge,
The most deliberate fighter! If he ventures
(As in Illyria once they say he did,

To storm a town), 'tis when he cannot choose,
When all the world have fixed their eyes upon him—
And then he lives on that for seven years.
But at a close revenge he never fails.
    Vent. I heard you challenged him.
    Ant. I did, Ventidius.
What think'st thou was his answer? 'Twas so tame,—
He said he had more ways than one to die:
I had not.
    Vent. Poor!
    Ant. He has more ways than one;
But he would choose them all before that one.
    Vent. He first would choose an ague, or a fever.
    Ant. No: it must be an ague, not a fever.
He has not warmth enough to die by that.
    Vent. Or old age and a bed.
    Ant. Ay, there's his choice.
He would live, like a lamp, to the last wink,
And crawl upon the utmost verge of life.
O, Hercules! why should a man like this,
Who dares not trust his fate for one great action,
Be all the care of heaven? Why should he lord it
O'er fourscore thousand men, of whom each one
Is braver than himself?
    Vent. You conquered for him:
Philippi knows it; there you shared with him
That empire, which your sword made all your own.
    Ant. Fool that I was; upon my eagle's wings
I bore this wren, till I was tired with soaring,
And now he mounts above me.
Good heavens! is this, is this the man who braves me?
Who bids my age make way? drives me before him
To the world's ridge, and sweeps me off like rubbish?
    Vent. Sir, we lose time; the troops are mounted all.
    Ant. Then give the word to march;
I long to leave this prison of a town,
To join the legions, and, in open field,
Once more to show my face. Lead, my deliverer.

Enter ALEXAS.

    Alex. Great Emperor,
In mighty arms renowned above mankind,

But, in soft pity to the oppress'd, a god—
This message sends the mournful Cleopatra
To her departing lord.

    Vent. Smooth sycophant!

    Alex. A thousand wishes, and ten thousand prayers,
Millions of blessings wait you to the wars,
Millions of sighs and tears she sends you, too,
And would have sent
As many dear embraces to your arms,
As many parting kisses to your lips,
But those, she fears, have wearied you already.

    Vent. [*Aside.*] False crocodile!

    Alex. And yet she begs not now you would not leave
That were a wish too mighty for her hopes,
Too presuming for her low fortune and your ebbing love;
That were a wish for her more prosp'rous days,
Her blooming beauty, and your growing kindness.

    Ant. [*Aside.*] Well, I must man it out; what would
        the Queen?

    Alex. First, to these noble warriors, who attend
Your daring courage in the chase of fame,
(Too daring, and too dangerous for her quiet,)
She humbly recommends all she holds dear,
All her own cares and fears, the care of you.

    Vent. Yes, witness Actium.

    Ant. Let him speak, Ventidius.

    Alex. You, when his matchless valour bears him forward,
With ardour too heroic, on his foes,
Fall down, as she would do, before his feet;
Lie in his way, and stop the paths of death;
Tell him, this god is not invulnerable,
That absent Cleopatra bleeds in him;
And, that you may remember her petition,
She begs you wear these trifles, as a pawn,
Which, at your wish'd return, she will redeem
                  [*Gives jewels to the commanders.*
With all the wealth of Egypt.
This, to the great Ventidius she presents,
Whom she can never count her enemy,
Because he loves her lord.

    Vent. Tell her I'll none on't;
I'm not ashamed of honest poverty:

Not all the diamonds of the East can bribe
Ventidius from his faith. I hope to see
These, and the rest of all her sparkling store,
Where they shall more deservingly be placed.
    Ant. And who must wear them, then ?
    Vent. The wronged Octavia.
    Ant. You might have spared that word.
    Vent. And he that bribe.
    Ant. But have I no remembrance ?
    Alex. Yes, a dear one :
Your slave, the Queen——
    Ant. My mistress.
    Alex. Then your mistress,
Your mistress would, she says, have sent her soul,
But that you had long since ; she humbly begs
This ruby bracelet, set with bleeding hearts
(The emblem of her own) may bind your arm.
                              [*Presenting a bracelet.*
    Vent. Now, my best lord, in honour's name, I ask you,
For manhood's sake, and for your own dear safety,
Touch not these poison'd gifts,
Infected by the sender ; touch them not :
Myriads of bluest plagues lie underneath them,
And more than aconite has dipp'd the silk.
    Ant. Nay, now you grow too cynical, Ventidius :
A lady's favours may be worn with honour.
What, to refuse her bracelet ! on my soul,
When I lie pensive in my tent alone,
'Twill pass the wakeful hours of winter nights
To tell those pretty beads upon my arm,
To count for every one a soft embrace,
A melting kiss at such and such a time ;
And now and then the fury of her love,
When—— And what harm's in this ?
    Alex. None, none, my lord,
But what's to her, that now 'tis past for ever.
    Ant. [*Going to tie it.*] We soldiers are so awkward—
            help me to tie it.
    Alex. In faith, my lord, we courtiers, too, are awkward
In these affairs ; so are all men, indeed—
Even I, who am not one. But shall I speak ?
    Ant. Yes, freely.

Alex. Then, my lord, fair hands alone
Are fit to tie it; she who sent it can.

Vent. Hell! death! this eunuch pander ruins you.
You will not see her?

> [ALEXAS *whispers an attendant, who goes out.*

Ant. But to take my leave.

Vent. Then I have washed an Ethiop. You're undone;
You're in the toils; you're taken; you're destroyed—
Her eyes do Cæsar's work.

Ant. You fear too soon.
I'm constant to myself: I know my strength;
And yet she shall not think me barbarous neither,
Born in the depths of Afric; I'm a Roman,
Bred to the rules of soft humanity.
A guest, and kindly used, should bid farewell.

Vent. You do not know
How weak you are to her; how much an infant;
You are not proof against a smile, or glance;
A sigh will quite disarm you.

Ant. See, she comes!
Now you shall find your error. Gods, I thank you:
I formed the danger greater than it was,
And now 'tis near, 'tis lessened.

Vent. Mark the end yet.

Enter CLEOPATRA, CHARMION, *and* IRAS.

Ant. Well, madam, we are met.

Cleo. Is this a meeting?
Then, we must part?

Ant. We must.

Cleo. Who says we must?

Ant. Our own hard fates.

Cleo. We make those fates ourselves.

Ant. Yes, we have made them; we have loved each
Unto our mutual ruin.   [other

Cleo. The gods have seen my joys with envious eyes;
I have no friends in heaven; and all the world
(As 'twere the business of mankind to part us)
Is armed against my love: even you, yourself
Join with the rest; you, you are armed against me.

Ant. I will be justified in all I do
To late posterity, and therefore hear me.

If I mix a lie
With any truth, reproach me freely with it:
Else, favour me with silence.

 Cleo. You command me,
And I am dumb.

 Vent. I like this well—he shows authority.

 Ant. That I derive my ruin
From you alone——

 Cleo. O heavens! I ruin you!

 Ant. You promised me your silence, and you break it
Ere I have scarce begun.

 Cleo. Well, I obey you.

 Ant. When I beheld you first, it was in Egypt,
Ere Cæsar saw your eyes; you gave me love,
And were too young to know it; that I settled
Your father in his throne, was for your sake,
I left the acknowledgment for time to ripen.
Cæsar stepp'd in, and with a greedy hand
Plucked the green fruit, ere the first blush of red,
Yet cleaving to the bough. He was my lord,
And was, beside, too great for me to rival.
But I deserved you first, though he enjoyed you.
When, after, I beheld you in Cilicia,
An enemy to Rome, I pardoned you.

 Cleo. I cleared myself——

 Ant. Again you break your promise.
I loved you still, and took your weak excuses,
Took you into my bosom, stained by Cæsar,
And not half mine. I went to Egypt with you,
And hid me from the business of the world,
Shut out inquiring nations from my sight,
To give whole years to you.

 Vent. Yes, to your shame be't spoken.   [*Aside.*

 Ant. How I loved,
Witness ye days and nights, and all ye hours,
That danced away with down upon your feet,
As all your business were to count my passion.
One day pass'd by, and nothing saw but love;
Another came, and still 'twas only love.
The suns were wearied out with looking on,
And I untired with loving.
I saw you every day, and all the day;

And every day was still but as the first—
So eager was I still to see you more.

Vent. 'Tis all too true.

Ant. Fulvia, my wife, grew jealous,
As she indeed had reason; raised a war
In Italy, to call me back.

Vent. But yet
You went not.

Ant. While within your arms I lay,
The world fell mouldering from my hands each hour,
And left me scarce a grasp (I thank your love for't).

Vent. Well push'd: that last was home.

Cleo. Yet may I speak?

Ant. If I have urged a falsehood, yes; else, not.
Your silence says I have not.   Fulvia died
(Pardon, you gods! with my unkindness died).
To set the world at peace, I took Octavia,
This Cæsar's sister; in her pride of youth,
And flower of beauty did I wed that lady,
Whom blushing I must praise, because i left her.
You called; my love obeyed the fatal summons:
This raised the Roman arms; the cause was yours.
I would have fought by land, where I was stronger:
You hindered it: yet when I fought at sea,
Forsook me fighting; and (O stain to honour!
O lasting shame!) I knew not that I fled;
But fled to follow you.

Vent. What haste she made to hoist her purple sails!
And, to appear magnificent in flight,
Drew half our strength away.

Ant. All this you caused.
And would you multiply more ruins on me?
This honest man, my best, my only friend,
Has gathered up the shipwreck of my fortunes;
Twelve legions I have left, my last recruits,
And you have watched the news, and bring your eyes
To seize them too.   If you have ought to answer,
Now speak, you have free leave.

Alex. [*Aside.*] She stands confounded:
Despair is in her eyes.

Vent. Now lay a sigh in th' way, to stop his passage:
Prepare a tear, and bid it for his legions;
'Tis like they shall be sold.

Cleo. How shall I plead my cause when you my judge,
Already have condemned me? Shall I bring
The love you bore me for my advocate?
That now is turned against me, that destroys me;
For love once past is, at the best, forgotten;
But oftener sours to hate: 'twill please my lord
To ruin me, and therefore I'll be guilty.
But, could I once have thought it would have pleased you,
That you would pry, with narrow searching eyes,
Into my faults, severe to my destruction,
And watching all advantages with care,
That serve to make me wretched? Speak, my lord,
For I end here. Though I deserve this usage,
Was it like you to give it?
    Ant. O, you wrong me,
To think I sought this parting, or desired
To accuse you more than what will clear myself,
And justify this breach.
    Cleo. Thus low I thank you.
And, since my innocence will not offend,
I shall not blush to own it.
    Vent. After this
I think she'll blush at nothing.
    Cleo. You seem grieved
(And therein you are kind) that Cæsar first
Enjoyed my love, though you deserved it better:
I grieve for that, my lord, much more than you.
For, had I first been yours, it would have saved
My second choice; I never had been his,
And ne'er had been but yours. But Cæsar first,
You say, possessed my love. Not so, my lord:
He first possessed my person, you my love;
Cæsar loved me; but I loved Antony.
If I endured him after, 'twas because
I judged it due to the first name of men;
And, half constrained, I gave, as to a tyrant,
What he would take by force.
    Vent. O syren! syren!
Yet grant that all the love she boasts were true,
Has she not ruined you? I still urge that,
The fatal consequence.
    Cleo. The consequence, indeed,

For I dare challenge him, my greatest foe,
To say it was designed ; 'tis true, I loved you,
And kept you far from an uneasy wife
(Such Fulvia was).
Yes, but he'll say, you left Octavia for me ;—
And, can you blame me to receive that love,
Which quitted such desert for worthless me ?
How often have I wished some other Cæsar,
Great as the first, and as the second young,
Would court my love, to be refused for you !

    Vent. Words, words ; but Actium, sir, remember
        Actium.

    Cleo. Even there, I dare his malice. True, I counselled
To fight at sea ; but I betrayed you not.
I fled, but not to the enemy. 'Twas fear ;
Would I had been a man, not to have feared,
For none would then have envied me your friendship,
Who envy me your love.

    Ant. We're both unhappy :
If nothing else, yet our ill fortune parts us.
Speak : would you have me perish by my stay ?

    Cleo. If as a friend you ask my judgment, go ;
If as a lover, stay. If you must perish :
'Tis a hard word ; but stay.

    Vent. See now the effects of her so boasted love !
She strives to drag you down to ruin with her ;
But, could she 'scape without you, oh how soon
Would she let go her hold, and haste to shore,
And never look behind !

    Cleo. Then judge my love by this.

                  [*Giving* Antony *a writing.*

Could I have borne
A life or death, a happiness or woe
From yours divided, this had given me means.

    Ant. By Hercules ! the writing of Octavius !
I know it well : 'tis that proscribing hand,
Young as it was, that led the way to mine,
And left me but the second place in murder——
See, see, Ventidius ! here he offers Egypt,
And joins all Syria to it, as a present,
So, in requital, she forsake my fortunes,
And join her arms with his.

Cleo. And yet you leave me !
You leave me, Antony ; and, yet I love you.
Indeed, I do : I have refused a kingdom ;
That's a trifle ;
For I could part with life—with any thing,
But only you.   O let me die but with you !
Is that a hard request?
    Ant. Next living with you,
'Tis all that heaven can give.
    Alex. He melts ; we conquer.   [*Aside.*
    Cleo. No: You shall go ; your interest calls you hence ;
Yes, your dear interest pulls too strong for these
Weak arms to hold you here——   [*Takes his hand.*
Go, leave me soldier,
(For you're no more a lover)—leave me dying :
Push me all pale and panting from your bosom,
And, when your march begins, let one run after
Breathless almost for joy, and cry, She's dead ;
The soldiers shout ; you then perhaps may sigh,
And muster all your Roman gravity ;
Ventidius chides ; and straight your brow clears up,
As I had never been.
    Ant. Gods, 'tis too much : too much for man to bear.
    Cleo. What is't for me, then,
A weak forsaken woman, and a lover?
Here let me breathe my last ; envy me not
This minute in your arms : I'll die apace,
As fast as e'er I can, and end your trouble.
    Ant. Die ! rather let me perish : loosened nature
Leap from its hinges, sink the props of heaven,
And fall the skies to crush the nether world.
My eyes, my soul, my all !   [*Embraces her.*
    Vent. And what's this toy,
In balance with your fortune, honour, fame?
    Ant. What is't, Ventidius ?   It outweighs them all :
Why we have more than conquered Cæsar now ;
My Queen's not only innocent, but loves me.
This, this is she who drags me down to ruin !
But, could she 'scape without me, with what haste
Would she let slip her hold, and make to shore,
And never look behind!
Down on thy knees, blasphemer as thou art,
And ask forgiveness of wronged innocence.

Vent. I'll rather die than take it.   Will you go?
Ant. Go! whither?   Go from all that's excellent!
Faith, honour, virtue,—all good things forbid,
That I should go from her, who sets my love
Above the price of kingdoms!   Give, you gods,
Give to your boy, your Cæsar,
This rattle of a globe to play withal—
This gewgaw world—and put him cheaply off;
I'll not be pleased with less than Cleopatra.
Cleo. She's wholly yours.   My heart's so full of joy
That I shall do some wild extravagance
Of love in public; and the foolish world,
Which knows not tenderness, will think me mad.
Vent. O women! women! women! all the gods
Have not such power of doing good to man,
As you of doing harm.   [*Exit.*
Ant. Our men are armed.
Unbar the gate that leads to Cæsar's camp;
I would revenge the treachery he meant me:
And long security makes conquest easy.
I'm eager to return before I go;
For, all the pleasures I have known, beat thick
On my remembrance: how I long for night!
That both the sweets of mutual love may try,
And triumph once o'er Cæsar ere we die.   [*Exeunt.*

ACT III.   SCENE I.

At one door, enter CLEOPATRA, CHARMION, IRAS, *and*
ALEXAS, *a train of* EGYPTIANS: *At the other* ANTONY
and ROMANS. *The entrance on both sides is prepared
by music; the trumpets first sounding on* ANTONY'S
part: then answered by timbrels, &c., on CLEOPATRA'S.
CHARMION *and* IRAS *hold a laurel wreath betwixt them.
A dance of* EGYPTIANS. *After the ceremony,* CLEO-
PATRA *crowns* ANTONY.

Ant. I thought how those white arms would fold me in,
And strain me close, and melt me into love;
So, pleased with that sweet image, I sprung forward,
And added all my strength to every blow.

Cleo. Come to me, come, my soldier, to my arms,
You've been too long away from my embraces;
But, when I have you fast, and all my own,
With broken murmurs, and with amorous sighs,
I'll say, you were unkind and punish you,
And mark you red with many an eager kiss.
    Ant. My brighter Venus!
    Cleo. O my greater Mars!
    Ant. Thou join'st us well, my love!
Suppose me come from the Phlegræan plains,
Where gasping giants lay, cleft by my sword:
And mountain tops pared off each other blow,
To bury those I slew: Receive me, goddess:
Let Cæsar spread his subtle nets, like Vulcan,
In thy embraces I would be beheld
By heaven and earth at once;
And make their envy what they meant their sport.
Let those who took us blush; I would love on
With awful state, regardless of their frowns,
As their superior god.
There's no satiety of love, in thee
Enjoyed, thou still art new: perpetual spring
Is in thy arms; the ripened fruit but falls,
And blossoms rise to fill its empty place;
And I grow rich by giving.

        Enter VENTIDIUS, *and stands apart.*

    Alex. O, now the danger's past, your general comes,
He joins not in your joys, nor minds your triumphs;
But, with contracted brows, looks frowning on,
As envying your success.
    Ant. Now, on my soul, he loves me; truly loves me;
He never flattered me in any vice,
But awes me with his virtue: even this minute
Methinks he has a right of chiding me.
Lead to the temple: I'll avoid his presence;
It checks too strong upon me.   [*Exeunt the rest.*
    [*As* ANTONY *is going,* VENTIDIUS *pulls him by the robe.*
    Vent. Emperor!
    Ant. 'Tis the old argument: I prithee spare me.
                                [*Looking back.*
    Vent. But this one hearing, Emperor.

Ant. Let go
My robe; or, by my father Hercules——
    Vent. By Hercules's father, that's yet greater,
I bring you somewhat you would wish to know.
    Ant. Thou see'st we are observed; attend me here,
And I'll return.   [*Exit.*
    Vent. I'm waning in his favour, yet I love him;
I love this man, who runs to meet his ruin;
And, sure the gods, like me, are fond of him:
His virtues lie so mingled with his crimes,
As would confound their choice to punish one,
And not reward the other.

              Enter ANTONY.

    Ant. We can conquer,
You see, without your aid.
We have dislodged their troops,
They look on us at a distance, and, like curs
Scap'd from the lion's paws, they bay far off,
And lick their wounds, and faintly threaten war.
Five thousand Romans with their faces upward
Lie breathless on the plain.
    Vent. 'Tis well: and he
Who lost them, could have spared ten thousand more.
Yet if, by this advantage you could gain
An easier peace, while Cæsar doubts the chance
Of arms!——
    Ant. O think not on't, Ventidius;
The boy pursues my ruin, he'll no peace;
His malice is confederate in advantage;
O, he's the coolest murderer, so stanch,
He kills, and keeps his temper.
    Vent. Have you no friend
In all his army, who has power to move him?
Mecænas or Agrippa might do much.
    Ant. They're both too much in Cæsar's interests.
We'll work it out by dint of sword, or perish.
    Vent. Fain would I find some other.
    Ant. Thank thy love.
Some four or five such victories as this
Will save thy farther pains.
    Vent. Expect no more; Cæsar is on his guard:

I know, Sir, you have conquered against odds;
But still you draw supplies from one poor town,
And of Egyptians: he has all the world,
And, at his beck, nations come pouring in,
To fill the gaps you make. Pray think again.

Ant. Why dost thou drive me from myself to search
For foreign aids, to hunt my memory,
And range all o'er a waste and barren place
To find a friend? The wretched have no friends—
Yet I had one, the bravest youth of Rome,
Whom Cæsar loves beyond the love of women;
He could resolve his mind, as fire does wax,
From that hard, rugged image melt him down
And mould him in what softer form he pleased.

Vent. Him would I see; that man, of all the world,
Just such a one we want.

Ant. He loved me too,
I was his soul, he lived not but in me;
We were so closed within each other's breasts,
The rivets were not found that joined us first.
That does not reach us yet: we were so mixed,
As meeting streams, both to ourselves were lost;
We were one mass; we could not give or take,
But from the same; for he was I, I he.

Vent. He moves as I would wish him. [*Aside.*

Ant. After this,
I need not tell his name; 'twas Dolabella.

Vent. He's now in Cæsar's camp.

Ant. No matter where,
Since he's no longer mine. He took unkindly
That I forbade him Cleopatra's sight,
Because I feared he loved her. He confessed
He had a warmth, which, for my sake he stifled;
For 'twere impossible that two, so one,
Should not have loved the same. When he departed,
He took no leave, and that confirmed my thoughts.

Vent. It argues that he loved you more than her.
Else he had stayed; but he perceived you jealous,
And would not grieve his friend. I know he loves you.

Ant. I should have seen him then ere now.

Vent. Perhaps
He has thus long been lab'ring for your peace.

D

Ant. Would he were here.

Vent. Would you believe he loved you?
I read your answer in your eyes you would.
Not to conceal it longer, he has sent
A messenger from Cæsar's camp, with letters.

Ant. Let him appear.

Vent. I'll bring him instantly.

Exit VENTIDIUS, *and re-enters immediately with*
DOLABELLA.

Ant. 'Tis he himself, himself, by holy friendship!
                    [*Runs to embrace him.*
Art thou returned at last, my better-half?
Come, give me all myself.
Let me not live,
If the young bridegroom, longing for his night,
Was ever half so fond.

Dola. I must be silent, for my soul is busy
About a nobler work; she's new come home,
Like a long-absent man, and wanders o'er
Each room, a stranger to her own, to look
If all be safe.

Ant. Thou hast what's left of me.
For I am now so sunk from what I was,
Thou find'st me at my lowest water-mark,
The rivers that ran in and raised my fortunes,
Are all dried up, or take another course;
What I have left is from my native spring:
I've still a heart that swells, in scorn of fate,
And lifts me to my banks.

Dola. Still you are lord of all the world to me.

Ant. Why, then I yet am so, for thou art all.
If I had any joy when thou wert absent,
I grudged it to myself, methought I robbed
Thee of thy part.   But, Oh my Dolabella!
Thou hast beheld me other than I am.
Hast thou seen my morning chamber filled
With sceptered slaves, who waited to salute me?
With Eastern monarchs, who forgot the sun,
To worship my uprising?   Menial kings
Ran courting up and down my palace-yard,
Stood silent in my presence, watched my eyes,

And at my least command, all started out,
Like racers to the goal.
   Dola. Slaves to your fortune.
   Ant. Fortune is Cæsar's now; and what am I?
   Vent. What you have made yourself; I will not flatter.
   Ant. Is this friendly done?
   Dola. Yes, when his end is so, I must join with him;
Indeed I must, and yet you must not chide:
Why am I else your friend?
   Ant. Take heed, young man,
How thou upbraid'st my love; the queen has eyes,
And thou too hast a soul. Canst thou remember
When, swelled with hatred, thou beheld'st her first
As accessary to thy brother's death?
   Dola. Spare my remembrance; 'twas a guilty day,
And still the blush hangs here.
   Ant. To clear herself,
For sending him no aid, she came from Egypt,
Her galley down the silver Cydnos rowed,
The tackling silk, the streamers waved with gold,
The gentle winds were lodged in purple sails;
Her nymphs, like Nereids, round her couch were placed;
Where she, another sea-born Venus, lay.
   Dola. No more, I would not hear it.
   Ant. Oh, you must!
She lay, and leant her cheek upon her hand,
And cast a look so languishingly sweet,
As if, secure of all beholders' hearts,
Neglecting she could take them; boys, like cupids,
Stood fanning, with their painted wings, the winds
That played about her face; but if she smiled,
A darting glory seemed to blaze abroad:
That men's desiring eyes were never wearied,
But hung upon the object: to soft flutes
The silver oars kept time; and while they played
The hearing gave new pleasure to the sight,
And both to thought. 'Twas heaven, or somewhat more
For she so charmed all hearts, that gazing crowds
Stood panting on the shore, and wanted breath
To give their welcome voice.
Then, Dolabella, where was then thy soul?
Was not thy fury quite disarmed with wonder?

Didst thou not shrink behind me from those eyes,
And whisper in my ear :—Oh tell her not
That I accused her of my brother's death ?

Dola. And should my weakness be a plea for yours?
Mine was an age when love might be excused,
When kindly warmth, and when my springing youth
Made it a debt to nature.   Yours——

Vent. Speak boldly.
Yours, he would say, in your declining age,
When no more heat was left but what you forced,
When all the sap was needful for the trunk,
When it went down, then they constrained the course,
And robbed from nature, to supply desire;
In you (I would not use so hard a word)
'Tis but plain dotage.

Ant. Ha!

Dola. 'Twas urged too home,
But yet the loss was private that I made;
'Twas but myself I lost; I lost no legions;
I had no world to lose, no people's love.

Ant. This from a friend?

Dola. Yes, Antony, a true one :
A friend so tender that each word I speak
Stabs my own heart, before it reach your ear.
O, judge me not less kind because I chide;
To Cæsar I excuse you.

Ant. O ye gods!
Have I then lived to be excused to Cæsar?

Dola. As to your equal.

Ant. Well, he's but my equal;
While I wear this he never shall be more.

Dola. I bring conditions from him.

Ant.   Are they noble ?
Methinks thou shouldst not bring them else; yet he
Is full of deep dissembling; knows no honour
Divided from his interest.   Fate mistook him:
For nature meant him for an usurer;
He's fit, indeed, to buy, not conquer kingdoms.

Vent. Then, granting this,
What power was theirs who wrought so hard a temper
To honourable terms?

Ant. It was my Dolabella, or some god.

Dola. Nor I; nor yet Mecænus, nor Agrippa:
They were your enemies; and I, a friend,
Too weak alone; yet 'twas a Roman deed.
Ant. 'Twas like a Roman done: show me that man
Who has preserved my life, my love, my honour;
Let me but see his face.
Vent. That task is mine,
And, heaven, thou know'st how pleasing.   [*Exit* VENT.
Dola. You'll remember
To whom you stand obliged?
Ant. When I forget it,
Be thou unkind, and that's my greatest curse.
My Queen shall thank him too.
Dola. I fear she will not.
Ant. But she shall do't: the Queen, my Dolabella!
Hast thou not still some grudgings of thy fever?
Dola. I would not see her lost.
Ant. When I forsake her,
Leave me, my better stars; for she has truth
Beyond her beauty. Cæsar tempted her,
At no less price than kingdoms, to betray me;
But she resisted all; and yet thou chidest me
For loving her too well. Could I do so?
Dola. Yes, there's my reason.

Re-enter VENTIDIUS, *with* OCTAVIA, *leading* ANTONY'S
two little daughters.

Ant. Where?——Octavia there!   [*Starting back.*
Vent. What, is she poison to you—a disease?
Look on her, view her well, and those she brings.
Are they all strangers to your eyes? Has nature
No secret call, no whisper they are yours?
Dola. For shame, my lord, if not for love, receive them
With kinder eyes. If you confess a man,
Meet them, embrace them, bid them welcome to you.
Your arms should open, even without your knowledge,
To clasp them in; your feet should turn to wings,
To bear you to them; and your eyes dart out,
And aim a kiss ere you could reach the lips.
Ant. I stood amazed to think how they came hither.
Vent. I sent for them, I brought them in, unknown
To Cleopatra's guards.

Dola. Yet, are you cold?

Oct. Thus long I have attended for my welcome;
Which, as a stranger, sure I might expect.
Who am I?

Ant. Cæsar's sister.

Oct. That's unkind!
Had I been nothing more than Cæsar's sister,
Know I had still remained in Cæsar's camp;
But your Octavia, your much injured wife,
Though banished from your bed, driven from your house,
In spite of Cæsar's sister, still is yours.
'Tis true, I have a heart disdains your coldness,
And prompts me not to seek what you should offer ;
But a wife's virtue still surmounts that pride ;
I come to claim you as my own ; to show
My duty first, to ask, nay beg, your kindness.
Your hand, my lord : 'tis mine, and I will have it.

[*Taking his hand.*

Vent. Do take it; thou deserv'st it.

Dola. On my soul,
And so she does ; she's neither too submissive
Nor yet too haughty : but so just a mean
Shows, as it ought, a wife and Roman too.

Ant. I fear, Octavia, you have begged my life.

Oct. Begged it, my lord ?

Ant. Yes, begged it, my ambassadress,
Poorly and basely begged it of your brother.

Oct. Poorly and basely I could never beg,
Nor could my brother grant.

Ant. Shall I, who to my kneeling slave could say,
Rise up and be a king—shall I fall down
And cry, Forgive me, Cæsar ?   Shall I set
A man, my equal, in the place of Jove,
As he could give me being ?   No ; that word,
Forgive, would choke me up,
And die upon my tongue.

Dola. You shall not need it.

Ant. I will not need it.   Come, you've all betrayed me ;
My friend, too ! to receive some vile conditions.
My wife has bought me with her prayers and tears ;
And now I must become her branded slave.
In every peevish mood she will upbraid

The life she gave ; if I but look awry,
She cries, I'll tell my brother.

Oct. My hard fortune
Subjects me still to your unkind mistakes.
But the conditions I have brought are such
You need not blush to take. I love your honour,
Because 'tis mine : it never shall be said
Octavia's husband was her brother's slave.
Sir, you are free—free, e'en from her you loathe ;
For, tho' my brother bargains for your love,
Makes me the price and cement of your peace,
I have a soul like yours ; I cannot take
Your love as alms, nor beg what I deserve.
I'll tell my brother we are reconciled ;
He shall draw back his troops, and you shall march
To rule the East : I may be dropt at Athens ;
No matter where, I never will complain,
But only keep the barren name of wife,
And rid you of the trouble.

Vent. Was ever such a strife of sullen honour !
Both scorn to be obliged.

Dola. O, she has touched him in the tenderest part;
See how he reddens with despite and shame
To be outdone in generosity !

Vent. See how he winks ! how he dries up a tear,
That fain would fall !

Ant. Octavia, I have heard you, and must praise
The greatness of your soul ;
But cannot yield to what you have proposed :
For I can ne'er be conquered but by love ;
And you do all for duty. You would free me,
And would be dropt at Athens ; was't not so ?

Oct. It was, my lord.

Ant. Then I must be obliged
To one who loves me not ; who, to herself,
May call me thankless and ungrateful man :
I'll not endure it ; no.

Vent. I'm glad it pinches there.

Oct. Would you triumph o'er poor Octavia's virtue?
That pride was all I had to bear me up ;
That you might think you owed me for your life,
And owed it to my duty, not my love.

I have been injured, and my haughty soul
Could brook but ill the man who slights my bed.
  Ant. Therefore, you love me not.
  Oct. Therefore, my lord,
I should not love you.
  Ant. Therefore, you would leave me?
  Oct. And, therefore, I should leave you—if I could.
  Dola. Her soul's too great, after such injuries,
To say she loves; and yet she lets you see it.
Her modesty and silence plead her cause.
  Ant. O, Dolabella, which way shall I turn?
I find a secret yielding in my soul;
But Cleopatra, who would die with me,
Must she be left? Pity pleads for Octavia,
But does it not plead more for Cleopatra?
  Vent. Justice and pity both plead for Octavia;
For Cleopatra, neither.
One would be ruined with you; but the first
Had ruined you: the other you have ruined,
And yet she would preserve you.
In everything their merits are unequal.
  Ant. O, my distracted soul!
  Oct. Sweet heaven, compose it.
Come, come, my lord: if I can pardon you,
Methinks you should accept it. Look on these;
Are they not yours? or stand they thus neglected
As they are mine? Go to him, children, go;
Kneel to him, take him by the hand, speak to him;
For you may speak, and he may own you, too,
Without a blush; and so he cannot all
His children: Go, I say, and pull him to me,
And pull him to yourselves, from that bad woman.
You, Agrippina, hang upon his arms;
And you, Antonia, clasp about his waist:
If he will shake you off, if he will dash you
Against the pavement, you must bear it, children;
For you are mine, and I was born to suffer.
                    [*Here the children go to him, &c.*
  Vent. Was ever sight so moving! Emperor!
  Dola. Friend!
  Oct. Husband!
  Both Child. Father!

Ant. I am vanquished : Take me,
Octavia; take me, children; share me all.   [*Embracing*
I've been a thriftless debtor to your loves,   [*them.*
And run out much in riot from your stock ;
But all shall be amended.

Oct. O blest hour !

Dola. O happy change !

Vent. My joy stops at my tongue,
But it has found two channels here for one,
And bubbles out above.

Ant. [*To Octavia.*] This is thy triumph: lead me where
Ev'n to thy brother's camp.   [thou wilt :

Oct. All there are yours.

      Enter ALEXAS *hastily.*

Alex. The Queen, my mistress, sir, and yours——

Ant. 'Tis past.   Octavia, you shall stay this night ;
To-morrow, Cæsar and we are one.

     [*Ex. leading* OCT. DOLA. *and the children follow.*

Vent. There's news for you ; run, my officious eunuch,
Be sure to be the first ; haste forward :
Haste, my dear eunuch, haste.   [*Exit.*

Alex. This downright fighting fool, this thick-sculled
This blunt, unthinking instrument of death,   [hero,
With plain, dull virtue, has out-gone my wit :
Pleasure forsook my earliest infancy,
The luxury of others robbed my cradle,
And ravished thence the promise of a man :
Cast out from Nature, disinherited
Of what her meanest children claim by kind ;
Yet, greatness kept me from contempt : that's gone.
Had Cleopatra followed my advice,
Then he had been betrayed, who now forsakes.
She dies for love ; but she has known its joys :
Gods is this just, that I, who know no joys,
Must die, because she loves ?

    Enter CLEOPATRA, CHARMION, IRAS, *and Train.*

Oh, madam, I have seen what blasts my eyes !
Octavia's here !

Cleo. Peace with that raven's note.
I know it too ; and now am in
The pangs of death.

Alex. You are no more a Queen;
Egypt is lost.
    Cleo. What tell'st thou me of Egypt?
My life, my soul, is lost! Octavia has him!
O fatal name to Cleopatra's love!
My kisses, my embraces, now are hers:
While I—— But thou hast seen my rival: speak,
Does she deserve this blessing? Is she fair?
Bright as a goddess? and is all perfection
Confined to her? It is. Poor I was made
Of that coarse matter which, when she was finished,
The gods threw by for rubbish.
    Alex. She's indeed a very miracle.
    Cleo. Death to my hopes, a miracle!
    Alex. A miracle;   *[Bowing.*
I mean of goodness; for in beauty, madam,
You make all wonders cease.
    Cleo. I was too rash:
Take this in part of recompense. But, oh,   *[Giving a*
I fear thou flatterest me.   *[ring.*
    Char. She comes! she's here!
    Iras. Fly, madam; Cæsar's sister!
    Cleo. Were she the sister of the Thunderer Jove,
And bore her brother's lightning in her eyes,
Thus would I face my rival.

Meets OCTAVIA *with* VENTIDIUS. OCTAVIA *bears up to her.*
    Their Trains come up on either side.

    Oct. I need not ask if you are Cleopatra,
Your haughty carriage——
    Cleo. Shows I am a Queen:
Nor need I ask who you are.
    Oct. A Roman:
A name that makes and can unmake a Queen.
    Cleo. Your lord, the man who serves me, is a Roman.
    Oct. He was a Roman, till he lost that name
To be a slave in Egypt; but I come
To free him thence.
    Cleo. Peace, peace, my lover's Juno.
When he grew weary of that household clog,
He chose my easier bonds.
    Oct. I wonder not

Your bonds are easy; you have long been practised
In that lascivious art. He's not the first
For whom you spread your snares: let Cæsar witness.

Cleo. I loved not Cæsar; 'twas but gratitude
I paid his love. The worst your malice can,
Is but to say the greatest of mankind
Has been my slave. The next, but far above him
In my esteem, is he whom law calls yours,
But whom his love made mine.

Oct. I would view nearer   [*Coming up close to her.*
That face which has so long usurped my right,
To find the inevitable charms that catch
Mankind so sure—that ruined my dear lord.

Cleo. O, you do well to search; for had you known
But half these charms, you had not lost his heart.

Oct. Far be their knowledge from a Roman lady,
Far from a modest wife. Shame of our sex,
Dost thou not blush to own those black endearments
That make sin pleasing?

Cleo. You may blush, who want them.
If bounteous nature, if indulgent heaven
Have given me charms to please the bravest man,
Should I not thank them?—should I not be ashamed,
And not be proud? I am, that he has loved me;
And when I love not him, heaven change this face
For one like that.

Oct. Thou lov'st him not so well.

Cleo. I love him better, and deserve him more.

Oct. You do not; cannot: you have been his ruin.
Who made him cheap at Rome, but Cleopatra?
Who made him scorned abroad, but Cleopatra?
At Actium, who betrayed him? Cleopatra.
Who made his children orphans? and poor me
A wretched widow? only Cleopatra.

Cleo. Yet she who loves him best is Cleopatra.
If you have suffered, I have suffered more.
You bear the specious title of a wife,
To gild your cause, and draw the pitying world
To favour it: the world contemns poor me;
For I have lost my honour, lost my fame,
And stained the glory of my royal house,
And all to bear the branded name of mistress.

There wants but life, and that, too, I would lose
For him I love.
    Oct. Be it so, then ; take thy wish.   [*Exit cum suis.*
    Cleo. And 'tis my wish,
Now he is lost for whom alone I lived.
My sight grows dim, and every object dances
And swims before me in the maze of death.
My spirits, while they were opposed, kept up ;
They could not sink beneath a rival's scorn :
But now she's gone, they faint.
    Alex. Mine have had leisure
To recollect their strength, and furnish counsel
To ruin her, who else must ruin you.
    Cleo. Vain promiser !
Lead me, my Charmion ; nay, your hand too, Iras.
My grief has weight enough to sink you both.
Conduct me to some solitary chamber,
And draw the curtains round ;
Then leave me to myself, to take alone
My fill of grief.
There I till death will his unkindness weep,
As harmless infants moan themselves asleep.

                           [*Exeunt.*

ACT IV. SCENE I.

Enter ANTONY *and* DOLABELLA.

    Dola. Why would you shift it from yourself on me ?
Can you not tell her you must part ?
    Ant. I cannot.
I could pull out an eye, and bid it go,
And t'other should not weep. Oh, Dolabella,
How many deaths are in this word, Depart !
I dare not trust my tongue to tell her so :
One look of hers would thaw me into tears,
And I should melt till I were lost again.
    Dola. Then let Ventidius ;
He's rough by nature.
    Ant. Oh, he'll speak too harshly ;
He'll kill her with the news : thou, only thou.
    Dola. Nature has cast me in so soft a mould,

That but to hear a story feigned for pleasure
Of some sad lover's death, moistens my eyes,
And robs me of my manhood.——I should speak
So faintly, with such fear to grieve her heart,
She'd not believe it earnest.

Ant. Therefore, therefore
Thou, only thou, art fit: think thyself me,
And when thou speak'st (but let it first be long)
Take off the edge from every sharper sound,
And let our parting be as gently made
As other loves begin. Wilt thou do this?

Dola. What you have said so sinks into my soul
That, if I must speak, I shall speak just so.

Ant. I leave you then to your sad task : farewell.
I sent her word to meet you.
                    [*Goes to the door, and comes back.*
I forgot ;
Let her be told, I'll make her peace with mine :
Her crown and dignity shall be preserved,
If I have power with Cæsar.—— Oh, be sure
To think on that.

Dola. Fear not, I will remember.
            [ANTONY *goes again to the door, and comes back.*
Ant. And tell her, too, how much I was constrained ;
I did not this but with extremest force :
Desire her not to hate my memory,
For I still cherish hers. Insist on that.

Dola. Trust me, I'll not forget it.
Ant. Then that's all.   [*Goes out and returns again.*
Wilt thou forgive my fondness this once more?
Tell her, though we shall never meet again,
If I should hear she took another love,
The news would break my heart.—Now I must go ;
For every time I have returned, I feel
My soul more tender ; and my next command
Would be to bid her stay, and ruin both: [*Exit.*

Dola. Men are but children of a larger growth,
Our appetites as apt to change as theirs,
And full as craving too, and full as vain ;
And yet the soul, shut up in her dark room,
Viewing so clear abroad, at home sees nothing ;
But, like a mole in earth, busy and blind,

Works all her folly up, and casts it outward
To the world's open view: thus I discovered,
And blamed the love of ruined Antony;
Yet wish that I were he, to be so ruined.

Enter VENTIDIUS *above.*

Vent. Alone, and talking to himself? concerned, too?
Perhaps my guess is right; he loved her once,
And may pursue it still.

Dola. O friendship! friendship!
Ill canst thou answer this; and reason, worse:
Unfaithful in the attempt; hopeless to win:
And, if I win, undone: mere madness all.
And yet the occasion's fair. What injury
To him, to wear the robe which he throws by?

Vent. None, none at all. This happens as I wish,
To ruin her yet more with Antony.

Enter CLEOPATRA, *talking with* ALEXAS; CHARMION, IRAS,
on the other side.

Dola. She comes! what charms have sorrow on that
face!
Sorrow seems pleased to dwell with so much sweetness;
Yet, now and then, a melancholy smile
Breaks loose, like lightning, in a winter's night,
And shows a moment's day.

Vent. If she should love him too! her eunuch there!
That porc'pisce bodes ill weather. Draw, draw nearer,
Sweet devil, that I may hear.

Alex. Believe me; try
        [DOLABELLA *goes over to* CHARMION *and* IRAS;
                seems to talk with them.
To make him jealous; jealousy is like
A polished glass held to the lips when life's in doubt:
If there be breath, 'twill catch the damp and show it.

Cleo. I grant you jealousy's a proof of love,
But 'tis a weak and unavailing medicine;
It puts out the disease, and makes it show,
But has no power to cure.

Alex. 'Tis your last remedy, and strongest too:
And then this Dolabella, who so fit
To practice on? He's handsome, valiant, young,

And looks as he were laid for Nature's bait,
To catch weak women's eyes.
He stands already more than half suspected
Of loving you. The least kind word or glance
You give this youth, will kindle him with love :
Then, like a burning vessel set adrift,
You'll send him down amain before the wind,
To fire the heart of jealous Antony.

Cleo. Can I do this? Ah no ; my love's so true,
That I can neither hide it where it is,
Nor show it where it is not. Nature meant me
A wife ; a silly, harmless, household dove,
Fond without art, and kind without deceit ;
But Fortune, that has made a mistress of me,
Has thrust me out to the wide world, unfurnished
Of falsehood to be happy.

Alex. Force yourself.
The event will be, your lover will return
Doubly desirous to possess the good
Which once he feared to lose.

Cleo. I must attempt it,
But Oh with what regret!

            [Exit ALEX. *She comes up to* DOLABELLA.

Vent. So now the scene draws near ; they're in my reach.

Cleo. [*To Dola.*] Discoursing with my women! might
Share in your entertainment?   [not I

Char. You have been
The subject of it, madam.

Cleo. How! and how?

Iras. Such praises of your beauty !

Cleo. Mere poetry.
Your Roman wits, your Gallus and Tibullus,
Have taught you this from Cytheris and Delia.

Dola. These Roman wits have never been in Egypt,
Cytheris and Delia else had been unsung :
I, who have seen—had I been born a poet,
Should choose a nobler name.

Cleo. You flatter me.
But 'tis your nation's vice : all of your country
Are flatterers and all false. Your friend's like you :
I'm sure he sent you not to speak these words.

Dola. No, madam ; yet he sent me——

Cleo. Well, he sent you——

Dola. Of a less pleasing errand.

Cleo. How less pleasing?
Less to yourself, or me?

Dola. Madam, to both;
For you must mourn, and I must grieve to cause it.

Cleo. You, Charmion, and your fellow, stand at
    distance.
Hold up, my spirits. [*Aside.*] Well, now your mournful
For I'm prepared; perhaps can guess it, too.   [matter;

Dola. I wish you would; for 'tis a thankless office
To tell ill news; and I, of all your sex,
Most fear displeasing you.

Cleo. Of all your sex,
I soonest could forgive you, if you should.

Vent. Most delicate advances! Woman! woman!
Dear, damned, inconstant sex!

Cleo. In the first place,
I am to be forsaken; is't not so?

Dola. I wish I could not answer to that question.

Cleo. Then pass it o'er, because it troubles you:
I should have been more grieved another time.
Next, I'm to lose my kingdom——Farewell, Egypt!
Yet, is there any more?

Dola. Madam, I fear
Your too deep sense of grief has turned your reason.

Cleo. No, no, I'm not run mad; I can bear fortune:
And love may be expelled by other love,
As poisons are by poisons.

Dola. You o'erjoy me, madam,
To find your griefs so moderately borne.
You've heard the worst; all are not false, like him.

Cleo. No; heaven forbid they should.

Dola. Some men are constant.

Cleo. And constancy deserves reward, that's certain.

Dola. Deserves it not; but give it leave to hope.

Vent. I'll swear thou hast my leave. I have enough;
But how to manage this! Well, I'll consider.   [*Exit.*

Dola. I came prepared
To tell you heavy news; news which I thought
Would fright the blood from your pale cheeks to hear;
But you have met it with a cheerfulness

That makes my talk more easy, and my tongue,
Which on another's message was employed,
Would gladly speak its own.

Cleo. Hold, Dolabella.
First tell me, were you chosen by my lord?
Or sought you this employment?

Dola. He picked me out, and, as his bosom friend,
He charged me with his words.

Cleo. The message, then,
I know was tender, and each accent smooth,
To mollify that rugged word Depart.

Dola. Oh, you mistake: he chose the harshest words,
With fiery eyes, and with contracted brows,
He coined his face in the severest stamp,
And fury shook his fabric like an earthquake;
He heaved for vent, and burst like bellowing Etna,
In sounds scarce human, " Hence, away for ever!
Let her begone, the blot of my renown
And bane of all my hopes:

> [*All the time of this speech,* CLEOPATRA *seems more*
> *and more concerned, till she sinks quite down.*

Let her be driven as far as man can think
From man's commerce: she'll poison to the centre."

Cleo. Oh, I can bear no more!

Dola. Help, help! Oh, wretch! Oh, cursed, cursed
What have I done! [wretch!

Char. Help! chafe her temples, Iras.

Iras. Bend, bend her forward quickly.

Char. Heaven be praised,
She comes again!

Cleo. Oh, let him not approach me.
Why have you brought me back to this loathed being,
The abode of falsehood, violated vows,
And injured love? For pity, let me go;
For, if there be a place of long repose,
I'm sure I want it. My disdainful lord
Can never break that quiet; nor awake
The sleeping soul, with hollowing in my tomb
Such words as fright her hence: Unkind, unkind.

Dola. Believe me, 'tis against myself I speak,
That sure deserves belief; I injured him: [*Kneeling.*
My friend ne'er spoke those words. Oh, had you seen

E

How often he came back, and every time
With something more obliging and more kind,
To add to what he said; what dear farewells,
How almost vanquished by his love he parted,
And leaned to what unwillingly he left:
I, traitor as I was, for love of you,
(But what can you not do, who made me false!)
I forged that lie; for whose forgiveness kneels
This self-accused, self-punished criminal.

　　Cleo. With how much ease believe we what we wish!
Rise, Dollabella; if you have been guilty,
I have contributed, and too much love
Has made me guilty too.
The advance of kindness which I made was feigned
To call back fleeting love by jealousy;
But 'twould not last.　Oh, rather let me lose,
Than so ignobly trifle with his heart.

　　Dola. I find your breast fenced round from human
Transparent as a rock of solid crystal;　　　　　[reach,
Seen through, but never pierced.　My friend, my friend,
What endless treasure hast thou thrown away,
And scattered, like an infant, in the ocean,
Vain sums of wealth which none can gather thence.

　　Cleo. Could you not beg
An hour's admittance to his private ear?
Like one who wanders through long barren wilds,
And yet foreknows no hospitable inn
Is near to succour hunger,
Eats his fill, before his painful march:
So would I feed awhile my famished eyes
Before we part; for I have far to go,
If death be far, and never must return.

VENTIDIUS, with OCTAVIA, behind.

　　Vent. From hence you may discover—O, sweet, sweet!
Would you indeed? the pretty hand in earnest?
　　Dola. I will, for this reward.　　　　[*Takes her hand.*
――Draw it not back,
'Tis all I e'er will beg.
　　Vent. They turn upon us.
　　Oct. What quick eyes has guilt!
　　Vent. Seem not to have observed them, and go on.

They enter.

Dola. Saw you the Emperor, Ventidius?

Vent. No.
I sought him, but I heard that he was private,
None with him but Hipparchus his freedman.

Dola. Know you his business?

Vent. Giving him instructions,
And letters to his brother Cæsar.

Dola. Well,
He must be found.   [*Exeunt* Dola. *and* Cleo.

Oct. Most glorious impudence!

Vent. She looked, methought,
As she would say, Take your old man, Octavia;
Thank you, I'm better here.
Well, but what use
Make we of this discovery?

Oct. Let it die.

Vent. I pity Dolabella; but she's dangerous:
Her eyes have power beyond Thessalian charms
To draw the moon from heaven; for eloquence,
The sea-green syrens taught her voice their flattery;
And, while she speaks, night steals upon the day,
Unmarked of those that hear. Then she's so charming,
Age buds at sight of her, and swells to youth;
The holy priests gaze on her when she smiles,
And with heav'd hands, forgetting gravity,
They bless her wanton eyes: even I, who hate her,
With a malignant joy behold such beauty;
And, while I curse, desire it. Antony
Must needs have some remains of passion still,
Which may ferment into a worse relapse,
If not now fully cured. I know, this minute,
With Cæsar he's endeavouring her peace.

Oct. You have prevailed:——But for a farther purpose
I'll prove how he will relish this discovery.   [*Walks off.*
What, make a strumpet's peace! it swells my heart;
It must not, shall not be.

Vent. His guards appear.
Let me begin, and you shall second me.

Enter Antony.

Ant. Octavia, I was looking you, my love:

What, are your letters ready?   I have given
My last instructions.

   Oct. Mine, my lord, are written.

   Ant. Ventidius!   [*Drawing him aside.*

   Vent. My lord?

   Ant. A word in private.
When saw you Dolabella?

   Vent. Now, my lord,
He parted hence; and Cleopatra with him.

   Ant. Speak softly.   'Twas by my command he went.
To bear my last farewell.

   Vent. It looked, indeed,   [*Aloud.*
Like your farewell.

   Ant. More softly—— My farewell?
What secret meaning have you in those words
Of my farewell?   He did it by my order.

   Vent. Then he obeyed your order. I suppose   [*Aloud.*
You bid him do it with all gentleness,
All kindness, and all—love.

   Ant. How she mourned,
The poor forsaken creature!

   Vent. She took it as she ought; she bore your parting
As she did Cæsar's, as she would another's,
Were a new love to come.

   Ant. Thou dost belie her;   [*Aloud.*
Most basely and maliciously belie her.

   Vent. I thought not to displease you; I have done.

   Oct. [*Coming up.*] You seem disturbed, my lord.

   Ant. A very trifle.
Retire, my love.

   Vent. It was indeed a trifle.
He sent——

   Ant. No more.   Look how thou disobeyest me;
Thy life shall answer it.   [*Angrily.*

   Oct. Then, 'tis no trifle.

   Vent. [*To Oct.*] 'Tis less: a very nothing; you, too,
As well as I, and therefore 'tis no secret.   [saw it,

   Ant. She saw it!

   Vent. Yes; she saw young Dolabella——

   Ant. Young Dolabella!

   Vent. Young—I think him young,
And handsome, too; and so do others think him.

But what of that? he went by your command;
Indeed, 'tis probable, with some kind message;
For she received it graciously. She smiled,
And then he grew familiar with her hand,
Squeez'd it, and worried it with ravenous kisses;
She blushed, and sighed, and smiled, and blushed again;
At last she took occasion to talk softly,
And brought her cheek up close, and leaned on his:
At which he whispered kisses back on hers;
And then she cried aloud, that constancy
Should be rewarded.

 Oct. This I saw and heard.

 Ant. What woman was it whom you heard and saw
So playful with my friend!
Not Cleopatra?

 Vent. Even she, my lord.

 Ant. My Cleopatra?

 Vent. Your Cleopatra;
Dolabella's Cleopatra;
Every man's Cleopatra.

 Ant. Thou liest.

 Vent. I do not lie, my lord.
Is this so strange? Should mistresses be left,
And not provide against a time of change?
You know she's not much used to lonely nights.

 Ant. I'll think no more on't.
I know 'tis false, and see the plot betwixt you.
You needed not have gone this way, Octavia.
What harms it you that Cleopatra's just?
She's mine no more. I see, and I forgive;
Urge it no farther, love.

 Oct. Are you concerned
That she's found false?

 Ant. I should be, were it so;
For, though 'tis past, I would not that the world
Should tax my former choice, that I loved one
Of so light note; but I forgive you both.

 · *Vent.* What has my age deserved, that you should think
I would abuse your ears with perjury?
If heaven be true, she's false.

 Ant. Though heaven and earth
Should witness it, I'll not believe her tainted.

Vent. I'll bring you then a witness
From hell to prove her so !   Nay, go not back ;
            [*Seeing* ALEXAS *just entering, and starting back.*
For stay you must and shall.
    Alex. What means my lord ?
    Vent. To make you do what most you hate—speak
You are of Cleopatra's private counsel,   [truth.
Of her bed-counsel, her lascivious hours ;
Are conscious of each nightly change she makes,
And watch her, as Chaldeans do the moon,
Can tell what signs she passes through, what day.
    Alex. My noble lord.
    Vent. My most illustrious pander,
No fine set speech, no cadence, no turned periods,
But a plain home-spun truth, is what I ask :
I did, myself, o'erhear your Queen make love
To Dolabella.   Speak ; for I will know,
By your confession, what more passed betwixt them ;
How near the business draws to your employment ;
And when the happy hour.
    Ant. Speak truth, Alexas ; whether it offend
Or please Ventidius, care not.   Justify
Thy injured Queen from malice : dare his worst.
    Oct. [*Aside.*] See, how he gives him courage, how he
To find her false ! and shuts his eyes to truth,   [fears
Willing to be misled !
    Alex. As far as love may plead for woman's frailty,
Urged by desert and greatness of the lover,
So far, divine Octavia, may my Queen
Stand even excused to you for loving him
Who is your lord : so far, from brave Ventidius,
May her past actions hope a fair report.
    Ant. 'Tis well, and truly spoken ; mark, Ventidius.
    Alex. To you, most noble Emperor, her strong passion
Stands not excused, but wholly justified.
Her beauty's charms alone, without her crown,
From Ind and Meroe drew the distant vows
Of fighting kings ; and at her feet were laid
The sceptres of the earth, exposed on heaps,
To choose where she would reign :
She thought a Roman only could deserve her ;
And, of all Romans, only Antony.

And, to be less than wife to you, disdained
Their lawful passion.

Ant. 'Tis but truth.

Alex. And yet, tho' love, and your unmatch'd desert,
Have drawn her from the due regard of honour,
At last, heaven opened her unwilling eyes
To see the wrongs she offered fair Octavia,
Whose holy bed she lawlessly usurped.
The sad effects of this improsperous war
Confirmed those pious thoughts.

Vent. [*Aside.*] O, wheel you there?
Observe him now; the man begins to mend,
And talk substantial reason. Fear not, eunuch,
The Emperor has given thee leave to speak.

Alex. Else had I never dared to offend his ears
With what the last necessity has urged
On my forsaken mistress; yet I must not
Presume to say her heart is wholly altered.

Ant. No, dare not for thy life; I charge thee, dare not
Pronounce that fatal word.

Oct. [*Aside.*] Must I bear this? Good heaven afford me
patience.

Vent. O, sweet eunuch; my dear half man, proceed.

Alex. Yet Dolabella
Has loved her long; he, next my god-like lord,
Deserves her best; and should she meet his passion,
Rejected as she is by him she loved——

Ant. Hence from my sight; for I can bear no more:
Let furies drag thee quick to hell; let all
The longer damned have rest; each torturing hand
Do thou employ, till Cleopatra comes,
Then join thou, too, and help to torture her.

[*Exit* ALEXAS, *thrust out by* ANTONY.

Oct. 'Tis not well,
Indeed, my lord, 'tis much unkind to me,
To show this passion, this extreme concernment
For an abandoned, faithless prostitute.

Ant. Octavia, leave me: I am much disordered;
Leave me, I say.

Oct. My lord!

Ant. I bid you leave me.

Vent. Obey him, madam; best withdraw a while,
And see how this will work.

Oct. Wherein have I offended you, my lord,
That I am bid to leave you?   Am I false,
Or infamous?   Am I a Cleopatra?
Were I she,
Base as she is, you would not bid me leave you;
But hang upon my neck, take slight excuses,
And fawn upon my falsehood.

Ant. 'Tis too much,
Too much, Octavia; I am press'd with sorrows
Too heavy to be borne, and you add more;
I would retire, and recollect what's left
Of man within, to aid me.

Oct. You would mourn
In private, for your love who has betrayed you.
You did but half return to me; your kindness
Lingered behind with her.   I hear, my lord,
You make conditions for her,
And would include her treaty.   Wondrous proofs
Of love to me!

Ant. Are you my friend, Ventidius?
Or are you turned a Dolabella too,
And let this fury loose?

Vent. Oh, be advised,
Sweet madam, and retire.

Oct. Yes, I will go; but never to return.
You shall no more be haunted with this fury.
My lord! my lord! love will not always last,
When urged with long unkindness and disdain.
Take her again whom you prefer to me;
She stays but to be called.   Poor cozened man!
Let a feigned parting give her back your heart,
Which a feigned love first got; for injured me,
Though my just sense of wrongs forbid my stay,
My duty shall be yours.
To the dear pledges of our former love,
My tenderness and care shall be transferred,
And they shall cheer, by turns, my widowed nights.
So take my last farewell: for I despair
To have you whole, and scorn to take you half.   [*Exit.*

Vent. I combat Heaven, which blasts my best designs;

My last attempt must be to win her back:
But O, I fear, in vain.   [*Exit.*
   Ant. Why was I framed with this plain honest heart,
Which knows not to disguise its griefs and weakness,
But bears its workings outward to the world?
I should have kept the mighty anguish in,
And forced a smile at Cleopatra's falschood:
Octavia had believed it, and had stayed.
But I am made a shallow-forded stream,
Seen to the bottom: all my clearness scorned,
And all my faults exposed.—See where he comes

     Enter DOLABELLA.

Who has profaned the sacred name of friend,
And worn it into vileness!
With how secure a brow, and specious form
He gilds the secret villain! Sure that face
Was meant for honesty; but Heaven mis-matched it,
And furnished treason out with nature's pomp,
To make its work more easy.
   Dola. O, my friend!
   Ant. Well, Dolabella, you performed my message?
   Dola. I did, unwillingly.
   Ant. Unwillingly?
Was it so hard for you to bear our parting?
You should have wished it.
   Dola. Why?
   Ant. Because you love me.
And she received my message with as true,
With as unfeigned a sorrow, as you brought it?
   Dola. She loves you, even to madness.
   Ant. Oh, I know it.
You, Dolabella, do not better know
How much she loves me. And should I
Forsake this beauty? this all-perfect creature?
   Dola. I could not, were she mine.
   Ant. And yet you first
Persuaded me: how come you altered since?
   Dola. I said at first I was not fit to go;
I could not hear her sighs and see her tears,
But pity must prevail; and so, perhaps,
It may again with you; for I have promised

That she should take her last farewell, and see,
She comes to claim my word.

Enter CLEOPATRA.

Ant. False Dolabella!

Dola. What's false, my lord?

Ant. Why, Dolabella's false,
And Cleopatra's false, both false and faithless.
Draw near, you well-joined wickedness, you serpents,
Whom I have in my kindly bosom warmed,
Till I am stung to death.

Dola. My lord, have I
Deserved to be thus used?

Cleo. Can Heaven prepare
A newer torment? Can it find a curse
Beyond our separation?

Ant. Yes, if fate
Be just, much greater; Heaven should be ingenious
In punishing such crimes. The rolling stone,
And gnawing vulture, were slight pains invented
When Jove was young, and no examples known
Of mighty ills; but you have ripened sin
To such a monstrous growth, 'twill pose the gods
To find an equal torture. Two, two such—
Oh, there's no farther name,—two such,—to me,
To me, who locked my soul within your breasts,
Had no desires, no joys, no life, but you;
When half the globe was mine, I gave it you
In dowry with my heart; I had no use,
No fruit of all, but you: A friend and mistress
Was what the world could give. Oh, Cleopatra!
Oh, Dolabella! how could you betray
This tender heart, which with an infant-fondness
Lay lull'd betwixt your bosoms, and there slept
Secure of injured faith?

Dola. If she has wronged you,
Heaven, hell, and you revenge it.

Ant. If she has wronged me!
Thou would'st evade thy part of guilt; but swear
Thou lov'st not her.

Dola. Not so as I love you.   [her.

Ant. Not so! swear, swear, I say, thou dost not love

Dola. No more than friendship will allow.

Ant. No more?
Friendship allows thee nothing.   Thou art perjured——
And yet thou did'st not swear thou loved'st her not;
But not so much, no more.   Oh, trifling hypocrite,
Who dar'st not own to her thou dost not love,
Nor own to me thou dost!   Ventidius heard it;
Octavia saw it.

Cleo. They are enemies.

Ant. Alexas is not so: he, he confessed it;
He who, next hell, best knew it, he avowed it.
Why do I seek a proof beyond yourself,   [*To Dola.*
You whom I sent to bear my last farewell,
Returned to plead her stay.

Dola. What shall I answer?
If to have loved be guilt, then I have sinned;
But if to have repented of that love
Can wash away my crime, I have repented.
Yet, if I have offended past forgiveness,
Let her not suffer: she is innocent.

Cleo. Ah, what will not a woman do who loves!
What means will she refuse, to keep that heart
Where all her joys are placed!   'Twas I encouraged,
'Twas I blew up the fire that scorched his soul,
To make you jealous, and by that regain you.
But all in vain; I could not counterfeit:
In spite of all the dams, my love broke o'er,
And drowned my heart again.   Fate took the occasion;
And thus one minute's feigning has destroyed
My whole life's truth.

Ant. Thin cobweb arts of falsehood;
Seen, and broke through at first.

Dola. Forgive your mistress.

Cleo. Forgive your friend.

Ant. You have convinced yourselves.
You plead each other's cause: what witness have you,
That you but meant to raise my jealousy?

Cleo. Ourselves and Heaven.

Ant. Guilt witnesses for guilt.   Hence love and friend-
You have no longer place in human breasts.   [ship!
These two have driven you out.   Avoid my sight;
I would not kill the man whom I have loved,

And cannot hurt the woman; but avoid me;
I do not know how long I can be tame,
For if I stay one minute more to think
How I am wronged, my justice and revenge
Will cry so loud within me, that my pity
Will not be heard for either.

    Dola. Heaven has but
Our sorrow for our sins; and then delights
To pardon erring man; sweet mercy seems
Its darling attribute, which limits justice;
As if there were degrees in infinite,
And infinite would rather want perfection,
Than punish to extent.

    Ant. I can forgive
A foe, but not a mistress and a friend;
Treason is there in its most horrid shape,
Where trust is greatest; and the soul resigned
Is stabbed by its own guards. I'll hear no more;
Hence from my sight, for ever.

    Cleo. How? for ever!
I cannot go one moment from your sight,
And must I go for ever?
My joys, my only joys, are centred here;
What place have I to go to? my own kingdom?
That I have lost for you; or to the Romans?
They hate me for your sake; or must I wander
The wide world o'er, a helpless, banished woman?
Banished for love of you; banished from you;
Ay, there's the banishment! Oh, hear me; hear me
With strictest justice, for I beg no favour;
And if I have offended you, then kill me,
But do not banish me.

    Ant. I must not hear you.
I have a fool within me takes your part;
But honour stops my ears.

    Cleo. For pity hear me!
Would you cast off a slave who followed you,
Who crouched beneath your spurn?—— He has no pity!
See, if he gives one tear to my departure;
One look, one kind farewell! Oh, iron heart!
Let all the gods look down, and judge betwixt us,
If he did ever love!

Ant. No more : Alexas !

Dola. A perjured villain !

Ant. [*To Cleo.*] Your Alexas ; yours.

Cleo. O 'twas his plot : his ruinous design
To engage you in my love by jealousy.
Hear him ; confront him with me ; let him speak.

Ant. I have ; I have.

Cleo. And if he clear me not——

Ant. Your creature ! one who hangs upon your smiles !
Watches your eye, to say or to unsay
Whate'er you please ! I am not to be moved.

Cleo. Then, must we part ?   Farewell, my cruel lord.
The appearance is against me ; and I go,
Unjustified, for ever from your sight.
How I have loved, you know ; how I yet love,
My only comfort is, I know myself ;
I love you more, e'en now you are unkind,
Than when you loved me most ; so well, so truly,
I'll never strive against it, but die pleased
To think you once were mine.

Ant. Good Heaven, they weep at parting.
Must I weep too ? that calls them innocent.
I must not weep ; and yet I must, to think
That I must not forgive——
Live ; but live wretched, 'tis but just you should,
Who made me so : live from each other's sight ;
Let me not hear you meet.   Set all the earth,
And all the seas, betwixt your sundered loves ;
View nothing common but the sun and skies.
Now, all take several ways ;
And each your own sad fate with mine deplore ;
That you were false, and I could trust no more.

[*Exeunt severally.*

ACT V.   SCENE I.

Enter CLEOPATRA, CHARMION, *and* IRAS.

Char. Be juster, Heaven ; such virtue punished thus,
Will make us think that chance rules all above,
And shuffles, with a random hand, the lots
Which man is forced to draw.

Cleo. I could tear out these eyes that gained his heart,
And had not power to keep it.   Oh, the curse
Of doting on, e'en when I find it dotage !
Bear witness, gods, you heard him bid me go ;
You whom he mocked with imprecating vows
Of promised faith.   I'll die ; I will not bear it.
You may hold me——
          [*She pulls out her dagger, and they hold her.*
But I can keep my breath ; I can die inward,
And choke this love.

Enter ALEXAS.

Iras. Help, O Alexas, help !
The Queen grows desperate, her soul struggles in her,
With all the agonies of love and rage,
And strives to force its passage.
     Cleo. Let me go.
Art thou there, traitor ?—— O,
O, for a little breath, to vent my rage !
Give, give me way, and let me loose upon him.
     Alex. Yes, I deserve it, for my ill-timed truth.
Was it for me to prop
The ruins of a falling majesty ?
To place myself beneath the mighty flaw,
Thus to be crushed, and pounded into atoms,
By its o'erwhelming weight ?   'Tis too presuming
For subjects to preserve that wilful power
Which courts its own destruction.
     Cleo. I would reason
More calmly with you.   Did you not o'er-rule,
And force my plain, direct, and open love
Into these crooked paths of jealousy ?
Now, what's the event ?   Octavia is removed,
But Cleopatra's banished.   Thou, thou, villain,
Hast pushed my boat to open sea, to prove,
At my sad cost, if thou can'st steer it back.
It cannot be ; I'm lost too far—I'm ruined.
Hence, thou impostor ! traitor ! monster ! devil !——
I can no more : thou, and my griefs, have sunk
Me down so low, that I want voice to curse thee.
     Alex. Suppose some shipwrecked seaman near the shore,
Dropping and faint with climbing up the cliff,

If, from above, some charitable hand
Pull him to safety, hazarding himself
To draw the other's weight—would he look back
And curse him for his pains?   The case is yours ;
But one step more, and you have gained the height.
    Cleo. Sunk, never more to rise.
    Alex. Octavia's gone, and Dolabella banished.
Believe me, madam, Antony is yours.
His heart was never lost, but started off
To jealousy, love's last retreat and covert,
Where it lies hid in shades, watchful in silence,
And listening for the sound that calls it back.
Some other, any man ('tis so advanced),
May perfect this unfinished work, which I
(Unhappy only to myself) have left
So easy to his hand.
    Cleo. Look well thou do it : else——
    Alex. Else—what your silence threatens—Antony
Is mounted up the Pharos ; from whose turret,
He stands surveying our Egyptian galleys
Engaged with Cæsar's fleet ; now death or conquest.
If the first happen, fate acquits my promise,
If we o'ercome, the conqueror is yours.
                     [*A distant shout within.*
    Char. Have comfort, madam ; did you mark that
        shout ?   [*Second shout nearer.*
    Iras. Hark ! they redouble it.
    Alex. 'Tis from the port.
The loudness shows it near ; good news, kind heavens.
    Cleo. Osiris make it so.

Enter SERAPION.

    Serap. Where, where's the Queen ?
    Alex. How frightfully the holy coward stares !
As if not yet recovered of the assault,
When all his gods, and, what's more dear to him,
His offerings were at stake.
    Serap. O, horror, horror !
Egypt has been ; our latest hour has come :
The Queen of Nations from her ancient seat
Is sunk for ever in the dark abyss.
Time has unrolled her glories to the last,
And now closed up the volume.

Cleo. Be more plain:
Say whence thou cam'st (though Fate is in thy face;
Which from thy haggard eyes looks wildly out,
And threatens ere thou speak'st).
    Serap. I came from Pharos:
From viewing (spare me, and imagine it)
Our land's last hope, your navy——
    Cleo. Vanquished?
    Serap. No.
They fought not.
    Cleo. Then they fled.
    Serap. Nor that. I saw,
With Antony, your well-appointed fleet
Row out; and thrice he waved his hand on high,
And thrice with cheerful cries they shouted back;
'Twas then false fortune, like a fawning strumpet,
About to leave the bankrupt prodigal,
With a dissembled smile would kiss at parting,
And flatter to the last; the well-timed oars
Now dipt from every bank, now smoothly run
To meet the foe; and soon, indeed, they met,
But not as foes. In few, we saw their caps
On either side thrown up; the Egyptian galleys
(Received like friends) pass'd through, and fell behind
The Roman rear; and now they all come forward,
And ride within the port.
    Cleo. Enough, Serapion;
I've heard my doom. This needed not, you gods;
When I lost Antony, your work was done;
'Tis but superfluous malice. Where's my lord?
How bears he this last blow?
    Serap. His fury cannot be expressed by words:
Thrice he attempted headlong to have fallen
Full on his foes, and aimed at Cæsar's galley;
Withheld, he raves on you; cries, he's betrayed.
Should he now find you——
    Alex. Shun him, seek your safety,
Till you can clear your innocence.
    Cleo. I'll stay.
    Alex. You must not; haste you to your monument,
While I make speed to Cæsar.
    Cleo. Cæsar! no,
I have no business with him.

Alex. I can work him
To spare your life, and let this madman perish.
  Cleo. Base, fawning wretch! would'st thou betray him
Hence, from my sight; I will not hear a traitor.   [too!
'Twas thy design brought all this ruin on us;
Serapion, thou art honest: counsel me;
But haste, each moment's precious.
  Serap. Retire; you must not yet see Antony.
He who began this mischief,
'Tis just he tempt the danger.   Let him clear you;
And, since he offered you his servile tongue,
To gain a poor precarious life from Cæsar,
Let him expose that fawning eloquence,
And speak to Antony.
  Alex. O Heavens! I dare not,
I meet my certain death.
  Cleo. Slave, thou deserv'st it.
Not that I fear my lord will I avoid him;
I know him noble; when he banished me,
And thought me false, he scorned to take my life,
But I'll be justified, and then die with him.
  Alex. Oh, pity me, and let me follow you.
  Cleo. To death, if thou stir hence.   Speak, if thou can'st.
Now for thy life, which basely thou would'st save;
While mine I prize at this.   Come, good Serapion.
                    [*Exeunt* CLEO. SERAP. CHAR. *and* IRAS.
  Alex. Oh that I less could fear to lose this being,
Which, like a snow-ball, in my coward hand,
The more 'tis grasped, the faster melts away.
Poor reason! what a wretched aid art thou!
For still, in spite of thee,
These two long lovers, soul and body, dread
Their final separation.   Let me think:
What can I say to save myself from death?
No matter what becomes of Cleopatra.
  Ant. [*Within.*] Which way? where?
  Vent. [*Within.*] This leads to the monument.
  Alex. Ah me! I hear him; yet I'm unprepared;
My gift of lying's gone,
And this court-devil, which I so oft have raised,
Forsakes me at my need.   I dare not stay;
Yet cannot far go hence.   [*Exit.*
                    F

Enter ANTONY *and* VENTIDIUS.

Ant. O happy Cæsar! thou hast men to lead.
Think not 'tis thou hast conquered Antony;
But Rome has conquered Egypt. I'm betrayed.
  Vent. Curse on this treacherous train!
Their soil and heaven infect them with all baseness;
And their young souls come tainted to the world
With the first breath they draw.
  Ant. The original villain sure no god created;
He was a bastard of the Sun, by Nile,
Ap'd into man, with all his mother's mud
Crusted about his soul.
  Vent. The nation is
One universal traitor, and their Queen
The very spirit and extract of them all.
  Ant. Is there yet left
A possibility of aid from valour?
Is there one god unsworn to my destruction?
The least unmortgaged hope? for, if there be,
Methinks I cannot fall beneath the fate
Of such a boy as Cæsar.
The world's one half is yet in Antony;
And from each limb of it that hewed away,
The soul comes back to me.
  Vent. There yet remain
Three legions in the town. The last assault
Lopt off the rest. If death be your design,
As I must wish it now, these are sufficient
To make a heap about us of dead foes,
An honest pile for burial.
  Ant. They're enough.
We'll not divide our stars; but side by side
Fight emulous, and with malicious eyes
Survey each other's acts; so every death
Thou giv'st, I'll take on me as a just debt,
And pay thee in a soul.
  Vent. Now you shall see I love you. Not a word
Of chiding more. By my few hours of life,
I am so pleased with this brave Roman fate,
That I would not be Cæsar, to outlive you.
When we put off this flesh and mount together,

I shall be shown to all the ethereal crowd:
Lo! this is he who died with Antony.   [troops,
    Ant. Who knows but we may pierce through all their
And reach my veterans yet? 'Tis worth the tempting,
To o'er-leap this gulph of fate,
And leave our wondering destinies behind.

Enter ALEXAS, *trembling.*

    Vent. See, see, that villain;
See Cleopatra stamped upon that face,
With all her cunning, all her arts of falsehood!
How she looks out through those dissembling eyes!
How he has set his countenance for deceit;
And promises a lie before he speaks!
Let me despatch him first.   [*Drawing.*
    Alex. Oh spare me, spare me.
    Ant. Hold! he's not worth your killing.   On thy life,
(Which thou may'st keep, because I scorn to take it),
No syllable to justify thy Queen;
Save thy base tongue its office.
    Alex. Sir, she's gone,
Where she shall never be molested more
By love, or you.
    Ant. Fled to her Dolabella!
Die, traitor! I revoke my promise; die!
                [*Going to kill him.*
    Alex. Oh, hold! she is not fled.
    Ant. She is; my eyes
Are open to her falsehood; my whole life
Has been a golden dream of love and friendship.
But, now I wake, I'm like a merchant roused
From soft repose to see his vessel sinking,
And all his wealth cast o'er.   Ungrateful woman!
Who followed me but as the swallow summer,
Hatching her young ones in my kindly beams,
Singing her flatteries to my morning wake.
But, now my winter comes, she spreads her wings,
And seeks the spring of Cæsar.
    Alex. Think not so;
Her fortunes have in all things mixed with yours.
Had she betrayed her naval force to Rome,
How easily might she have gone to Cæsar,
Secure by such a bribe!

Vent. She sent it first,
To be more welcome after.

Ant. 'Tis too plain;
Else would she have appeared to clear herself.

Alex. Too fatally she has; she could not bear
To be accused by you; but shut herself
Within her monument, looked down and sighed;
While, from her unchanged face, the silent tears
Dropp'd, as they had not leave, but stole their parting.
Some undistinguished words she inly murmured;
At last, she raised her eyes; and, with such looks
As dying Lucrece cast——

Ant. My heart forebodes——

Vent. All for the best; go on.

Alex. She snatched her poniard,
And, ere we could prevent the fatal blow,
Plunged it within her breast: Then turned to me,
Go, bear my lord (said she) my last farewell;
And ask him if he yet suspect my faith.
More she was saying, but death rushed betwixt.
She half pronounced your name with her last breath,
And buried half within her.

Vent. Heaven be praised!

Ant. Then, art thou innocent, my poor dear love?
And art thou dead?
O, these two words! their sound should be divided:
Had'st thou been false, and died; or had'st thou lived,
And had'st been true—— But innocence and death!
This shows not well above.   Then what am I?
The murderer of this truth, this innocence!
Thoughts cannot form themselves in words so horrid
As can express my guilt!

Vent. Is't come to this?   The gods have been too
And thus you thank them for't.   [gracious;

Ant. [*To Alex.*] Why stay'st thou here?
Is it for thee to spy upon my soul,
And see its inward mourning?   Get thee hence;
Thou art not worthy to behold what now
Becomes a Roman Emperor to perform.

Alex. He loves her still: [*Aside.*
His grief betrays it.   Good! the joy to find
She's yet alive, completes the reconcilement.

I've saved myself and her.   But oh, the Romans !
Fate comes too fast upon my wit,
Hunts me too hard, and meets me at each double.   [*Exit.*

Vent. Would she had died a little sooner, though,
Before Octavia went ; you might have treated :
Now 'twill look tame, and would not be received.
Come, rouse yourself, and let's die warm together.

Ant. I will not fight ; there's no more work for war.
The business of my angry hours is done.

Vent. Cæsar is at your gates.

Ant. Why, let him enter ;
He's welcome now.

Vent. What lethargy has crept into your soul ?

Ant. 'Tis but a scorn of life, and just desire
To free myself from bondage.

Vent. Do it bravely.

Ant. I will ; but not by fighting.   O, Ventidius !
What should I fight for now ?   My Queen is dead.
I was but great for her ; my power, my empire,
Were but my merchandise to buy her love ;
And conquered kings, my factors.   Now she's dead,
Let Cæsar take the world—
An empty circle, since the jewel's gone
Which made it worth my strife.   My being's nauseous,
For all the bribes of life are gone away.

Vent. Would you be taken ?

Ant. Yes, I would be taken ;
But, as a Roman ought—dead, my Ventidius !
For I'll convey my soul from Cæsar's reach,
And lay down life myself.   'Tis time the world
Should have a lord, and know whom to obey.
We two have kept its homage in suspense,
And bent the globe on whose each side we trod,
Till it was dinted inwards.   Let him walk
Alone upon't ; I'm weary of my part.
My torch is out ; and the world stands before me
Like a black desert at the approach of night.
I'll lay me down, and stray no farther on.

Vent. I could be grieved,
But that I'll not out-live you.   Choose your death ;
For I have seen him in such various shapes,
I care not which I take.   I'm only troubled,

The life I bear is worn to such a rag,
'Tis scarce worth giving.   I could wish, indeed,
We threw it from us with a better grace ;
That, like a lion taken in the toils,
We might at least thrust out our paws, and wound
The hunters that enclose us.
    Ant. I have thought on't.
Ventidius, you must live.
    Vent. I must not, sir.
    Ant. Wilt thou not live to speak some good of me?
To stand by my fair fame, and guard the approaches
From the ill tongues of men ?
    Vent. Who shall guard mine
For living after you ?
    Ant. Say, I command it.
    Vent. If we die well, our deaths will speak themselves,
And need no living witness.
    Ant. Thou hast loved me,
And fain I would reward thee.   I must die ;
Kill me, and take the merit of my death
To make thee friends with Cæsar.
    Vent. Thank your kindness.
You said I loved you, and, in recompense,
You bid me turn a traitor ; did I think
You would have used me thus ? that I should die
With a hard thought of you ?
    Ant. Forgive me, Roman.
Since I have heard of Cleopatra's death
My reason bears no rule upon my tongue,
But lets my thoughts break all at random out :
I've thought better ; do not deny me twice.
    Vent. By Heaven, I will not,
Let it not be to out-live you.
    Ant. Kill me first,
And then die thou ; for 'tis but just thou serve
Thy friend before thyself.
    Vent. Give me your hand.
We soon shall meet again.   Now, farewell, Emperor.
                            [Embraces.
Methinks that word's too cold to be my last ;
Since death sweeps all distinctions, farewell, friend.
That's all——

I will not make a business of a trifle ;
And yet I cannot look on you, and kill you.
Pray turn your face.
    Ant. I do ; strike home, be sure.
    Vent. Home, as my sword will reach.   [*Kills himself.*
    Ant. O, thou mistak'st ;
That wound was none of thine : give it me back ;
Thou robb'st me of my death.
    Vent. I do indeed ;
But, think 'tis the first time I e'er deceived you ;
If that may plead my pardon.   And you, gods,
Forgive me, if you will ; for I die perjured,
Rather than kill my friend.   [*Dies.*
    Ant. Farewell.   Ever my leader, even in death !
My Queen and thou have got the start of me ;
And I'm the lag of honour—— Gone so soon ?
Is death no more ? He used him carelessly,
With a familiar kindness ; ere he knocked,
Ran to the door, and took him in his arms,
As who should say, You're welcome at all hours,
A friend need give no warning.   Books had spoiled him ;
For all the learned are cowards by profession.
'Tis not worth
My further thought ; for death, for aught I know,
Is but to think no more.   Here's to be satisfied.
                     [*Falls on his sword.*
I've miss'd my heart.   O, unperforming hand !
Thou never could'st have err'd in a worse time.
My fortune jades me to the last ; and Death,
Like a great man, takes state, and makes me wait
For my admittance——   [*Trampling within.*
Some perhaps from Cæsar ;
If he should find me living, and suspect
That I played booty with my life !   I'll mend
My work, ere they can reach me.   [*Rises upon his knees.*

   Enter CLEOPATRA, CHARMION, *and* IRAS.

    Cleo. Where is my lord ? where is he ?
    Char. There he lies,
And dead Ventidius by him.
    Cleo. My fears were prophets ; I am come too late.
O that accurs'd Alexas !   [*Runs to him.*

Ant. Art thou living?
Or am I dead before I knew? and thou
The first kind ghost that meets me?
   Cleo. Help me seat him.
Send quickly, send for help.　　[*They place him in a chair.*
   Ant. I am answered.
We live both.　Sit thee down, my Cleopatra:
I'll make the most I can of life, to stay
A moment more with thee.
   Cleo. How is it with you?
   Ant. 'Tis as with a man
Removing in a hurry; all packed up,
But one dear jewel that his haste forgot;
And he, for that, returns upon the spur:
So I come back, for thee.
   Cleo. Too long, ye heavens, you have been cruel to me;
Now show your mended faith, and give me back
His fleeting life.
   Ant. It will not be, my love.
I keep my soul by force.
Say but thou art not false.
   Cleo. 'Tis now too late
To say I'm true: I'll prove it, and die with you.
Unknown to me, Alexas feigned my death,
Which, when I knew, I hasted to prevent
This fatal consequence.　My fleet betrayed
Both you and me.
   Ant. And Dolabella——
   Cleo. Scarce esteemed before he loved; but hated now.
   Ant. Enough: my life's not long enough for more.
Thou sayest thou wilt come after: I believe thee;
For I can now believe whate'er thou sayest,
That we may part more kindly.
   Cleo. I will come:
Doubt not, my life, I'll come, and quickly too;
Cæsar shall triumph o'er no part of thee.
   Ant. But grieve not, while thou stayest,
My last disastrous times;
Think we have had a clear and glorious day;
And Heaven did kindly to delay the storm
Just till our close of evening.　Ten years love,
And not a moment lost, but all improved

To the utmost joys: what ages have we lived!
And now to die each other's; and, so dying,
While hand in hand we walk in groves below,
Whole troops of lovers' ghosts shall flock about us,
And all the train be ours.

Cleo. Your words are like the notes of dying swans,
Too sweet to last. Were there so many hours
For your unkindness, and not one for love?

Ant. No, not a minute—this one kiss—more worth
Than all I leave to Cæsar. [*Dies.*

Cleo. O, tell me so again,
And take ten thousand kisses for that word.
My lord, my lord: speak if you yet have being;
Sigh to me, if you cannot speak; or cast
One look: do anything that shows you live.

Iras. He's gone too far to hear you;
And this you see, a lump of senseless clay,
The leavings of a soul.

Char. Remember, madam,
He charged you not to grieve.

Cleo. And I'll obey him.
I have not loved a Roman, not to know
What should become his wife—his wife, my Charmion;
For 'tis to that high title I aspire,
And now I'll not die less. Let dull Octavia
Survive, to mourn him dead: my noble fate
Shall knit our spousals with a tie too strong
For Roman laws to break.

Iras. Will you then die?

Cleo. Why should'st thou make that question?

Iras. Cæsar is merciful.

Cleo. Let him be so
To those that want his mercy: my poor lord
Made no such covenant with him, to spare me
When he was dead. Yield me to Cæsar's pride?
What, to be led in triumph through the streets,
A spectacle to base plebeian eyes;
While some dejected friend of Antony's,
Close in a corner, shakes his head, and mutters
A secret curse on her who ruined him?
I'll none of that.

Char. Whatever you resolve,
I'll follow even to death.

Iras. I only feared
For you; but more should fear to live without you.
  Cleo. Why, now 'tis as it should be. Quick, my friends,
Despatch; ere this the town's in Cæsar's hands:
My lord looks down concerned, and fears my stay,
Lest I should be surprised;
Keep him not waiting for his love too long.
You, Charmion, bring my crown and richest jewels,
With them, the wreath of victory I made
(Vain augury!) for him who now lies dead;
You, Iras, bring the cure of all our ills.
  Iras. The aspicks, madam?
  Cleo. Must I bid you twice?   [*Ex.* CHAR. *and* IRAS.
'Tis sweet to die, when they would force life on me,
To rush into the dark abode of death,
And seize him first; if he be like my love,
He is not frightful sure.
We're now alone, in secrecy and silence;
And is not this like lovers? I may kiss
These pale, cold lips; Octavia does not see me;
And, oh! 'tis better far to have him thus,
Than see him in her arms—— O welcome, welcome.

Enter CHARMION *and* IRAS.

  Char. What must be done?
  Cleo. Short ceremony, friends;
But yet it must be decent. First, this laurel
Shall crown my hero's head; he fell not basely,
Nor left his shield behind him.   Only thou
Could'st triumph o'er thy self; and thou alone
Wert worthy so to triumph.
  Char. To what end
These ensigns of your pomp and royalty?
  Cleo. Dull, that thou art! why, 'tis to meet my love;
As when I saw him first, on Cydnos bank,
All sparkling, like a goddess; so adorned,
I'll find him once again: my second spousals
Shall match my first, in glory.   Haste, haste, both,
And dress the bride of Antony.
  Char. 'Tis done.
  Cleo. Now set me by my lord, I claim this place;
For I must conquer Cæsar too, like him,

And win my share o' the world.   Hail, you dear relics
Of my immortal love!
O let no impious hand remove you hence,
But rest for ever here; let Egypt give
His death that peace which it denied his life.
Reach me the casket.
   Iras. Underneath the fruit the aspick lies.
   Cleo. Welcome, thou kind deceiver!
                       [Putting aside the leaves.
Thou best of thieves, who, with an easy key,
Dost open life, and, unperceived by us,
Even steal us from ourselves: discharging so
Death's dreadful office, better than himself,
Touching our limbs so gently into slumber,
That death stands by, deceived by his own image,
And thinks himself but sleep.
   Serap. [*Within.*] The Queen, where is she?
The town is yielded, Cæsar's at the gates.
   Cleo. He comes too late to invade the rights of death.
Haste, bare my arm, and rouse the serpent's fury.
               [Holds out her arm, and draws it back.
Coward flesh——
Would'st thou conspire with Cæsar to betray me
As thou wert none of mine? I'll force thee to it,
And not be sent by him,
But bring myself my soul to Antony.
        [Turns aside, and then shows her arm bloody.
Take hence; the work is done.
   Serap. [*Within.*] Break open the door,
And guard the traitor well.
   Char. The next is ours.
   Iras. Now, Charmion, to be worthy
Of our great Queen and mistress. [*They apply the aspicks.*
   Cleo. Already, death, I feel thee in my veins;
I go with such a will to find my Lord,
That we shall quickly meet.
A heavy numbness creeps through every limb.
And now 'tis at my head: my eye-lids fall,
And my dear love is vanished in a mist.
Where shall I find him, where? O turn me to him,
And lay me on his breast—Cæsar, thy worst;
Now part us, if thou canst.   *[Dies.*

[IRAS *sinks down at her feet, and dies;* CHARMION
stands behind her chair, as dressing her head.

Enter SERAPION, *two Priests,* ALEXAS *bound,* EGYPTIANS.

2 Priests. Behold, Serapion, what havoc death has
Serap. 'Twas what I feared. [made!
Charmion, is this well done?
Char. Yes, 'tis well done, and like a Queen, the last
Of her great race: I follow her. [*Sinks down; dies.*
Alex. 'Tis true,
She has done well; much better thus to die,
Than live to make a holiday in Rome.
Serap. See, how the lovers sit in state together,
As they were giving laws to half mankind.
The impression of a smile left in her face,
Shows she died pleased with him for whom she lived,
And went to charm him in another world.
Cæsar's just entering; grief has now no leisure.
Secure that villain, as our pledge of safety,
To grace the Imperial triumph. Sleep, blest pair,
Secure from human chance, long ages out,
While all the storms of fate fly o'er your tomb;
   And fame, to late posterity, shall tell,
   No lovers lived so great, or died so well. [*Exeunt.*

EPILOGUE.

Poets, like disputants, when reasons fail,
Have one sure refuge left, and that's to rail.
Fop, coxcomb, fool, are thundered through the pit,
And this is all their equipage of wit.
We wonder how the devil this difference grows,
Betwixt our fools in verse, and yours in prose;
For, faith, the quarrel rightly understood,
'Tis civil war with their own flesh and blood.
The threadbare author hates the gaudy coat,
And swears at the gilt coach, but swears afoot:
For 'tis observed of every scribbling man,
He grows a fop as fast as e'er he can;
Prunes up, and asks his oracle, the glass,
If pink or purple best become his face.

For our poor wretch, he neither rails nor prays,
Nor likes your wit just as you like his plays;
He has not yet so much of Mr. Bays.
He does his best; and if he cannot please,
Would quietly sue out his writ of ease.
Yet, if he might his own grand jury call,
By the fair sex he begs to stand or fall.
Let Cæsar's power the men's ambition move,
But grace you him who lost the world for love.
Yet if some antiquated lady say,
The last age is not copied in his play;
Heaven help the man who for that face must drudge,
Which only has the wrinkles of a judge.
Let not the young and beauteous join with those;
For should you raise such numerous hosts of foes,
Young wits and sparks he to his aid must call;
'Tis more than one man's work to please you all.

DON SEBASTIAN,

KING OF PORTUGAL.

DRAMATIS PERSONÆ.

———

DON SEBASTIAN, *King of Portugal.*

MULEY-MOLUCH, *Emperor of Barbary.*

DORAX, *a Noble Portuguese, now a Renegade, formerly Don Alonza de Sylvera, Alcade, or Governor, of Alcazar.*

BENDUCAR, *Chief Minister, and favourite of the Emperor.*

ABDALLA, *the Mufti.*

MULEY-ZEYDAN, *Brother to the Emperor.*

DON ANTONIA, *a young, noble Portuguese, now a Slave.*

DON ALVAREZ, *an old Councillor to Don Sebastian, now a Slave also.*

MUSTAPHA, *Captain of the Rabble.*

ALMEYDA, *a Captive Queen of Barbary.*

MORAYMA, *Daughter to the Mufti.*

JOHAYMA, *Chief wife to the Mufti.*

Two Merchants.

Rabble.

A Servant to Benducar.

A Servant to the Mufti.

———

"Commonly esteemed either the first or second of Dryden's dramatic performances."—JOHNSON, *Lives of the Poets.*

"Brought out in 1690; it was his first appearance on the stage after the Revolution, which had deprived him of Court favour, and of his offices of Poet Laureate and Historiographer-Royal."—CHRISTIE, Editor of *Dryden's Poems,* Globe Edition.

DON SEBASTIAN,

KING OF PORTUGAL.

PROLOGUE.

THE judge removed, though he's no more my lord,
May plead at bar, or at the council board ;
So may cast poets write ; there's no pretension
To argue loss of wit, from loss of pension.
Your looks are cheerful ; and in all this place
I see not one that wears a damning face.
The British nation is too brave to show
Ignoble vengeance on a vanquished foe.
At least be civil to the wretch imploring ;
And lay your paws upon him without roaring.
Suppose our poet was your foe before ;
Yet now, the business of the field is o'er ;
'Tis time to let your civil wars alone,
When troops are into winter quarters gone.
Jove was alike to Latian and to Phrygian,
And you well know a play's of no religion.
Take good advice, and please yourselves this day,
No matter from whose hands you have the play.
Among good fellows every health will pass,
That serves to carry round another glass:
When, with full bowls of Burgundy you dine,
Though at the mighty monarch you repine,
You grant him still most Christian in his wine.
  Thus far the poet ; but his brains grow addle :
And all the rest is purely from this noddle.
You've seen young ladies at the Senate door,
Prefer petitions, and your grace implore ;
However grave the legislators were,
Their cause went ne'er the worse for being fair.
Reasons as weak as theirs, perhaps, I bring ;
But I could bribe you with as good a thing.

I heard him make advances of good nature,
That he, for once, would sheath his cutting satire :
Sign but his peace, he vows he'll ne'er again
The sacred names of fops and beaux profane.
Strike up the bargain quickly, for I swear,
As times go now, he offers very fair.
Be not too hard on him with statutes neither ;
Be kind, and do not set your teeth together,
To stretch the laws, as cobblers do their leather.
Horses by Papists are not to be ridden,
But sure the muses' horse was ne'er forbidden.
For in no rate-book it was ever found
That Pegasus was valued at five pound ;
Fine him to daily drudging and inditing,
And let him pay his taxes out in writing.

ACT I.   Scene I.

*The Scene at Alcazar, representing a Market-place under
the Castle.*

Enter Muley-Zeydan *and* Benducar.

Mul. Zeyd. Now Africa's long wars are at an end,
And our parch'd earth is drenched in Christian blood ;
My conquering brother will have slaves enough
To pay his cruel vows for victory.
What hear you of Sebastian, King of Portugal ?
  Bend. He fell among a heap of slaughtered Moors ;
Though yet his mangled carcass is not found.
The rival of our threatened empire, Mahomet,
Was hot pursued : and in the general rout,
Mistook a swelling current for a ford,
And in Mucazer's flood was seen to rise.
Thrice was he seen ; at length his courser plunged,
And threw him off ; the waves whelm'd over him,
And, helpless in his heavy arms, he drowned.
  Mul. Zeyd. Thus, then, a doubtful title is extinguished ;
Thus Moluch, still the favourite of fate,
Swims in a sanguine torrent to the throne,
As if our Prophet only worked for him ;
The heavens and all the stars are his hired servants,

As Muley-Zeydan were not worth their care,
And younger brothers but the draff of nature.
Bend. Be still, and learn the soothing arts of Court;
Adore his fortune, mix with flattering crowds,
And when they praise him most, be you the loudest;
Your brother is luxurious, close, and cruel,
Generous by fits, but permanent in mischief.
The shadow of a discontent would ruin us;
We must be safe before we can be great.
These things observed, leave me to shape the rest.
Mul. Zeyd. You have the key; he opens inward to you.
Bend. So often tried, and ever found so true,
Has given me trust, and trust has given me means
Once to be false for all. I trust not him:
For, now his ends are served, and he grown absolute,
How am I sure to stand who served those ends?
I know your nature open, mild, and grateful;
In such a prince the people may be blest,
And I be safe.
Mul. Zeyd. My father!   [*Embracing him.*
Bend. My future King, auspicious Muley-Zeydan,
Shall I adore you? No, the place is public;
I worship you within, the outward act
Shall be reserved till nations follow me,
And Heaven shall envy you the kneeling world.
You know the Alcade of Alcazar, Dorax?
Mul. Zeyd. The gallant renegade, you mean?
Bend. The same.
That gloomy outside, like a rusty chest,
Contains the shining treasure of a soul
Resolved and brave; he has the soldiers' hearts,
And time shall make him ours.
Mul. Zeyd. He's just upon us.
Bend. I know him from afar,
By the long stride, and by the sullen port:
Retire my lord.
Wait on your brother's triumph, yours is next,
His growth is but a wild and fruitless plant,
I'll cut his barren branches to the stock,
And graft you on to bear.
Mul. Zeyd. My oracle!   [*Exit* MUL. ZEYD.
Bend. Yes, to delude your hopes, poor credulous fool,

To think that I would give away the fruit
Of so much toil, such guilt, and such damnation;
If I am damn'd it shall be for myself:
This easy fool must be my stale, set up
To catch the people's eyes; he's tame and merciful,
Him I can manage, till I make him odious
By some unpopular act, and then dethrone him.

Enter DORAX.

Now Dorax!
    Dor. Well, Benducar!
    Bend. Bare Benducar!
    Dor. Thou wouldst have titles, take them then, Chief
First Hangman of the State.   [Minister,
    Bend. Some call me favourite.
    Dor. What's that, his minion?
Thou art too old to be a catamite!
Now prithee tell me, and abate thy pride,
Is not Benducar bare a better name,
In a friend's mouth, than all those gaudy titles.
Which I disdain to give the man I love?
    Bend. But always out of humour——
    Dor. I have cause,
Though all mankind is cause enough for satire.
    Bend. Why, then, thou hast revenged thee on mankind;
They say, in fight thou hadst a thirsty sword,
And well 'twas glutted there.
    Dor. I spitted frogs, I crushed a heap of emmets,
A hundred of them to a single soul,
And that but scanty weight too. The great devil
Scarce thanked me for my pains; he swallows the vulgar
Like whipped cream, feels them not in going down.
    Bend. Brave renegade! couldst thou not meet Sebastian?
Thy master had been worthy of thy sword.
    Dor. My master? By what title?
Because I happened to be born where he
Happened to be King? And yet I served him,
Nay, I was fool enough to love him too. .
You know my story, how I was rewarded
For fifteen hard campaigns, still hooped in iron,
And why I turned Mahometan. I'm grateful;
But whosoever dares to injure me,
Let that man know, I dare to be revenged.

Bend. Still you run off from bias; say what moves
Your present spleen?
Dor. You marked not what I told you;
I killed not one that was his Maker's image;
I met with none but vulgar two-legged brutes,
Sebastian was my aim; he was a man.
Nay, though he hated me, and I hate him,
Yet I must do him right; he was a man,
Above man's height, even towering to divinity;
Brave, pious, generous, great, and liberal,
Just as the scales of Heaven that weigh the seasons.
He loved his people, him they idolized;
And thence proceeds my mortal hatred to him,
That thus unblameable to all besides,
He erred to me alone.
His goodness was diffused to human kind,
And all his cruelty confined to me.
   Bend. You could not meet him then?
   Dor. No, though I fought
Where ranks fell thickest; 'twas, indeed, the place
To seek Sebastian. Through a track of death
I followed him, by groans of dying foes,
But still I came too late, for he was flown
Like lightning, swift before me to new slaughters.
I mowed across, and made irregular harvest,
Defaced the pomp of battle, but in vain,
For he was still supplying death elsewhere.
This mads me, that perhaps ignoble hands
Have overlaid him, for they could not conquer:
Murdered by multitudes, whom I alone
Had right to slay; I too would have been slain,
That catching hold upon his flitting ghost,
I might have robbed him of his opening heaven,
And dragged him down with me, spite of predestination.
   Bend. 'Tis of as much import as Afric's worth,
To know what came of him, and of Almeyda,
The sister of the vanquished Mahomet,
Whose fatal beauty to her brother drew
The land's third part, as Lucifer did heaven's.
   Dor. I hope she died in her own female calling.
As for Sebastian, we must search the field,
And where we see a mountain of the slain,

Send one to climb, and looking down below,
There he shall find him at his manly length,
With his face up to heaven, in the red monument,
Which his true sword has digged.
    Bend. Yet we may possibly hear further news;
For while our Africans pursued the chase,
The captain of the rabble issued out,
With a black shirtless train to spoil the dead,
And seize the living.
    Dor. Each of them an host,
A million strong of vermin every villain;
No part of government, but lords of anarchy,
Chaos of power, and privileged destruction.
    Bend. Yet I must tell you, friend, the great must use
Sometimes as necessary tools of tumult.   [them,
    Dor. I would use them
Like dogs in times of plague, outlaws of nature,
Fit to be shot and brained, without a process,
To stop infection, that's their proper death.
    Bend. No more,
Behold the Emperor coming to survey
The slaves, in order to perform his vow.

    Enter MULEY-MOLUCH, *the Emperor, with attendants.*
        the MUFTI, *and* MULEY-ZEYDAN.

    Mul. Mol. Our armours now may rust, our idle scimitars
Hang by our sides for ornament, not use;
Children shall beat our atabals and drums,
And all the noisy trades of war no more
Shall wake the peaceful morn.   The Xeriff's blood
No longer in divided channels runs,
The younger house took end in Mahomet.
Nor shall Sebastian's formidable name
Be longer used, to lull the crying babe!
    Muf. For this victorious day our mighty prophet
Expects your gratitude, the sacrifice
Of Christian slaves, devoted, if you won.
    Mul. Mol. The purple present shall be richly paid;
That vow performed, fasting shall be abolished;
None ever served Heaven well with a starved face.
Preach abstinence no more; I tell thee Mufti,
Good feasting is devout.   And thou our head

Hast a religious, ruddy countenance.
We will have learned luxury; our lean faith
Gives scandal to the Christians; they feed high.
Then look for shoals of converts, when thou hast
Reformed us into feasting.

Muf. Fasting is but the letter of the law,
Yet it shows well to preach it to the vulgar.
Wine is against our law, that's literal too.
But not denied to Kings and to their guides;
Wine is a holy liquor for the great.

Dor. [*Aside.*] This Mufti in my conscience is some
English renegado, he talks so favourably of toping.

Mul. Mol. Bring forth the unhappy relics of the war.

Enter MUSTAPHA, *Captain of the Rabble, with his followers
of the Black Guard, &c., and other Moors. With
them a company of Portuguese slaves, without any
of the chief persons.*

Mul. Mol. These are not fit to pay an Emperor's vow;
Our bulls and rams had been more noble victims;
These are but garbage, not a sacrifice.

Muf. The prophet must not pick and choose his offerings;
Now he has given the day, 'tis past recalling,
And he must be content with such as these.   [masters.

Mul. Mol. But are these all? Speak you that are their
Must. All upon my honour. If you'll take them as
their fathers got them, so. If not, you must stay till
they get a better generation. These Christians are mere
bunglers; they procreate nothing but out of their own
wives, and these have all the looks of eldest sons.

Mul. Mol. Pain of your lives, let none conceal a
slave.

Must. Let every man look to his own conscience; I am
sure mine shall never hang me.

Bend. Thou speak'st as if thou wert privy to conceal-
ments; then thou art an accomplice.

Must. Nay, if accomplices must suffer, it may go hard
with me; but here's the devil on't: there's a great man,
and a holy man, too, concerned with me. Now, if I
confess, he'll be sure to escape between his greatness and
his holiness, and I shall be murdered because of my
poverty and rascality.

Muf. [*Winking at him.*] Then, if thy silence save the
    great and holy,
'Tis sure thou shalt go straight to Paradise.

Must. 'Tis a fine place, they say; but doctor, I am not
worthy on't; I am contented with this homely world; 'tis
good enough for such a poor rascally Mussulman as I am.
Besides, I have learned so much good manners, doctor, as
to let my betters be served before me.

Mul. Mol. Thou talk'st as if the Mufti were concerned.

Must. Your majesty may lay your soul on't. But for
my part, though I am a plain fellow, yet I scorn to be
tricked into Paradise. I would he should know it. The
truth on't is, an't like you, his reverence bought of me
the flower of all the market; these—these are but dogs-
meat to them; and a round price he paid me, too; I'll
say that for him; but not enough for me to venture my
neck for. If I get Paradise when my time comes, I can't
help myself; but I'll venture nothing beforehand upon a
blind bargain.

Mul. Mol. Where are those slaves? produce them.

Muf. They are not what he says.

Mul. Mol. No more excuses.

                    [*One goes out to fetch them.*
Know thou may'st better dally
With a dead prophet, than a living king.

Muf. I but reserved them to present thy greatness
An offering worthy thee.

Must. By the same token, there was a dainty virgin
(virgin, said I! but I would not be too positive of that,
neither), with a roguish leering eye! he paid me down
upon the nail a thousand golden sultanins, or he had
never had her, I can tell him that. Now, is it very
likely he would pay so dear for such a delicious morsel,
and give it away out of his own mouth; when it had
such a farewell with it too?

Enter SEBASTIAN *conducted in mean habit, with* ALVAREZ,
    ANTONIA, *and* ALMEYDA, *her face veiled with a
    barnus.*

Mul. Mol. Ay; these look like the workmanship of
This is the porcelain clay of human kind,   [heaven;
And therefore cast into these noble moulds.

Dor. [*Aside, while the Emperor whispers* BENDUCAR.] By
 all my wrongs,
'Tis he! Damnation seize me, but 'tis he!
My heart heaves up and swells; he's poison to me.
My injured honour and my ravished love
Bleed at their murderer's sight.
 Bend. [*To* DORAX *aside.*] The Emperor would learn
You know them.   [these prisoners' names;
 Dor. Tell him, no;
And trouble me no more—— I will not know them.
Shall I trust Heaven, that Heaven which I renounced,
            [*Aside.*
With my revenge? Then, where's my satisfaction?
No, it must be my own; I scorn a proxy.
 Mul. Mol. 'Tis decreed,
These of a better aspect, with the rest,
Shall share one common doom, and lots decide it.
For every numbered captive put a ball
Into an urn, three only black be there,
The rest, all white, are safe.
 Muf. Hold, sir, the woman must not draw.
 Mul. Mol. O Mufti,
We know your reason; let her share the danger.
 Muf. Our law says plainly, women have no souls.
 Mul. Mol. 'Tis true, their souls are mortal; set her by;
Yet, were Almeyda here, though fame reports her
The fairest of her sex, so much unseen
I hate the sister of our rival house,
Ten thousand such dry notions of our Alcoran
Should not protect her life; if not immortal,
Die as she could, all of a piece, the better
That none of her remain.

 [*Here is an urn brought in; the prisoners approach
  with great concernment, and amongst the rest* SEBAS-
  TIAN, ALVAREZ, *and* ANTONIA, *who come more cheerfully.*

 Dor. [*Aside.*] Poor abject creatures, how they fear to die!
These never knew one happy hour in life,
Yet shake to lay it down. Is load so pleasant?
Or has Heaven hid the happiness of death,
That men may dare to live?—— Now for our heroes.
          [*The three approach.*

O, these come up with spirits more resolved!
Old venerable Alvarez, well I know him,
The favourite once of this Sebastian's father;
Now Minister (too honest for his trade);
Religion bears him out, a thing taught young,
In age ill practised, yet his prop in death.
O, he has drawn a black; and smiles upon't,
As who should say, my faith and soul are white,
Though my lot swarthy.   Now, if there be hereafter,
He's bless'd; if not, well cheated, and dies pleased.

   Ant. [*Holding his lot in his clenched hand.*] Here I have
Be what thou wilt: I will not look too soon.   [thee,
Thou hast a colour; if thou prov'st not right,
I have a minute good ere I behold thee.
Now let me roll and grubble thee.
Blind men say white feels smooth, and black feels rough;
Thou hast a rugged skin; I do not like thee.

   Dor. There's the amorous airy spark, Antonia;
The wittiest woman's toy in Portugal.
Lord, what a loss of treats and serenades!
The whole she nation will be in mourning for him.

   Ant. I've a moist, sweaty palm, the more's my sin;
If it be black—yet only dyed—not odious,
Damned natural ebony—there's hopes in rubbing
To wash this Ethiop white.—— [*Looks.*] Pox of the
As black as hell—another lucky saying!   [proverb!
I think the devil's in me——good again,
I cannot speak one syllable, but tends
To death or to damnation.   [*Holds up his ball.*

   Dor. [*Aside.*] He looks uneasy at his future journey,
And wishes his boots off again, for fear
Of a bad road, and a worse inn at night.
Go to bed, fool, and take secure repose,
For thou shalt wake no more.

                [SEBASTIAN *comes up to draw.*

   Mul. Mol. [*To* BEND.] Mark him who now approaches
                       [to the lottery,
He looks secure of death, superior greatness,
Like Jove when he made fate, and said, Thou art
The slave of my creation; I admire him.

   Bend. He looks as man was made, with face erect,
That scorns his brittle corps, and seems ashamed

He's not all spirit; his eyes with a dumb pride
Accusing fortune that he fell not warm;
Yet now disdains to live.   [SEBASTIAN *draws a black.*
Mul. Mol. He has his wish;
And I have failed of mine.

Dor. [*Aside.*] Robb'd of my vengeance, by a trivial
Fine work above, that their anointed care   [chance.
Should die such little death; or did his genius
Know mine the stronger demon, feared the grapple,
And looking round him, found this nook of fate
To skulk behind my sword? Shall I discover him?
Still he would not die mine; no thanks to my
Revenge: reserved but to more royal shambles.
'Twere base, too, and below those vulgar souls
That shared his danger, yet not one disclosed him,
But struck with reverence, kept an awful silence.
I'll see no more of this; dog of a prophet!   [*Exit.*

Mul. Mol. One of these three is a whole hecatomb,
And therefore only one of them shall die.
The rest are but mute cattle; and when death
Comes like a rushing lion, couch like spaniels,
With lolling tongues, and tremble at the paw.
Let lots again decide it.
    [*The three draw again, and the lot falls on* SEBASTIAN.

Sebas. Then there's no more to manage! If I fall,
It shall be like myself; a setting sun
Should leave a track of glory in the skies.
Behold Sebastian, King of Portugal.

Mul. Mol. Sebastian! ha! it must be he; no other
Could represent such suffering majesty;
I saw him, as he terms himself, a sun
Struggling in dark eclipse, and shooting day
On either side of the black orb that veiled him.

Sebas. Not less even in this despicable now,
Than when my name filled Afric with afrights,
And froze your hearts beneath your torrid zone.

Bend. [*To* MUL. MOL.] Extravagantly brave! even to
Of greatness.   [an impudence

Sebas. Here satiate all your fury;
Let fortune empty her whole quiver on me,
I have a soul, that like an ample shield
Can take in all, and verge enough for more.

I would have conquered you; and ventured only
A narrow neck of land for a third world,
To give my loosened subjects room to play.
Fate was not mine,
Nor am I Fate's; now I have pleased my longing,
And trod the ground which I beheld from far,
I beg no pity for this mouldering clay!
For if you give it burial, there it takes
Possession of your earth;
If burn'd and scattered in the air, the winds
That strew my dust diffuse my royalty,
And spread me o'er your clime : for where one atom
Of mine shall light, know there Sebastian reigns.

    Mul. Mol. What shall I do to conquer thee?
    Sebas. Impossible!
Souls know no conquerors.
    Mul. Mol. I'll show thee for a monster thro' my Afric.
    Sebas. No, thou canst only show me for a man;
Afric is stored with monsters; man's a prodigy
Thy subjects have not seen.
    Mul. Mol. Thou talk'st as if
Still at the head of battle.
    Sebas. Thou mistak'st,
For then I would not talk.
    Bend. Sure he would sleep—
    Sebas. Till doom's-day; when the trumpet sounds to
For that's a soldier's call.   [rise;
    Mul. Mol. Thou'rt brave too late;
Thou should'st have died in battle like a soldier.
    Sebas. I fought and fell like one, but death deceived
I wanted weight of feeble Moors upon me,   [me;
To crush my soul out.
    Mul. Mol. Still untameable!
In what a ruin has thy headstrong pride,
And boundless thirst of empire, plunged thy people!
    Sebas. What say'st thou? ha! no more of that.
    Mul. Mol. Behold,
What carcasses of thine thy crimes have strewed,
And left our Afric vultures to devour.
    Bend. Those souls were those thy God entrusted with
To cherish, not destroy.   [thee,
    Sebas. Witness, O Heaven, how much

This sight concerns me ! Would I had a soul
For each of these, how gladly would I pay
The ransom down ; but since I have but one,
'Tis a king's life, and freely 'tis bestowed.
Not your false prophet, but eternal justice
Has destined me the lot, to die for these ;
'Tis fit a sovereign so should pay such subjects,
For subjects such as they are seldom seen,
Who not forsook me at my greatest need,
Nor for base lucre sold their loyalty ;
But shared my dangers to the last event,   [you :
And fenced them with their own. These thanks I pay
                               [*Wipes his eyes.*
And know that when Sebastian weeps, his tears
Come harder than his blood.
  Mul. Mol. They plead too strongly
To be withstood ! My clouds are gathering too,
In kindly mixture with his royal shower.
Be safe, and owe thy life not to my gift,
But to the greatness of thy mind, Sebastian.
Thy subjects, too, shall live ; a due reward
For their untainted faith in thy concealment.
  Muf. Remember, sir, your vow.   [*A general shout.*
  Mul. Mol. Do thou remember
Thy function, mercy, and provoke not blood.
  Mul. Zeyd. One of his generous fits, too strong to last.
                         [*Aside to* BENDUCAR.
  Bend. The Mufti reddens : mark that holy cheek.
                              [*To him.*
He frets within, froths treason at his mouth,
And churns it through his teeth ; leave me to work him.
  Sebas. A mercy unexpected, undesired,
Surprises more. You've learned the art to vanquish :
You could not (give me leave to tell you, sir)
Have given me life but in my subjects' safety ;
Kings, who are fathers, live but in their people.
  Mul. Mol. Still great, and grateful, that's thy character.
Unveil the woman ; I would view the face
That warmed our Mufti's zeal :
These pious parrots peck the fairest fruit ;
Such tasters are for kings.
         [*Officers go to* ALMEYDA *to unveil her.*

Alm. Stand off, ye slaves; I will not be unveiled.

Mul. Mol. Slave is thy title; force her.

Sebas. On your lives, approach her not.

Mul. Mol. How's this?

Sebas. Sir, pardon me,
And hear me speak——

Alm. Hear me: I will be heard.
I am no slave; the noblest blood of Afric
Runs in my veins, a purer stream than thine;
For, tho' derived from the same source, thy current
Is puddled and defiled with tyranny.

Mul. Mol. What female fury have we here!

Alm. I should be one,
Because of kin to thee; would'st thou be touched
By the presuming hands of saucy grooms?
The same respect, nay more, is due to me:
More for my sex; the same for my descent.
These hands are only fit to draw the curtain.
Now, if thou dar'st, behold Almeyda's face.

                                 [*Unveils herself.*

Bend. [*Aside.*] Would I had never seen it.

Alm. She whom thy Mufti taxed to have no soul;
Let Afric now be judge;
Perhaps thou think'st I meanly hope to 'scape,
As did Sebastian, when he owned his greatness.
But to remove that scruple, know, base man,
My murdered father and my brother's ghost
Still haunt this breast, and prompt it to revenge.
Think not I could forgive, nor dare thou pardon.

Mul. Mol. Would'st thou revenge thee, trait'ress, had'st
        thou power?

Alm. Traitor, I would; the name's more justly thine;
Thy father was not more than mine the heir
Of this large empire; but with arms united
They fought their way, and seized the crown by force:
And equal as their danger was their share;
For where was eldership, where none had right
But that which conquest gave? 'Twas thy ambition
Pulled from my peaceful father what his sword
Helped thine to gain; surprised him and his kingdom,
No provocation given, no war declared.

Mul. Mol. I'll hear no more.

Alm. This is the living coal, that burning in me
Would flame to vengeance, could it find a vent ;
My brother, too, that lies yet scarcely cold
In his deep wat'ry bed ; my wand'ring mother,
Who in exile died.
O that I had the fruitful heads of Hydra,
That one might bourgeon where another fell !
Still would I give thee work ; still, still, thou tyrant,
And hiss thee with the last.

Mul. Mol. Something, I know not what, comes over
Whether the toils of battle, unrepaired   [me ;
With due repose, or other sudden qualm.
Benducar, do the rest. [*Goes off ; the Court follows him.*

Bend. Strange! in full health! this pang is of the soul;
The body's unconcerned ; I'll think hereafter.
Conduct these royal captives to the castle ;
Bid Dorax use them well, till further order.

[*Going off ; stops.*

The inferior captives their first owners take,
To sell, or to dispose.   You, Mustapha,
Set ope the market for the sale of slaves.   [*Exit.* BEN.

[*The masters and slaves come forward, and buyers of
    several qualities come in and chaffer about the several
    owners, who make their slaves do tricks.*

Must. My chattels are come into my hands again, and
my conscience will serve me to sell them twice over ; any
price now, before the Mufti comes to claim them.

1st Mer. [*To* MUST.] What dost thou hold that old
        fellow at ?   [*Pointing to* ALVAREZ.
He's tough, and has no service in his limbs.

Must. I confess he's somewhat tough ; but I suppose
you would not boil him.   I ask for him a thousand
crowns.

1st Mer. Thou mean'st a thousand maravedies,

Must. Prithee, friend, give me leave to know my own
meaning.

1st Mer. What virtues has he to deserve that price?

Must. Marry come up, sir ! virtues quotha ! I took
him in the king's company ; he's of a great family, and
rich ; what other virtues would'st thou have in a noble-
man ?

1st Mer. I buy him with another man's purse, that's

my comfort. My Lord Dorax, the Governor, will have
him at any rate. There's hansel. Come, old fellow, to
the castle.

Alva. [*Aside.*] To what is miserable age reserved!
But oh the King! and oh the fatal secret!
Which I have kept thus long to time it better,
And now I would disclose, 'tis past my power.

[Exit with his master.

Must. Something of a secret and of the King I heard
him mutter. A pimp, I'll warrant him, for I am sure he
is an old courtier. Now to put off t'other remnant of
my merchandise,—Stir up, sirrah.   [*To* ANTONIO.

Ant. Dog, what would'st thou have?

Must. Learn better manners, or I shall serve you a
dog-trick: come down upon all four immediately; I'll
make you know your rider.

Ant. Thou wilt not make a horse of me?

Must. Horse or ass, that's as thy mother made thee,—
but take earnest in the first place for thy sauciness.
[*Lashes him with his whip.*]   Be advised, friend, and
buckle to thy gears: Behold my ensign of royalty dis-
played over thee.

Ant. I hope one day to use thee worse in Portugal.

Must. Ay, and good reason, friend; if thou catchest
me a conquering on thy side of the water, lay me on
lustily; I'll take it as kindly as thou dost this.

[Holds up his whip.

Ant. [*Lying down.*] Hold, my dear thrum-cap; I obey
thee cheerfully. I see the doctrine of non-resistance is
never practised thoroughly but when a man can't help
himself.

Enter a Second Merchant.

2nd Mer. You, friend, I would see that fellow do his
postures.

Must. [*Bridling* ANT.] Now, sirrah, follow; for you
have rope enough. To your paces, villain; amble, trot,
and gallop. Quick about, there—— Yeap, the more
money's bidden for you, the more your credit.

[ANTONIA *follows at the end of his bridle on his hands
and feet, and does all his postures.*

2nd Mer. He's well chin'd, and has a tolerable good

back; that's half in half. [*To* Must.] I would see him
strip; has he no diseases about him?

Must. He's the best piece of man's flesh in the market;
not an eye-sore in his whole body. Feel his legs, master,
neither splint, spavin, nor wind-gall.

[*Claps him on the shoulder.*

2nd Mer. [*Feeling about him, and then putting his hand
on his side.*] Out upon him, how his flank heaves! The
whorson's broken winded.

Must. Thick breathed a little; nothing but a sorry
cold with lying out a nights in trenches; but sound wind
and limb, I warrant him. Try him at a loose trot a
little.

[*Puts the bridle into his hand; he strokes him.*

Ant. For Heaven's sake, owner, spare me; you know
I am but new broken.

2nd Mer. 'Tis but a washy jade, I see; what do you
ask for this bauble?

Must. Bauble do you call him? he's a substantial true-
bred beast; bravely forehanded: mark but the cleanness
of his shapes too: his dam may be a Spanish gennet, but
a true barb by the sire, or I have no skill in horseflesh.
Marry, I ask six hundred xeriffs for him.

Enter Mufti.

Muf. What's that you are asking, sirrah?

Must. Marry, I ask your reverence six hundred par-
dons; I was doing you a small piece of service here,
putting off your cattle for you.

Muf. And putting the money into your own pocket.

Must. Upon vulgar reputation, no, my lord; it was for
your profit and emolument. What, wrong the head of
my religion? I was sensible you would have damned me,
or any man that should have injured you in a single
farthing; for I knew that was sacrifice.

Muf. Sacrilege you mean, sirrah, —— and damning
shall be the least part of your punishment: I have taken
you in the manner, and will have the law upon you.

Must. Good my lord, take pity upon a poor man in
this world, and damn me in the next.

Muf. No, sirrah, so you may repent, and 'scape punish-

H

ment.   Did you not sell this very slave amongst the rest
to me, and take money for him?

Must. Right, my lord.

Muf. And selling him again, take money twice for the
same commodity?   Oh, villain!   But did you not know
him to be my slave, sirrah?

Must. Why should I lie to your honour?   I did know
him; and thereupon seeing him wander about, took him
up for a stray and impounded him, with intention to
restore him to the right owner.

Muf. And yet at the same time was selling him to
another: how rarely the story hangs together!

Must. Patience, my lord.   I took him up, as your
herriot, with intention to have made the best of him, and
then have brought the whole product of him in a purse
to you; for I know you would have spent half of it upon
your pious pleasures, have hoarded up the other half, and
given the remainder in charities to the poor.

Muf. And what's become of my other slave?   Thou
hast sold him too, I have a villanous suspicion.

Must. I know you have, my lord; but while I was
managing this young robustious fellow, that old spark,
who was nothing but skin and bone, and by consequence
very nimble, slipt thro' my fingers like an eel, for there
was no hold-fast of him, and ran away to buy himself a
new master.

Muf. [*To* Ant.] Follow me home, sirrah.   [*To* Must.]
I shall remember you some other time.

[*Exit* Mufti *with* Antonia.

Must. I never doubted your lordship's memory for an
ill turn.   And I shall remember him, too, in the next
rising of the mobile for this act of resumption, and more
especially for the ghostly counsel he gave me before the
Emperor, to have hanged myself in silence to have saved
his reverence.   The best on't is, I am beforehand with
him for selling one of his slaves twice over.   And if he
had not come just in the nick, I might have pocketed up
the other.   For what should a poor man do that gets his
living by hard labour, but pray for bad times when he
may get it easily?   O for some incomparable tumult!
Then should I naturally wish that the beaten party might

prevail, because we have plundered the other side already, and there's nothing more to get of them.

Both rich and poor for their own interest pray,
'Tis ours to make our fortune while we may;
For kingdoms are not conquered every day.　　[*Exit.*

ACT II. Scene I.

Supposed to be a Terrace Walk, on the side of the Castle of Alcazar.

Enter Emperor *and* Benducar.

Emp. And think'st thou not it was discovered?
Bend. No;
The thoughts of kings are like religious groves,
The walks of muffled gods: sacred retreat,
Where none but whom they please to admit approach.
Emp. Did not my conscious eyes flash out a flame
To lighten those brown horrors, and disclose
The secret path I trod?
Bend. I could not find it, till you lent a clue
To that close labyrinth; how, then, should they?
Emp. I would be loath they should; it breeds contempt
For herds to listen, or presume to pry,
When the hurt lion groans within his den.
But is't not strange?
Bend. To love? not more than 'tis to live—a tax
Imposed on all by nature, paid in kind,
Familiar as our being.
Emp. Still, 'tis strange
To me. I know my soul as wild as wind
That sweeps the deserts of our moving plains.
Love might as well be sowed upon our sands,
As in a breast so barren.
To love an enemy, the only one
Remaining too, whom yester sun beheld
Mustering her charms, and rolling, as she pass'd
By every squadron, her alluring eyes,
To edge her champions' swords, and urge my ruin.
The shouts of soldiers, and the burst of cannon,

Maintain even still a deaf and murmuring noise;
Nor is Heaven yet recovered of the sound
Her battle roused. Yet, spite of me, I love.
    Bend. What, then, controls you?
Her person is as prostrate as her party.
    Emp. A thousand things control this conqueror—
My native pride to own the unworthy passion,
Hazard of interest, and my people's love.
To what a storm of fate am I exposed!
What if I had her murdered? 'tis but what
My subjects all expect, and she deserves.
Would not the impossibility
Of ever, ever seeing or possessing,
Calm all this rage, this hurricane of soul?
    Bend. That ever, ever—
I marked the double—shows extreme reluctance
To part with her for ever.
    Emp. Right, thou hast me.
I would, but cannot kill; I must enjoy her.
I must, and what I must, be sure I will.
What's royalty, but power to please myself?
And if I dare not, then am I the slave,
And my own slaves the sovereigns. 'Tis resolved.
Weak princes flatter when they want the power
To curb their people: tender plants must bend;
But when a Government is grown to strength,
Like some old oak, rough with its armed bark,
It yields not to the tug, but only nods,
And turns to sullen state.
    Bend. Then you resolve
To implore her pity, and to beg relief?
    Emp. Death, must I beg the pity of my slave?
Must a king beg? Yes, love's a greater king;
A tyrant, nay, a devil that possesses me;
He tunes the organs of my voice, and speaks
Unknown to me within me; pushes me,
And drives me on by force.
Say I should wed her, would not my wise subjects
Take check, and think it strange? perhaps revolt?
    Bend. I hope they would not.
    Emp. Then thou doubt'st they would?
    Bend. To whom?

Emp. To her
Perhaps, or to my brother, or to thee.   [I tremble!
Bend. [*In disorder.*] To me! me did you mention? how
The name of treason shakes my honest soul.
If I am doubted, sir,
Secure yourself this moment; take my life.
Emp. No more: if I suspected thee—I would.
Bend. I thank your kindness. Guilt had almost lost
          me.   [*Aside.*
Emp. But clear my doubts. Think'st thou they may
Bend. [*Aside.*] This goes as I would wish.   [rebel?
'Tis possible.
A secret party still remains, that lurks
Like embers raked in ashes—wanting but
A breath to blow aside the involving dust,
And then they blaze abroad.
Emp. They must be trampled out.
Bend. But first be known.
Emp. Torture shall force it from them.
Bend. You would not put a nation to the rack?
Emp. Yes, the whole world; so I be safe, I care not.
Bend. Our limbs and lives
Are yours, but mixing friends with foes is hard.
Emp. All may be foes; or how to be distinguished,
If some be friends?
Bend. They may with ease be winnowed.
Suppose some one who has deserved your trust,
Some one who knows mankind, should be employed
To mix among them, seem a malcontent,
And dive into their breasts, to try how far
They dare oppose your love!
Emp. I like this well; 'tis wholesome wickedness.
Bend. Whomever he suspects, he fastens there,
And leaves no cranny of his soul unsearched:
Then, like a bee bagg'd with his honey'd venom,
He brings it to your hive: if such a man
So able and so honest may be found;
If not, my project dies.
Emp. By all my hopes, thou hast described thyself.
Thou, thou alone art fit to play that engine
Thou only could'st contrive.
Bend. Sure I could serve you;

I think I could—but here's the difficulty,
I'm so entirely yours,
That I should scurvily dissemble hate ;
The cheat would be too gross.

    Emp. Art thou a statesman,
And canst not be a hypocrite ? impossible :
Do not distrust thy virtues.

    Bend. If I must personate this seeming villain,
Remember 'tis to serve you.

    Emp. No more words :
Love goads me to Almeyda, all affairs
Are troublesome but that; and yet that most.   [*Going.*
Bid Dorax treat Sebastian like a king ;
I had forgot him ; but this love mars all,
And takes up my whole breast.   [*Exit Emperor.*

    Bend. [*To the Emp.*] Be sure I'll tell him—
With all the aggravating circumstances   [*Alone.*
I can, to make him swell at that command.
The tyrant first suspected me ;
Then with a sudden gust he whirled about
And trusted me too far.   Madness of power!
Now, by his own consent I ruin him.
For, should some feeble soul, for fear or gain,
Bolt out to accuse me, even the king is cozened,
And thinks he's in the secret.
How sweet is treason when the traitor's safe?

         [*Sees the* MUFTI *and* DORAX *entering, and
           seeming to confer.*

The Mufti, and with him my sullen Dorax ;
That first is mine already.
'Twas easy work to gain a covetous mind,
Whom rage to lose his prisoners had prepared :
Now, caught himself,
He would seduce another ; I must help him—
For Churchmen, though they itch to govern all,
Are silly, woeful, awkward politicians.
They make lame mischief, though they mean it well ;
Their interest is not finely drawn and hid.
But seams are coarsely bungled up and seen.

    Muf. He'll tell you more.

    Dor. I've heard enough already
To make me loathe thy morals.

Bend. [*To Dor.*] You seem warm ;
The good man's zeal perhaps has gone too far.

Dor. Not very far: not farther than zeal goes
Of course ; a small day's journey short of treason.

Muf. By all that's holy, treason was not named,
I spared the Emperor's broken vows, to save
The slaves from death, though it was cheating Heaven,
But I forgave him that.

Dor. And slighted o'er   [*Scornfully.*
The wrongs himself sustained in property :
When his bought slaves were seized by force, no loss
Of his considered, and no cost repaid.

Muf. Not wholly slighted o'er, not absolutely.
Some modest hints of private wrongs I urged.

Dor. Two thirds of all he said: there he began
To show the fulness of his heart; there ended.
Some short excursions of a broken vow
He made indeed, but flat insipid stuff;
But when he made his loss the theme, he flourished,
Relieved his fainting rhetoric with new figures,
And thundered at oppressing tyranny.

Muf. Why not, when sacrilegious power would seize
My property !   'Tis an affront to Heaven,
Whose person, tho' unworthy, I sustain.

Dor. You've made such strong alliances above,
That 'twere profaneness in us laity
To offer earthly aid.
I tell thee, Mufti, if the world were wise,
They would not wag one finger in your quarrels.
Your heaven you promise, but our earth you covet :
The phaetons of mankind, who fire that world
Which you were sent by preaching but to warm.

Bend. This goes beyond the mark.

Muf. No, let him rail ;
His prophet works within him.
He's a rare convert.

Dor. Now his zeal yearns
To see me burnt ; he damns me from his church,
Because I would restrain him to his duty.
Is not the care of souls a load sufficient ?
Are not your holy stipends paid for this ?
Were you not bred apart from worldly noise,

To study souls, their cures and their diseases?
If this be so, we ask you but our own ;
Give us your whole employment, all your care ;
The province of the soul is large enough
To fill up every cranny of your time,
And leave you much to answer if one wretch
Be damned by your neglect.
    Bend. [*To the* MUFTI.] He speaks but reason.
    Dor. Why then these foreign thoughts of State-employ-
Abhorrent to your function and your breeding?   [ments,
Poor droning truants of unpractised cells,
Bred in the fellowship of bearded boys,
What wonder is it if you know not men !
Yet there you live demure, with downcast eyes,
And humble as your discipline requires ;
But, when let loose from thence to live at large,
Your little tincture of devotion dies.
Then luxury succeeds, and sets agog
With a new scene of yet untasted joys,
You fall with greedy hunger to the feast.
Of all your college virtues nothing now
But your original ignorance remains ;
Bloated with pride, ambition, avarice,
You swell to counsel kings and govern kingdoms.
    Muf. He prates as if kings had not consciences,
And none required directors but the crowd.
    Dor. As private men they want you, not as kings;
Nor would you care to inspect their public conscience,
But that it draws dependencies of power,
And earthly interest which you long to sway.
Content you with monopolising heaven,
And let this little hanging ball alone.
For, give you but a foot of conscience there,
And you, like Archimedes, toss the globe.
We know your thoughts of us, that laymen are
Lag souls, and rubbish of remaining clay,
Which heaven, grown weary of more perfect work,
Set upright with a little puff of breath,
And bid us pass for men.
    Muf. I will not answer,
Base, foul-mouthed renegade ; but I'll pray for thee,
To show my charity.   [*Exit.* MUFTI.

Dor. Do; but forget not him who needs it most;
Allow thyself some share. He's gone too soon;
I had to tell him of his holy jugglings—
Things that would startle faith, and make us deem
Not this, or that, but all religions false.

Bend. [*Aside.*] Our holy orator has lost the cause,
But I shall yet redeem it. [*To* DORAX.] Let him go;
For I have secret orders from the Emperor,
Which none but you must hear: I must confess
I could have wished some other hand had brought them.
When did you see your prisoner, great Sebastian?

Dor. You might as well have asked me, when I saw
A crested dragon, or a basilisk:
Both are less poison to my eyes and nature.
He knows not I am I; nor shall he see me,
Till time has perfected a labouring thought,
That rolls within my breast.

Bend. 'Twas my mistake:
I guessed, indeed, that time, and his misfortunes,
And your returning duty, had effaced
The memory of past wrongs; they would in me,
And I judged you as tame and as forgiving.

Dor. Forgive him! no: I left my foolish faith,
Because it would oblige me to forgiveness.

Bend. I can't but grieve to find you obstinate;
For you must see him: 'tis our Emperor's will,
And strict command.

Dor. I laugh at that command. [him.

Bend. You must do more than see; serve and respect

Dor. See, serve him, and respect, and after all
My yet uncancelled wrongs, I must do this!
But I forget myself.

Bend. Indeed you do.

Dor. The Emperor is a stranger to my wrongs;
I need but tell my story to revoke
This hard commission.

Bend. Can you call me friend,
And think I could neglect to speak at full
The affronts you had from your ungrateful master?

Dor. And yet enjoined my service and attendance?

Bend. And yet enjoined them both. Would that were
He screwed his face into a hardened smile, [all;
And said Sebastian knew to govern slaves.

Dor. Slaves are the growth of Afric, not of Europe;
By Heaven, I will not lay down my commission;
Not at his foot, I will not stoop so low;
But if there be a part in all his face
More sacred than the rest, I'll throw it there.

Bend. You may; but then you lose all future means
Of vengeance on Sebastian, when no more
Alcade of this fort.

Dor.   That thought escaped me.

Bend. Keep your command, and be revenged on both:
Nor soothe yourself; you have no power to affront him;
The Emperor's love protects him from insults.
And he who spoke that proud, ill-natured word,
Following the bent of his impetuous temper,
May force your reconcilement to Sebastian:
Nay, bid you kneel and kiss the offending foot,
That kicked you from his presence.
But think not to divide their punishment;
You cannot touch a hair of loathed Sebastian,
While Muley-Moluch lives.

Dor.   What means this riddle?

Bend. 'Tis out: there needs no Œdipus to solve it.
Our Emperor is a tyrant, feared and hated;
I scarce remember in his reign one day
Pass guiltless o'er his execrable head.
He thinks the sun is lost that sees not blood:
When none is shed we count it holiday.
We, who are most in favour, cannot call
This hour our own. You know the younger brother,
Mild Muley-Zeydan?——

Dor.   Hold, and let me think.

Bend. The soldiers idolise you,
He trusts you with the castle,
The key of all his kingdom.

Dor. Well; and he trusts you too.

Bend. Else I were mad,
To hazard such a daring enterprise.

Dor. He trusts us both; mark that, shall we betray
A master who reposes life and empire   [him;
On our fidelity? I grant he is a tyrant,
That hated name my nature most abhors;
More, as you say, has loaded me with scorn,

Even with the last contempt, to serve Sebastian.
Yet more he knows he vacates my revenge;
Which but by this revolt I cannot compass;
But, while he trusts me, 'twere so base a part
To fawn and yet betray: I should be hissed
And whooped in hell for that ingratitude.

Bend. Consider well what I have done for you.

Dor. Consider thou what thou wouldst have me do.

Bend. You've too much honour for a renegade.

Dor. And thou too little faith to be a favourite.
Is not the bread thou eat'st, the robe thou wear'st,
Thy wealth and honours, all the pure indulgence
Of him thou wouldst destroy?
And would his creature, nay, his friend, betray him?
Why then no bond is left on human kind:
Distrusts, debates, immortal strifes ensue;
Children may murder parents, wives their husbands;
All must be rapine, wars, and desolation,
When trust and gratitude no longer bind.

Bend. Well have you argued in your own defence;
You who have burst asunder all those bonds,
And turned a rebel to your native Prince.

Dor. True, I rebelled; but when did I betray?
Indignities which man could not support,
Provoked my vengeance to this noble crime:
But he had stripped me first of my command,
Dismissed my service, and absolved my faith;
And, with disdainful language, dared my worst.
I but accepted war, which he denounced:
Else had you seen not Dorax, but Alonzo,
With his couched lance against your foremost Moors;
Perhaps, too, turned the fortune of the day;
Made Afric mourn, and Portugal triumph.

Bend. Let me embrace thee.

Dor. Stand off, sycophant,
And keep infection distant.

Bend. Brave and honest.

Dor. In spite of thy temptations.

Bend. Call them trials:
They were no more: thy faith was held in balance,
And nicely weighed by jealousy of power,
Vast was the trust of such a royal charge;

And our wise Emperor might justly fear
Sebastian might be freed and reconciled
By new obligements to thy former love.
   Dor. I doubt thee still; thy reasons were too strong,
And driven too near the head, to be but artifice:
And after all, I know thou art a statesman,
Where truth is rarely found.
   Bend. Behold the Emperor;

     Enter EMPEROR, SEBASTIAN, *and* ALMEYDA.

Ask him, I beg thee, to be justified,
If he employed me not to ford thy soul,
And try the footing whether false or firm.
   Dor. Death to my eyes, I see Sebastian with him!
Must he be served? avoid him; if we meet,
It must be like the crash of heaven and earth,
To involve us both in ruin.   [*Exit.*
   Bend. 'Twas a bare saving game I made with Dorax,
But better so than lost: he cannot hurt me,
That I precautioned; I must ruin him.
But now this love; ay, there's the gathering storm!
The tyrant must not wed Almeyda; no,
That ruins all the fabric I am raising.
Yet seeming to approve it gave me time,
And gaining time gains all.

   [BENDUCAR *goes and waits behind the Emperor.*

The Emperor, SEBASTIAN, *and* ALMEYDA, *advance to the
   front of the stage: guards and attendants.*

   Emp. [*To* SEBAS.] I bade them serve you, and if they
I keep my lions keen within their dens,   [obey not,
To stop their maws with disobedient slaves.
   Sebas. If I had conquered,
They could not have with more observance waited:
Their eyes, hands, and feet,
Are all so quick, they seem to have but one motion,
To catch my flying words.   Only the Alcade
Shuns me, and, with a grim civility,
Bows, and declines my walks.
   Emp. A renegade!
I know no more of him, but that he's brave,
And hates your Christian sect.   If you can frame

A farther wish, give wing to your desires,
And name the thing you want.
    Sebas. My liberty;
For were even Paradise itself my prison,
Still I should long to leap the crystal walls.
    Emp. Sure our two souls have somewhere been ac-
In former beings; or struck out together,   [quainted
One spark to Afric flew, and one to Portugal.
Expect a quick deliverance. [*Turning to* ALM.] Here's a
Of kindred soul to both.   Pity our stars   [third,
Have made us foes!   I should not wish her death.
    Alm. I ask no pity: if I thought my soul
Of kin to thine, soon would I rend my heart-strings,
And tear out that alliance.   But thou, viper,
Hast cancelled kindred, made a rent in nature,
And through her holy bowels gnawed thy way,
Through thy own blood to empire.
    Emp. This again;
And yet she lives, and only lives to upbraid me.
    Sebas. What honour is there in a woman's death!
Wronged as she says, but helpless to revenge;
Strong in her passion, impotent of reason,
Too weak to hurt, too fair to be destroyed.
Mark her majestic fabric: she's a temple
Sacred by birth, and built by hands divine;
Her soul's the deity that lodges there,
Nor is the pile unworthy of the god.
    Emp. She's all that thou can'st say, or I can think.
But the perverseness of her clamorous tongue
Strikes pity deaf.
    Sebas. Then only hear her eyes;
Tho' they are mute they plead; nay, more, command:
For beauteous eyes have arbitrary power.
All females have prerogative of sex,
The she's even of the savage herd are safe:
All when they snarl or bite have no return
But courtship from the male.
    Emp. Were she not she, and I not Muley-Moluch,
She's mistress of inevitable charms
For all but me; nor am I so exempt,
But that—I know not what I was to say—
But I am too obnoxious to my friends,
And swayed by your advice.

Sebas. Sir, I advised not ;
By Heaven, I never counselled love, but pity.
  Emp. By Heaven, thou did'st. Deny it not, thou did'st;
For what was all that prodigality
Of praise, but to enslave me—
  Sebas. Sir—
  Emp. No more :
Thou hast convinced me that she's worth my love.
  Sebas. [*Aside.*] Was ever man so ruined by himself?
  Alm. Thy love ! that odious mouth was never framed
To speak a word so soft.
Name death again, for that thou canst pronounce
With horrid grace, becoming of a tyrant.
Love is for human hearts, and not for thine,
Where the brute beast extinguishes the man.
  Emp. Such if I were, yet rugged lions love,
And grapple, and compel their savage dames.
Mark, my Sebastian, how that sullen frown, [*She frowns.*
Like flashing lightning, opens angry heaven;
And while it kills, delights. But yet, insult not
Too soon, proud beauty.   I confess no love.
  Sebas. No sir, I said so, and I witness for you.
Not love, but noble pity moved your mind :
Interest might urge you, too, to save her life ;
For those who wish her party lost, might murmur
At shedding royal blood.
  Emp. Right, thou instructest me.
Interest of state requires not death, but marriage,
To unite the jarring titles of our line.
  Sebas. [*Aside.*] Let me be dumb for ever; all I plead,
Like wildfire thrown against the winds, returns
With double force to burn me.
  Emp. Could I but bend to make my beauteous foe
The partner of my throne and of my bed—
  Alm. Still thou dissemblest; but I read thy heart,
And know the power of my own charms ; thou lov'st,
And I am pleased for my revenge thou dost.
  Emp. And thou hast cause.
  Alm. I have, for I have power to make thee wretched.
Be sure I will, and yet despair of freedom.
  Emp. Well, then, I love—
And 'tis below my greatness to disown it ;

Love thee implacably, yet hate thee, too;
Would hunt thee bare-foot in the mid-day sun
Through the parched desert and the scorching sands,
To enjoy thy love, and once enjoyed, to kill thee.

Alm. 'Tis a false courage, when thou threat'nest me;
Thou canst not stir a hand to touch my life—
Do not I see thee tremble when thou speak'st?
Lay by thy lion's hide, vain conqueror,
And take the distaff, for thy soul's my slave.

Emp. Confusion! how thou view'st my very heart!
I could as soon
Stop a spring-tide, blown in, with my bare hand,
As this impetuous love. Yes, I will wed thee:
In spite of thee and of myself, I will.

Alm. For what? To people Africa with monsters,
Which that unnatural mixture must produce?
No, were we joined, even tho' it were in death,
Our bodies burning in one funeral pile,
The prodigy of Thebes would be renewed,
And my divided flame should break from thine.

Emp. Serpent, I will engender poison with thee;
Join hate with hate, add venom to the birth.
Our offspring, like the seed of dragon's teeth,
Shall issue armed, and fight themselves to death.

Alm. I'm calm again; thou canst not marry me.

Emp. As gleams of sunshine soften storms to showers,
So if you smile, the loudness of my rage
In gentle whispers shall return, but this—
That nothing can divert my love but death.

Alm. See how thou art deceived—I am a Christian;
'Tis true, unpractised in my new belief,
Wrongs I resent, nor pardon yet with ease:
Those fruits come late, and are of slow increase
In haughty hearts like mine. Now, tell thyself
If this one word destroy not thy design,
The law permits thee not to marry me.

Emp. 'Tis but a specious tale, to blast my hopes,
And baffle my pretensions. Speak, Sebastian,
And, as a king, speak true.

Sebas. Then, thus adjured,
On a king's word, 'tis truth, but truth ill-timed:
For her dear life is now exposed anew;

Unless you wholly can put on divinity,
And graciously forgive.
  Alm. Now, learn by this
The little value I have left for life,
And trouble me no more.
  Emp. I thank the woman;
Thou hast restored me to my native rage,
And I will seize my happiness by force. [tempt——
  Sebas. Know, Mulcy-Moluch, when thou dar'st at-
  Emp. Beware! I would not be provoked to use
A conqueror's right, and therefore charge thy silence.
If thou would'st merit to be thought my friend,
I leave thee to persuade her to compliance.
If not, there's a new gust in ravishment,
Which I have never tried.
  Bend. [*Aside.*] They must be watched;
For something I observed creates a doubt.
          [*Exit* EMP. *and* BEND.
  Sebas. I've been too tame, have basely borne my wrongs,
And not exerted all the king within me.
I heard him, O sweet Heaven, he threatened rape;
Nay, insolently urged me to persuade thee,
Even thee, thou idol of my soul and eyes,
For whom I suffer life, and drag this being.
  Alm. You turn my prison to a paradise;
But I have turned your empire to a prison.
In all your wars good fortune flew before you;
Sublime you sat in triumph on her wheel,
Till in my fatal cause your sword was drawn.
The weight of my misfortunes dragged you down.
  Sebas. And is't not strange, that Heaven should bless
In common causes, and desert the best? [my arms
Now in your greatest, last extremity,
When I would aid you most, and most desire it,
I bring but sighs, the succours of a slave.
  Alm. Leave then the luggage of your fate behind
To make your flight more easy, leave Almeyda:
Nor think me left a base, ignoble prey,
Exposed to this inhuman tyrant's lust;
My virtue is a guard beyond my strength,
And death, my last defence, within my call.
  Sebas. Death may be called in vain, and cannot come;

Tyrants can tie him up from your relief:
Nor has a Christian privilege to die.
Alas, thou art too young in thy new faith;
Brutus and Cato might discharge their souls,
And give them furloughs for another world:
But we, like sentries, are obliged to stand
In starless nights, and wait the appointed hour.

Alm. If shunning ill be good
To those who cannot shun it but by death,
Divines but peep on undiscovered worlds,
And draw the distant landscape as they please:
But who has e'er returned from those bright regions,
To tell their manners, and relate their laws?
I'll venture landing on that happy shore
With an unsullied body and white mind;
If I have erred, some kind inhabitant
Will pity a strayed soul, and take me home.

Sebas. Beware of death, thou canst not die unperjured.
And leave an unaccomplished love behind.
Thy vows are mine; nor will I quit my claim:
The tie of minds are but imperfect bonds,
Unless the bodies join to seal the contract.

Alm. What joys can you possess, or can I give,
Where groans of death succeed the sighs of love?
Our Hymen has not on his saffron robe;
But, muffled up in mourning, downward holds
His drooping torch, extinguished with his tears.

Sebas. The god of love stands ready to revive it
With his ethereal breath.

Alm. 'Tis late to join, when we must part so soon.

Sebas. Nay, rather let us haste it, ere we part:
Our souls, for want of that acquaintance here,
May wander in the starry walks above,
And, forced on worse companions, miss ourselves.

Alm. The tyrant will not long be absent hence;
And soon I shall be ravished from your arms.

Sebas. Wilt thou thyself become the greater tyrant,
And give not love while thou hast love to give?
In dangerous days, when riches are a crime,
The wife betimes make over their estates:
Make o'er thy honour, by a deed of trust,
And give me seizure of the mighty wealth.

I

Alm. What shall I do! O teach me to refuse!
i would; and yet I tremble at the grant.
For dire presages fright my soul by day,
And boding visions haunt my nightly dreams;
Sometimes, methinks, I hear the groans of ghosts;
Thin, hollow sounds, and lamentable screams;
Then, like a dying echo, from afar,
My mother's voice, that cries, Wed not, Almeyda!
Forewarned Almeyda, marriage is thy crime.

Sebas. Some envious demon, to delude our joys;
Love is not sin, but where 'tis sinful love.

Alm. Mine is a flame so holy and so clear,
That the white taper leaves no soot behind;
No smoke of lust; but chaste as sisters' love,
When coldly they return a brother's kiss,
Without the zeal that meets at lovers' mouths.

Sebas. Laugh then at fond presages; I had some;
Famed Nostradamus, when he took my horoscope,
Foretold my father, I should wed with incest:
Ere this unhappy war my mother died;
And sisters I had none; vain augury!
A long religious life, a holy age,
My stars assigned me too; impossible:
For how can incest suit with holiness,
Or priestly orders with a princely state?

Alm. Old venerable Alvarez! ——   [*Sighing.*

Sebas. But why that sigh in naming that good man?

Alm. Your father's counsellor and confidant ——

Sebas. He was; and, if he lives, my second father.

Alm. Marked our farewell when going to the fight,
You gave Almeyda for the word of battle;
'Twas in that fatal moment he discovered
The love that long we laboured to conceal.
I know it; tho' my eyes stood full of tears,
Yet thro' the mist I saw him stedfast gaze,
Then knocked his aged breast and inward groaned,
Like some sad prophet that foresaw the doom
Of those whom best he loved, and could not save.

Sebas. It startles me, and brings to my remembrance
That, when the shock of battle was begun,
He would have much complained (but had not time)
Of our hid passion; then, with lifted hands,

He begg'd me by my father's sacred soul,
Not to espouse you, if he died in fight;
For if he lived, and we were conquerors,
He had such things to urge against our marriage,
As, now declared, would blunt my sword in battle,
And dastardise my courage.

Alm. My blood curdles,
And cakes about my heart.

Sebas. I'll breathe a sigh so warm into thy bosom,
Shall make it flow again. My love, he knows not
Thou art a Christian; that produced his fear,
Lest thou shouldst soothe my soul with charms so strong,
That Heaven might prove too weak.

Alm. There must be more:
This could not blunt your sword.

Sebas. Yes, if I drew it with a curst intent,
To take a misbeliever to my bed;
It must be so.

Alm. Yet—.

Sebas. No, thou shalt not plead
With that fair mouth, against the cause of love.
Within this castle is a captive priest,
My holy confessor, whose free access
Not even the barb'rous victors have refused;
This hour his hands shall make us one.

Alm. I go, with love and fortune, two blind guides,
To lead my way, half loath and half consenting;
If, as my soul forebodes, some dire event
Pursue this union, or some crime unknown,
Forgive me Heaven; and all ye blest above,
Excuse the frailty of unbounded love. [*Exeunt ambo.*

SCENE II.—*Supposed a Garden, with Lodging Rooms behind it, or on the sides.*

Enter MUFTI, ANTONIA *as a Slave, and* JOHAYMA, *the* MUFTI's *Wife.*

Muf. And how do you like him? look upon him well;
he's a personable fellow of a Christian dog. Now I think
you are fitted for a gardener. Ha! what say'st thou,
Johayma?

Joh. He may make shift to sow lettuce, raise melons, and water a garden-plot; but otherwise a very filthy fellow; how odiously he smells of his country garlic! fugh, how he stinks of Spain.

Muf. Why, honey-bird, I bought him on purpose for thee; didst thou not say thou long'dst for a Christian slave?

Joh. Ay, but the sight of that loathsome creature has almost cured me; and how can I tell that he's a Christian? and he were well searched he may prove a Jew for aught I know.

Ant. I was never taken for one in my own country; and not very peaceable, neither, when I am well provoked.

Muf. To your occupation, dog; bind up the jessamines in yonder arbour, and handle your pruning-knife with dexterity; tightly I say, go tightly to your business; you have cost me much, and must earn it in your work: here's plentiful provision for you, rascal, saladding in the garden, and water in the tank, and on holidays the licking of a platter of rice when he deserves it.

Joh. What have you been bred up to, sirrah, and what can you do to recommend you to my service?

Ant. Why, madam, I can perform as much as any man in a fair lady's service. I can play upon the flute and sing; I can carry your umbrella, and fan your lady-ship, and cool you when you are too hot; in fine, no service shall come amiss to me; and besides, am of so quick an apprehension, that you need but wink upon me at any time to make me understand my duty.

Joh. The whelp may come to something in time, when I have entered him into his business.

Muf. A very malapert cur, I can tell him that; I do not like his fawning; you must be taught your distance, sirrah.   [*Strikes him.*

Joh. Hold, hold! He has deserved it, I confess; but for once let his ignorance plead his pardon; we must not discourage a beginner. Your reverence has taught us charity even to birds and beasts; here, you filthy brute, you —— take this little alms to buy you plaisters.

[*Gives him a piece of money.*

Ant. [*Aside.*] Money, and a love-pinch in the inside of my palm into the bargain.

Enter a Servant.

Serv. Sir, my Lord Benducar is coming to wait on you, and is already at the palace gate.

Muf. Come in Johayma, regulate the rest of my wives and concubines, and leave the fellow to his work.

Joh. How stupidly he stares about him, like a calf new come into the world. I shall teach you, sirrah, to know your business a little better. This way, you awkward rascal, here lies the arbour; must I be showing you eternally? [*Turning him about.*

Muf. Come away, minion; you shall show him nothing.

Joh. I'll but bring him into the arbour, where a rose-tree and a myrtle-tree are just falling for want of a prop; if they were bound together, they would help to keep up one another. He's a raw gardener, and 'tis but charity to teach him.

Muf. No more deeds of charity to-day. Come in, or I shall think you a little better disposed than I could wish you.

Joh. Well, go before, I will follow my pastor.

Muf. So you may cast a sheep's eye behind you. In before me; and you, sauciness, mind your pruning-knife, or I may chance to use it for you.

[*Exeunt* MUFTI *and* JOHAYMA.

Ant. [*Alone.*] Thank you for that, but I am in no such haste to be made a Mussulman. For his wedlock, for all her haughtiness, I find her coming. Now have I a strange temptation to try what other females are belonging to this family; I am not far from the women's apartment I am sure, and if these birds are within distance, here's that will chuckle them together.

[*He pulls out his flute and plays: a grate opens and* MORAYMA, *the* MUFTI's *daughter appears at it.*

Ay, there's an apparition! This is the mystery of his Alcoran, that must be reserved from the knowledge of the profane vulgar. This is the holiday devotion; see, she beckons, too. [*She beckons to him.*

Mor. Come a little nearer, and speak softly.

Ant. I come, I come, I warrant thee; the least twinkle had brought me to thee; such another kind syllable or two would turn me to a meteor, and draw me up to thee,

Mor. I dare not speak, for fear of being overheard, but

if you think my person worth your hazard, and can deserve my love—the rest this note shall tell you. [*Throws down a handkerchief.*] No more; my heart goes with you.   [*Exit from the grate.*

Ant. O thou pretty little heart; art thou flown hither? I'll keep it warm I warrant it, and brood upon it in the new nest: but now upon my treasure trove, that's wrapt up in the handkerchief. No peeping here, though I long to be spelling her Arabic scrawls and pot-hooks. But I must carry off my prize as robbers do; and not think of sharing the booty before I am free from danger, and out of eye-shot from the other windows. If her wit be as poignant as her eyes, I am a double slave. Our northern beauties are mere dough to these: insipid white earth, mere tobacco-pipe clay: with no more soul and motion in them than a fly in winter.

Here the warm planet ripens and sublimes
The well-baked beauties of the southern climes;
Our Cupid's but a bungler in his trade;
His keenest arrows are in Afric made.   [*Exit.*

ACT III.   Scene I.

A Terrace-Walk; or some other Public Place in the Castle of Alcazar.

Enter Emperor MULEY-MOLUCH *and* BENDUCAR.

Emp. Married! I'll not believe it; 'tis imposture;.
Improbable they should presume to attempt,
Impossible they should effect their wish.
    Bend. Have patience till I clear it.
    Emp. I have none:
Go, bid our moving plains of sand lie still,
And stir not, when the stormy south blows high:
From top to bottom thou hast tossed my soul,
And now 'tis in the madness of the whirl,
Requir'st a sudden stop? unsay thy lie,
That may in time do somewhat.
    Bend. I have done:
For, since it pleases you it should be forged,

'Tis fit it should: far be it from your slave
To raise disturbance in your sacred breast.

Emp. Sebastian is my slave as well as thou;
Nor durst offend my love by that presumption.

Bend. Most sure he ought not.

Emp. Then all means were wanting;
No priest, no ceremonies of their sex;
Or, grant we these defects could be supplied,
How could our prophet do an act so base,
So to resume his gifts, and curse my conquests,
By making me unhappy? No, the slave
That told thee so absurd a story, lied.

Bend. Yet till this moment I have found him faithful:
He said he saw it, too.

Emp. Despatch; what saw he?

Bend. Truth is, considering with what earnestness
Sebastian pleaded for Almeyda's life,
Enhanced her beauty, dwelt upon her praise—

Emp. O stupid, and unthinking as I was!
I might have marked it, too; 'twas gross and palpable!

Bend. Methought I traced a lover ill disguised;
And sent my spy, a sharp, observing slave,
To inform me better, if I guessed aright.
He told me that he saw Sebastian's page
Run 'cross the marble square, who soon returned,
And after him there lagged a puffing friar;
Close wrapp'd he bore some secret instrument
Of Christian superstition in his hand;
My servant followed fast, and, through a chink,
Perceiv'd the royal captives hand in hand:
And heard the hooded father mumbling charms
That make those misbelievers man and wife;
Which done, the spouses kiss'd with such a fervour,
And gave such furious earnest of their flames,
That their eyes sparkled, and their mantling blood
Flew flushing o'er their faces.

Emp. Hell confound them!

Bend. The reverend father, with a holy leer,
Saw he might well be spared, and soon withdrew:
This forc'd my servant to a quick retreat,
For fear to be discovered; guess the rest.

Emp. I do. My fancy is too exquisite,

And tortures me with their imagined bliss.
Some earthquake should have risen and rent the ground,
Have swallowed him, and left the longing bride
In agony of unaccomplish'd love.   [*Walks disorderly.*

Enter the MUFTI.

Bend. In an unlucky hour   [*Aside.*
That fool intrudes, raw in this great affair,
And uninstructed how to stem the tide.
        [*Coming up to the* MUFTI, *aside.*
The emperor must not marry, nor enjoy;
Keep to that point; stand firm, for all's at stake.
        Emp. [*seeing him.*] You druggerman of heaven, must
            I attend
Your droning prayers? Why came ye not before?
Dost thou not know the captive king has dar'd
To wed Almeyda? Cancel me that marriage,
And make her mine; about the business, quick.
Expound thy Mahomet; make him speak my sense,
Or he's no prophet here, and thou no Mufti,
Unless thou know'st the trick of thy vocation,
To wrest and rend the law to please thy prince.
        Muf. Why, verily the law is monstrous plain:
There's not one doubtful text in all the Alcoran,
Which can be wrench'd in favour to your project.
        Emp. Forge one, and foist it into some by-place
Of some old rotten roll; do it, I command thee:
Must I teach thee thy trade?
        Muf. It cannot be.
For matrimony being the dearest point
Of law, the people have it all by heart:
A cheat on procreation will not pass.
Besides, the offence is so exorbitant   [*In a higher tone.*
To mingle with a misbelieving race,
That speedy vengeance would pursue your crime,
And holy Mahomet launch himself from heaven
Before the unready thunderbolts were form'd.
        [*Emperor taking him by the throat with one hand,
            snatches out his sword with the other, and points
            it to his breast.*
        Emp. Slave, have I raised thee to this pomp and power,
To preach against my will? Know I am law;

And thou, not Mahomet's messenger, but mine;
Make it, I charge thee, make my pleasure lawful:
Or, first I strip thee of thy ghostly greatness,
Then send thee post to tell thy tale above;
And bring thy vain memorials to thy prophet
Of justice done below for disobedience.

Muf. For heaven's sake, hold! the respite of a moment—
To think for you—

Emp. And for thyself—

Muf. For both.

Bend. Disgrace, and death, and avarice have lost
     him!   [*Aside.*

Muf. 'Tis true, our law forbids to wed a Christian;
But it forbids you not to ravish her.
You have a conqueror's right upon your slave;
And then the more despite you do a Christian,
You serve the prophet more, who loathes that sect.

Emp. O now it mends; and you talk reason, Mufti.
But stay! I promis'd freedom to Sebastian.
Now, should I grant it, his revengeful soul
Would ne'er forgive his violated bed.

Muf. Kill him, for then you give him liberty:
His soul is from his earthly prison freed.

Emp. How happy is the prince who has a churchman
So learned and pliant to expound his laws!

Bend. Two things I humbly offer to your prudence.

Emp. Be brief, but let not either thwart my love.

Bend. First, since our holy man has made rape lawful,
Fright her with that; proceed not yet to force:
Why should you pluck the green, distasteful fruit
From the unwilling bough,
When it may ripen of itself, and fall?

Emp. Grant her a day; though that's too much to give
Out of a life which I devote to love.

Bend. Then next, to bar
All future hopes of her desired Sebastian,
Let Dorax be enjoin'd to bring his head.

Emp. [*To the* MUFTI.] Go, Mufti, call him to receive
     his orders.   [*Exit* MUFTI.
I taste thy counsel; her desires new roused,
And yet unslaked, will kindle in her fancy,
And make her eager to renew the feast.

Bend. [*Aside.*] Dorax, I know before, will disobey;
There's a foe's head well cropt.
But this hot love precipitates my plot,
And brings it to projection ere its time.

Enter SEBASTIAN *and* ALMEYDA, *hand in hand; upon sight
of the Emperor they separate, and seem disturbed.*

Alm. He breaks at unawares upon our walks,
And like a midnight wolf invades the fold;
Make speedy preparation of your soul,
And bid it arm apace.   He comes for answer,
And brutal mischief sits upon his brow.
Sebas. Not the last sounding could surprise me more,
That summons drowsy mortals to their doom,
When called in haste they fumble for their limbs,
And tremble unprovided for their charge;
My sense has been so deeply plunged in joys,
The soul out-slept her hour; and scarce awake,
Would think too late, and cannot.   But brave minds
At worst can dare their fate.
Emp. [*Coming up to them.*] Have you performed
Your embassy, and treated with success?
Sebas. I had not time.
Emp. No, not for my affairs,
But for your own too much.
Sebas. You talk in clouds, explain your meaning, sir.
Emp. Explain yours first: what meant you hand in
And when you saw me, with a guilty start   [hand,
You loosed your hold, affrighted at my presence?
Sebas. Affrighted!
Emp. Yes, astonished and confounded.
Sebas. What mak'st thou of thyself, and what of me!
Art thou some ghost, some demon, or some god,
That I should stand astonished at thy sight?
If thou couldst deem so meanly of my courage,
Why didst thou not engage me man for man,
And try the virtue of that Gorgon face,
To stare me into statue?
Emp. O, thou art now recovered, but by Heaven,
Thou wert amazed at first, as if surprised
At unexpected baseness brought to light.
For know, ungrateful man, that kings, like gods,

Are everywhere : walk in the abyss of minds,
And view the dark recesses of the soul.

Sebas. Base and ungrateful never was I thought,
Nor, till this turn of fate, durst thou have called me ;
But, since thou boastest the omniscience of a god,
Say in what cranny of Sebastian's soul,
Unknown to me, so loathed a crime is lodged ?

Emp. Thou hast not broke my trust reposed in thee ?

Sebas. Imposed, but not received ; take back that false-
     hood.

Emp. Thou art not married to Almeyda ?

Sebas. Yes.

Emp. And own'st the usurpation of my love ?

Sebas. I own it, in the face of Heaven and thee,
No usurpation, but a lawful claim,
Of which I stand possess'd.

Emp. She has chosen well,
Betwixt a captive and a conqueror.

Alm. Betwixt a monster and the best of men.
He was the envy of his neighbouring kings ;
For him their sighing queens despised their lords,
And virgin daughters blushed when he was named.
To share his noble chains is more to me
Than all the savage greatness of thy throne.

Sebas. Were I to choose again, and knew my fate,
For such a night I would be what I am.
The joys I have possessed are ever mine ;
Out of thy reach behind eternity,
Hid in the sacred treasure of the past ;
But blest remembrance brings them hourly back.

Emp. Hourly, indeed, who hast but hours to live.
O mighty purchase of a boasted bliss !
To dream of what thou hadst one fugitive night,
And never shall have more.

Sebas. Barbarian, thou canst part us but a moment :
We shall be one again in thy despite.
Life is but air,
That yields a passage to the whistling sword,
And closes when 'tis gone.

Alm. How can we better die than close embraced.
Sucking each other's souls while we expire ?
Which so transfused, and mounting both at once,

The saints deceived, shall by a sweet mistake
Hand up thy soul for mine, and mine for thine.
 Emp. No, I'll outwit you.
I have occasion for your stay on earth;
Let him mount first, and beat upon the wing,
And wait an age for what I here detain;
Or sicken at immortal joys above,
And languish for the heaven he left below. [joined?
 Alm. Thou wilt not dare to break what Heaven has
 Emp. Not break the chain, but change a rotten link,
And rivet one to last.
Think'st thou I come to argue right and wrong?
Why lingers Dorax thus? Where are my guards,
   [BENDUCAR *goes out for the guards, and returns.*
To drag that slave to death? [*Pointing to* SEBASTIAN.
Now storm and rage,
Call vainly on thy prophet, then defy him
For wanting power to save thee.
 Sebas. That were to gratify thy pride; I'll show thee
How a man should, and how a king dare die:
So even, that my soul shall walk with ease
Out of its flesh, and shut out life as calmly
As it does words; without a sigh to note
One struggle in the smooth dissolving frame.
 Alm. [*To the Emp.*] Expect revenge from Heaven,
   inhuman wretch;
Nor hope to ascend Sebastian's holy bed.
Flames, daggers, poisons, guard the sacred steps;
Those are the promised pleasures of my love.
 Emp. And these might fright another, but not me;
Or me, if I designed to give you pleasure:
I seek my own, and while that lasts, you live.

   Enter two of the Guards.

Go, bear the captive to a speedy death,
And set my soul at ease.
 Alm. I charge you hold, ye ministers of death;
Speak, my Sebastian;
Plead for thy life; Oh, ask it of the tyrant;
'Tis no dishonour, trust me, love, 'tis none.
I would die for thee, but I cannot plead—
My haughty heart disdains it, even for thee.

Still silent! will the King of Portugal
Go to his death like a dumb sacrifice?
Beg him to save my life in saving thine.
    Sebas. Farewell, my life's not worth another word.
    Emp. [*To the guards.*] Perform your orders.
    Alm. Stay, take my farewell too.
Farewell the greatness of Almeyda's soul!
Look, tyrant, what excess of love can do,
It pulls me down thus low, as to thy feet; [*Kneels to him.*
Nay, to embrace thy knees with loathing hands,
Which blister when they touch thee; yet even thus,
Thus far I can, to save Sebastian's life.
    Emp. A secret pleasure trickles through my veins:
It works about the inlets of my soul!
To feel thy touch; and pity tempts the pass,
But the tough metal of my heart resists;
'Tis warmed with the soft fire, not melted down.
    Alm. A flood of scalding tears will make it run.
Spare him, Oh spare; can you pretend to love,
And have no pity? Love and that are twins.
Here will I grow;
Thus compass you with these supplanting cords,
And pull so long till the proud fabric falls.
    Emp. Still kneel, and still embrace; 'tis double pleasure
So to be hugged, and see Sebastian die.
    Alm. Look, tyrant, when thou nam'st Sebastian's death,
Thy very executioners turn pale.
Rough as they are, and hardened in their trade
Of death, they start at an anointed head,
And tremble to approach.——He hears me not,
Nor minds the impression of a God on kings,
Because no stamp of Heaven was on his soul,
But the resisting mass drove back the seal.
Say, though thy heart be rock of adamant,
Yet rocks are not impregnable to bribes:
Instruct me how to bribe thee: name thy price;
Lo, I resign my title to the crown;
Send me to exile with the man I love,
And banishment is empire.
    Emp. Here's my claim;
                   [*Clapping his hand to his sword.*
And this extinguished thine; thou giv'st me nothing.

Alm. My father's, mother's, brother's death I pardon:
That's somewhat sure; a mighty sum of murder,
Of innocent and kindred blood struck off.
My prayers and penance shall discount for these,
And beg of Heaven to charge the bill on me:
Behold what price I offer, and how dear
To buy Sebastian's life.

Emp. Let after-reckonings trouble fearful fools;
I'll stand the trial of those trivial crimes:
But, since thou begg'st me to prescribe my terms,
The only I can offer are thy love;
And this one day of respite to resolve.
Grant or deny; for thy next word is fate;
And fate is deaf to prayer.

Alm. May Heaven be so   [*Rising up.*
At thy last breath to thine: I curse thee not;
For who can better curse the plague or devil,
Than to be what they are? That curse be thine.
Now, do not speak, Sebastian, for you need not;
But die, for I resign your life: look, Heaven,
Almeyda dooms her dear Sebastian's death!
But is there Heaven? for I begin to doubt;
The skies are hushed, no grumbling thunders roll;
Now take your swing, ye impious; sin unpunished;
Eternal Providence seems over-watched,
And with a slumbering nod assents to murder.

Enter DORAX, *attended by three soldiers.*

Emp. Thou mov'st a tortoise pace to my relief.
Take hence that, once a king; that sullen pride
That swells to dumbness; lay him in the dungeon,
And sink him deep with irons; that, when he would,
He shall not groan to hearing: when I send,
The next commands are death.

Alm. Then prayers are vain as curses.

Emp. Much at one
In a slave's mouth, against a monarch's power.
This day thou hast to think;
At night, if thou wilt curse, thou shalt curse kindly;
Then I'll provoke thy lips; lay siege so close,
That all thy sallying breath shall turn to blessings.
Make haste, seize, force her, bear her hence.

Alm. Farewell, my last Sebastian!
I do not beg, I challenge justice now;
O Powers, if kings be your peculiar care,
Why plays this wretch with your prerogative?
Now flash him dead, now crumble him to ashes;
Or henceforth live confined in your own palace;
And look not idly out upon a world
That is no longer yours.

    [*She is carried off struggling,* EMP. *and* BEND. *follow.*
    SEBASTIAN *struggles in his guards' arms, and shakes*
    off one of them; but two others come in, and hold
    him: he speaks not all the while.

    Dor. [*Aside.*] I find I'm but a half-strained villain yet;
But mongrel-mischievous; for my blood boiled,
To view this brutal act; and my stern soul
Tugged at my arm to draw in her defence.
Down thou rebelling Christian in my heart;
Redeem thy fame on this Sebastian first; [*Walks a turn.*
Then think on other's wrongs when thine are righted.
But how to right them? on a slave disarmed;
Defenceless and submitted to my rage?
A base revenge is vengeance on myself;   [*Walks again.*
I have it, and I thank thee honest head,
Thus present to me at my great necessity:—

                    [*Comes up to* SEBASTIAN.

You know me not?
    Sebas. I hear men call thee Dorax.
    Dor. 'Tis well, you know enough for once, you speak
You were struck mute before.   [too;
    Sebas. Silence became me then.
    Dor. Yet we may talk hereafter.
    Sebas. Hereafter is not mine:—
Despatch thy work, good executioner.   [hood
    Dor. None of my blood were hangmen: add that false-
To a long bill that yet remains unreckon'd.
    Sebas. A king and thou can never have a reckoning.
    Dor. A greater sum perhaps than you can pay.
Meantime I shall make bold to increase your debt.

                    [*Gives him his sword.*

Take this, and use it at your greatest need.
    Sebas. This hand and this have been acquainted well:

                    [*Looks on it.*

It should have come before into my grasp,
To kill the ravisher.
    Dor. Thou heard'st the tyrant's orders; guard thy life
When 'tis attacked, and guard it like a man.
    Sebas. I'm still without thy meaning, but I thank thee.
    Dor. Thank me when I ask thanks, thank me with
    Sebas. Such surly kindness did I never see!   [that.
Dor. [*To the captain of his guards*] Muza, draw out a
    file, pick man by man,
Such who dare die, and dear will sell their death.
Guard him to the utmost; now conduct him hence,
And treat him as my person.
    Sebas. Something like
That voice methinks I should have somewhere heard:
But floods of woes have hurried it far off
Beyond my ken of soul.   [*Exit* SEBAS. *with the soldiers.*
    Dor. But I shall bring him back, ungrateful man.
                                   [*Solus.*
I shall, and set him full before thy sight,
When I shall 'front thee, like some staring ghost,
With all my wrongs about me.   What, so soon
Returned? this haste is boding.

       Enter to him EMPEROR, BENDUCAR, *and* MUFTI.

    Emp. She's still inexorable, still imperious,
And loud, as if, like Bacchus, born in thunder.
Be quick, ye false physicians of my mind,
Bring speedy death, or cure.
    Bend. What can be counselled while Sebastian lives?
The vine will cling, while the tall poplar stands,
But that cut down, creeps to the next support,
And twines as closely there.
    Emp. That's done with ease, I speak him dead; proceed.
    Muf. Proclaim your marriage with Almeyda next,
That civil wars may cease; this gains the crowd:
Then you may safely force her to your will:
For people side with violence and injustice,
When done for public good.
    Emp. Preach thou that doctrine.
    Bend. The unreasonable fool has broached a truth
                                   [*Aside.*
That blasts my hopes; but, since 'tis gone so far,

He shall divulge Almeyda is a Christian:
If that produce no tumult, I despair.
 Emp. Why speaks not Dorax?
 Dor. Because my soul abhors to mix with him.
Sir, let me bluntly say, you went too far,
To trust the preaching power on State affairs
To him or any heavenly demagogue.
'Tis a limb lopped from your prerogative,
And so much of heaven's image blotted from you.
 Muf. Sure thou hast never heard of holy men
(So Christians call them) fam'd in State affairs;
Such as in Spain, Ximenes, Albornez;
In England, Wolsey; match me these with laymen.
 Dor. How you triumph in one or two of these,
Born to be statesmen, happening to be churchmen!
Thou call'st them holy: so their function was:
But, tell me, Mufti, which of them were saints?
Next, sir, to you; the sum of all is this,
Since he claims powers from heaven, and not **from**
  kings,
When 'tis his interest, he can interest heaven
To preach you down; and ages oft depend
On hours, uninterrupted, in the chair.
 Emp. I'll trust his preaching while I rule his pay,
And I dare trust my Africans, to hear
Whatever he dare preach.
 Dor. You know them not.
The genius of your Moors is mutiny;
They scarcely want a guide to move their madness:
Prompt to rebel on every weak pretence,
Blustering when courted, crouching when oppressed;
Wise to themselves, and fools to all the world;
Restless in change, and perjured to a proverb.
They love religion sweetened to the sense,
A good, luxurious, palatable faith.
Thus vice and godliness, preposterous pair,
Ride cheek by jowl; but churchmen hold the reins.
And whene'er kings would lower clergy greatness,
They learn too late what power the preachers have,
And whose the subjects are. The Mufti knows it,
Nor dares deny what passed betwixt us two.
 Emp. No more; whate'er he said was my command.

Dor. Why, then, no more, since you will hear no more;
Some kings are resolute to their own ruin.

Emp. Without your meddling where you are not asked,
Obey your orders, and despatch Sebastian.

Dor. Trust my revenge ; be sure I wish him dead.

Emp. What mean'st thou ? What's thy wishing to my
Dispatch him, rid me of the man I loathe.   [will ?

Dor. I hear you, sir, I'll take my time and do't.

Emp. Thy time ? what's all thy time, what's thy whole
To my one hour of ease ?   No more replies,   [life
But see thou doest it, or——

Dor. Choke in that threat ; I can say Or as loud.

Emp. 'Tis well, I see my words have no effect,
But I may send a message to dispose you. [*Is going off.*

Dor. Expect an answer worthy of that message.

Muf. [*Aside.*] The prophet owed him this,
And thanked be heaven, he has it.

Bend. By holy Allah, I conjure you stay,
And judge not rashly of so brave a man.

            [*Draws the Emperor aside, and whispers him.*
I'll give you reasons why he cannot execute
Your orders now, and why he will hereafter.

Muf. [*Aside.*] Benducar is a fool to bring him off,
I'll work my own revenge, and speedily.

Bend. The fort is his, the soldiers' hearts are his ;
A thousand Christian slaves are in the castle,
Which he can free to reinforce his power ;
Your troops far off, beleaguering Lararche,
Yet in the Christian hands.

Emp. I grant all this ;
But grant me he must die.

Bend. He shall by poison ;
'Tis here, the deadly drug prepared in powder,
Hot as hell-fire :—then, to prevent his soldiers
From rising to revenge their general's death,
While he is struggling with his mortal pangs,
The rabble on the sudden may be rais'd
To seize the castle.

Emp. Do't ; 'tis left to thee.

Bend. Yet more ; but clear your brow ; for he
        observes.   [*They whisper again.*

Dor. What, will the fav'rite prop my falling fortunes?

[Aside.] O prodigy of court!

*[*Emp. *and* Bend. *return to* Dor.

Emp. Your friend has fully cleared your innocence;
I was too hasty to condemn unheard:
And you, perhaps, too prompt in your replies.
As far as fits the majesty of kings,
I ask excuse.

Dor. I'm sure I meant it well.

Emp. I know you did; this to our love renewed.

*[*Emp. *drinks.*

Benducar, fill to Dorax.

*[*Bend. *turns, and mixes a powder in it.*

Dor. Let it go round, for all of us have need
To quench our heats; 'tis the king's health, Benducar.
And I would pledge it, though I knew 'twere poison.

[He drinks.

Bend. Another bowl; for what the king has touched,
And you have pledged, is sacred to your loves.

[Drinks out of another bowl.

Muf. Since charity becomes my calling, thus
Let me provoke your friendship: and Heaven bless it,
As I intend it well.

*[Drinks, and turning aside, pours some drops out of a
little viol into the bowl; then presents it to* Dorax.

Dor. Heaven make thee honest,
On that condition we shall soon be friends. *[Drinks.*

Muf. *[Aside]* Yes, at our meeting in another world;
For thou hast drunk thy passport out of this.
Not the Nonacrian Font, nor Lethe's lake,
Could sooner numb thy nimble faculties,
Than this, to sleep eternal.

Emp. Now farewell, Dorax, this was our first quarrel,
And, I dare prophesy, will prove our last.

[Exit Emp. *with* Bend. *and the* Mufti.

Dor. It may be so: I'm strangely discompos'd:
Quick shootings through my limbs, and pricking pains,
Qualms at my heart, convulsions in my nerves,
Shiverings of cold, and burnings of my entrails,
Within my little world make medley-war,
Lose and regain, beat, and are beaten back,
As momentary victors quit their ground.
Can it be poison! poison's of one tenor,

Or hot, or cold; this neither, and yet both.
Some deadly draught, some enemy of life
Boils in my bowels, and works out my soul.
Ingratitude's the growth of every clime;
Afric, the scene removed, is Portugal.
    Of all court service learn the common lot;
    To-day 'tis done, to-morrow 'tis forgot.
    Oh, were that all! my honest corpse must lie
    Exposed to scorn and public infamy:
    My shameful death will be divulged alone;
    The worth and honour of my soul unknown.   [*Exit.*

SCENE II.   *A Night-Scene of the* MUFTI'S *Garden,
where an Arbour is Discovered.*

Enter ANTONIO.

Ant. She names herself Morayma; the Mufti's only
daughter, and a virgin! This is the time and place that
she appointed in her letter; yet she comes not. Why,
thou sweet, delicious creature, why so torture me with
thy delay! Dar'st thou be false to thy assignation?
What, in the cool and silence of the night, and to a new
lover? Pox on the hypocrite, thy father, for instructing
thee so little in the sweetest point of his religion. Hark,
I hear the rustling of her silk mantle. Now she comes,
now she comes; no, hang it, that was but the whistling
of the wind through the orange trees. Now again, I
hear the pit-a-pat of a pretty foot through the dark
alley. No, 'tis the son of a mare that's broken loose,
and munching upon the melons. Oh, the misery of an
expecting lover.   [*Goes to the arbour, and lies down.*

Enter JOHAYMA, *wrapped up in a Moorish mantle.*

Joh. Thus far my love has carried me, almost without
my knowledge whither I was going. Shall I go on, shall
I discover myself? [*She comes a little nearer the arbour.*

Ant. [*raising himself a little, and looking.*] At last
'tis she; this is no illusion, I am sure.

Joh. He's young and handsome.

Ant. [*Aside.*] Yes, well enough, I thank nature.

Joh. And I am yet neither old nor ugly.

Ant. [*Aside.*] Most divinely argued; she's the best
casuist in all Afric.   [*He rushes out and embraces her.*

I can hold no longer from embracing thee, my dear Morayma.

Joh. What nonsense do you talk? do you take me for the Mufti's daughter? *barnus.*

Ant. Why, are you not, madam? [*Throwing off her*

Joh. I find you had an appointment with Morayma.

Ant. [*Aside.*] By all that's good, the nauseous wife.

Joh. What, you are confounded, and stand mute?

Ant. Somewhat nonplussed I confess, to hear you deny your name so positively; why, are not you Morayma the Mufti's daughter? Did not I see you with him, did not he present me to you? Were you not so charitable as to give me money? Ay, and to tread upon my foot, and squeeze my hand too, if I may be so bold to remember you of past favours?

Joh. And you see I am come to make them good, but I am neither Morayma nor the Mufti's daughter.

Ant. Nay, I know not that; but I am sure he is old enough to be your father, and either father, or reverend father, I heard you call him.

Joh. Once again, how came you to name Morayma?

Ant. Another mistake of mine. For asking one of my fellow-slaves, who were the chief ladies about the house, he answered me, Morayma and Johayma; but she, it seems, is his daughter, with a pox to her, and you are his beloved wife.

Joh. This moon-shine grows offensive to my eyes; come, shall we walk into the arbour?

Ant. That's close and dark.

Joh. And are those faults to lovers?

Ant. But there I cannot please myself with the sight of your beauty.

Joh. Perhaps not. But you may hear my voice.

Ant. There's not a breath of air stirring.

Joh. The breath of lovers is the sweetest air; but you are fearful.

Ant. I am considering, indeed, that if I am taken with you——

Joh. The best way to avoid it is to retire, where we may not be heard.

Ant. Where lodges your husband?

Joh. Just against the face of this open walk.

Ant. Then he has seen us already, for aught I know.

Joh. You make so many difficulties, I fear I am displeasing to you.

Ant. [*Aside.*] If Morayma comes, and takes me in the arbour with her, I have made a fine exchange of that diamond for this pebble.

Joh. You are much fallen off, let me tell you, from your first ardour.

Ant. I confess I was somewhat too excited at first, but you will forgive the transport of my passion; now I have considered it better, I have a qualm of conscience.

Joh. Of conscience! Why, what has conscience to do with two young lovers?

Ant. Why, truly, conscience is something to blame for interposing in our matters; but how can I help it, if I have a scruple to betray my master?

Joh. There must be something more in it, for your conscience was very quiet when you took me for Morayma.

Ant. I grant you, madam, when I took you for his daughter.

Joh. You Christians are such peeking sinners, you tremble at a shadow in the moonshine.

Ant. And you Africans are such termagants, you stop at nothing. I must be plain with you: you are married, and to a holy man, the head of your religion. Go back to your chamber, go back I say. I will be true to you. I can tell you that for your comfort.

Joh. Flesh without blood I think thou art; or, if any, 'tis as cold as that of fishes. But I'll teach thee, to thy cost, what vengeance is in store for refusing a lady who has offered thee her love —— Help, help, there; will nobody come to my assistance?

Ant. What do you mean, madam? For Heaven's sake peace; your husband will hear you; think of your own danger, if you will not think of mine.

Joh. Ungrateful wretch, thou deservest no pity; help, help, husband, or I shall be ravished: the villain will be too strong for me. Help, help, for pity of a poor distressed creature.

Ant. Then I have nothing but impudence to assist me. I must drown her clamour, whatever comes of it.

[*He takes out his flute, and plays as loud as he can possibly, and she continues crying out.*

Enter the MUFTI *in his night-gown, and two Servants.*

Muf. O thou villain, what horrible impiety art thou committing? What, ravishing the wife of my bosom! Take him away, ganch him, impale him, rid the world of such a monster. [*Servants seize him.*

Ant. Mercy, dear master, mercy. Hear me first, and after, if I have deserved hanging, spare me not. What have you seen to provoke you to this cruelty?

Muf. I have heard the outcries of my wife; the bleatings of the poor innocent lamb: seen nothing, sayest thou! If I see the lamb lie bleeding, and the butcher by her with his knife drawn, and bloody, is not that evidence sufficient of the murder?

Ant. Pray think in reason, sir, is a man to be put to death for a similitude? No violence has been committed; none intended: the lamb's alive: and if I durst tell you so, no more a lamb than I am a butcher.

Joh. How's that, villain, dar'st thou accuse me?

Ant. Be patient, madam, and speak but truth, and I'll ever be thy grateful servant.

Joh. [*Aside.*] Ah! I fear 'tis now too late to save him: —— Pray hear him speak, husband; perhaps he may say something for himself; I know not.

Muf. Speak thou, has he not violated thy honour?

Joh. I forgive him freely, for he has done nothing.

Muf. But did he mean no mischief? Was he endeavouring nothing?

Joh. In my conscience, I begin to doubt he did not.

Muf. 'Tis impossible; then what meant all these outcries?

Joh. I heard music in the garden, and at an unseasonable time of night, and I stole softly out of my bed, as imagining it might be he.

Muf. How's that, Johayma? Imagining it was he, and yet you went?

Joh. Why not, my lord, am not I the mistress of the family? and is it not my place to see good order kept in it? I thought he might have allured some of the she-slaves to him, and was resolved to prevent what might have been betwixt him and them; when, on the sudden, he rushed out upon me, caught me in his arms with such a fury——

Muf. I have heard enough, away with him——

Joh. Mistaking me, no doubt, for one of his fellow-slaves. With that, affrighted as I was, I discovered myself, and cried aloud. But, as soon as ever he knew me, the villain let me go; and I must needs say, he started back, as if I were some serpent, and was more afraid of me than I of him.

Muf. O thou corrupter of my family, that's cause enough of death; once again, away with him.

Joh. What, for an intended trespass? No harm has been done, whatever may be. He cost you five hundred crowns, I take it.

Muf. Thou sayest true, a very considerable sum. He shall not die, though he had committed folly with a slave; 'tis too much to lose by him.

Ant. My only fault has ever been to love playing in the dark, and the more she cried the more I played, that it might be seen I intended nothing to her.

Muf. To your kennel, sirrah, mortify your flesh, and consider in whose family you are.

Joh. And one thing more, remember from henceforth to obey better.

Muf. [*Aside.*] For all her smoothness, I am not quite cured of my jealousy; but I have thought of a way that will clear my doubts.

[*Exit* MUFTI *with* JOHAYMA *and Servants.*

Ant. I am mortified sufficiently already, without the help of his ghostly counsel. Fear of death has gone further with me in two minutes than my conscience would have gone in two months. I find myself in a very dejected condition, and if Morayma should now appear——

[MORAYMA *comes out of the arbour; she steals behind him, and claps him on the back.*

Mor. And if Morayma should appear, as she does appear, alas you say for her and you!

Ant. Art thou there, my sweet temptation! my eyes, my life, my soul, my all!

Mor. A mighty compliment, when all these, by your own confession, are just nothing.

Ant. Nothing till thou cam'st to new create me; thou dost not know the power of thy own charms. Let me embrace thee.

Mor. [*Stepping back.*] Nay, 'tis best keeping you at a distance; I have no mind to warm a frozen snake in my bosom; he may chance to recover, and sting me for my pains.

Ant. Consider what I have suffered for thy sake already, and make me some amend; two disappointments in a night! O cruel creature!

Mor. And you may thank yourself for both; I came before my time, through the back walk behind the arbour; and you, like a fresh-water soldier, stood guarding the pass before. If you missed the enemy, you may thank your own dulness.

Ant. Nay, if you will be using stratagems, you shall give me leave to make use of my advantages.

Mor. By your favour, sir, we meet upon treaty now, and not upon defiance.

Ant. If that be all, you shall have *carte blanche* immediately; for I long to be ratifying.

Mor. No, now I think on't, you are already entered into articles with my enemy Johayma. Was that like a cavalier of honour?

Ant. Not very heroic: but self-preservation is a point above honour and religion too. Antonia was a rogue, I must confess; but you must give me leave to love him.

Mor. To beg your life so basely, and to present your sword to the enemy. Oh recreant!

Ant. If I had died honourably, my fame indeed would have sounded loud, but I should never have heard the blast. Come, don't make yourself worse natured than you are.

Mor. Yes, if I were sure you would listen to me.

Ant. Can you suspect I would leave you for Johayma?

Mor. No, but I can expect you would have both of us. Love is covetous; I must have all of you: heart for heart is an equal truck. In short, I am younger, I think handsomer, and am sure I love you better. She has been my stepmother these fifteen years. You think that's her face you see, but 'tis only a daub'd vizard. She wears an armour of proof upon't; an inch thick of paint, besides the wash. Her face is so fortified that you can make no approaches to it without a shovel. But for her constancy, I can tell you for your comfort, she will love till death—

I mean till yours; for when she cares not for you, she will certainly dispatch you to another world, as she has already served three slaves, your predecessors of happy memory.

Ant. Prithee prevent her then.

Mor. No, I'll have a butcher's pennyworth of you; first secure the carcass, and then take the fleece into the bargain.

Ant. Why, sure you did not put yourself and me to all this trouble. By this hand—— [*Taking it.*

Mor. Which you shall never touch but upon better assurances than you imagine. [*Pulling her hand away.*

Ant. I'll marry thee, and make a Christian of thee, thou pretty infidel.

Mor. I mean you shall, but no earnest, till the bargain be made before witness; there's love enough to be had, and as much as you can turn you to, never doubt, but all upon honourable terms.

Ant. I vow and swear by Love; and he's a Deity in all religions.

Mor. But never to be trusted in any; he has another name, too, of a worse sound. Shall I trust an oath when I see your eyes languishing, your cheeks flushing, and can hear your heart throbbing? No, I'll not come near you. He's a foolish physician who will feel the pulse of a patient that has the plague-spots upon him.

Ant. Did one ever hear a little moppet argue so?

Mor. You would fain be fingering your rents before-hand; but that makes a man an ill husband ever after. Consider, marriage is a painful vocation, as you shall prove it; manage your income as thriftily as you can, you shall find a hard task on't to make even at the year's end, and yet to live decently.

Ant. I came with a Christian intention to revenge myself upon thy father, for being the head of a false religion.

Mor. And so you shall; I offer you his daughter for your second. Meet me under my window to-morrow night, body for body, about this hour; I'll slip down out of my lodging, and bring my father in my hand.

Ant. How, thy father!

Mor. I mean all that's good of him; his pearls and

jewels, his whole contents, his heart and soul; as much
as ever I can carry! I'll leave him his Alcoran; that's
revenue enough for him. Every page of it is gold and
diamonds. He has the turn of an eye, a demure smile,
and a godly cant, that are worth millions to him. I forgot to tell you that I will have a slave prepared at the
postern gate, with two horses ready saddled. No more,
for fear I may be missed; and think I hear them calling
for me. If you have constancy and courage——

Ant. Never doubt it; and love in abundance, to wander
with thee all the world over.

Mor. The value of twelve hundred thousand crowns in
a casket?

Ant. A heavy burden, Heaven knows! but we must
pray for patience to support it.

Mor. Besides a willing titt that will venture her corpse
with you. Come, I know you long to have a parting
blow, and therefore to show I am in charity——

[He kisses her.

Ant. Once more, for pity; that I may keep the flavour
upon my lips till we meet again.

Mor. No; frequent charities make bold beggars. And
besides, I have learned of a falconer never to feed up a
hawk when I would have him fly. That's enough—but
if you would be nibbling, here's a hand to stay thy
stomach. *[Kissing her hand.*

Ant. Thus conquered infidels, that wars may cease,
    Are forced to give their hands and sign the peace.

Mor. Thus Christians are outwitted by the foe;
    You had her in your power, and let her go.
    If you release my hand, the fault's not mine;
    You should have made me seal as well as sign.

[*She runs off, he follows her to the door, then comes
back again, and goes out at the other.*

ACT IV. SCENE I.

BENDUCAR's *Palace in the Castle of Alcazar.*

Bend. My future fate, the colour of my life,   [*Solus.*
My all depends on this important hour:
This hour my lot is weighing in the scales,

And Heaven, perhaps, is doubting what to do.
Almeyda and a crown have pushed me forward:
'Tis fixed, the tyrant must not ravish her:
He and Sebastian stand betwixt my hopes:
He most; and therefore first to be dispatched.
These and a thousand things are to be done
In the short compass of this rolling night,
And nothing yet performed,
None of my emissaries yet returned.

Enter HALY, *first servant.*

Oh Haly, thou hast kept me long in pain.
What hast thou learnt of Dorax? is he dead?
 Haly. Two hours I warily have watched his palace;
All doors are shut, no servant peeps abroad;
Some officers with striding haste passed in,
While others outward went on quick dispatch;
Sometimes hushed silence seemed to reign within;
Then cries confused, and a joint clamour followed;
Then lights went gliding by, from room to room,
And shot like thwarting meteors cross the house.
Not daring further to enquire, I came
With speed to bring you this imperfect news.
 Bend. Hence I conclude him either dead or dying:
His mournful friends, summoned to take their leave,
Are thronged about his couch, and sit in council.
What those caballing captains may design,
I must prevent by being first in action.
To Muley-Zeydan fly with speed, desire him
To take my last instructions; tell the importance,
And haste his presence here.   [*Exit* HALY.
How has this poison lost its wonted way?
It should have burnt its passage, not have lingered
In the blind labyrinths and crooked turnings
Of human composition; now it moves
Like a slow fire that works against the wind,
As if his stronger stars had interposed.

Enter HAMET.

Well, Hamet, are our friends the rabble raised?
From Mustapha what message?
 Ham. What you wish.

The streets are thicker in this noon of night,
Than at the mid-day sun. A drowsy horror
Sits on their eyes, like fear not well awake.
All crowd in heaps, as at a night alarm,
The bees drive out upon each other's backs,
To emboss their hives in clusters; all ask news.
Their busy captain runs the weary round
To whisper orders, and commanding silence,
Makes not noise cease, but deafens it to murmurs.

Bend. Night wastes apace. When, when will he ap-
Ham. He only waits your summons. [pear?
Bend. Haste their coming.
Let secrecy and silence be enjoined
In their close march. What news from the lieutenant?
Ham. I left him at the gate, firm to your interest,
To admit the townsmen at their first appearance.
Bend. Thus far 'tis well. Go hasten Mustapha.
                                        [*Exit* HAMET.

Enter ORCHAN, *the third Servant.*

O, Orchan, did I think thy diligence
Would lag behind the rest? what from the Mufti?
    Orc. I sought him round his palace, made enquiry
Of all the slaves; in short, I used your name,
And urged the importance home, but had for answer,
That since the shut of evening none had seen him.
    Bend. O the curs'd fate of all conspiracies!
They move on many springs; if one but fail,
The restive machine stops. In an ill hour he's absent:
'Tis the first time, and sure will be the last
That e'er a Mufti was not in the way,
When tumults and rebellion should be broach'd.
Stay by me; thou art resolute and faithful;
I have employment worthy of thy arm. [*Walks.*

Enter MULEY-ZEYDAN.

Mul.-Zeyd. You see me come impatient of my hopes,
And eager as the courser for the race.
Is all in readiness?
    Bend. All but the Mufti.
    Mul.-Zeyd. We must go on without him.
    Bend. True, we must;

For 'tis ill stopping in the full career,
Howe'er the leap be dangerous and wide.
 Orc. [*Looking out.*] I see the blaze of torches from afar;
This way they move.
 Bend. No doubt, the Emperor.
We must not be surprised in conference.
Trust to my management the tyrant's death;
And haste yourself to join with Mustapha.
The officer who guards the gate is yours:
When you have gained that pass, divide your force;
Yourself in person head one chosen half,
And march to oppress the faction in consult
With dying Dorax. Fate has driven them all
Into the net: you must be bold and sudden:
Spare none, and if you find him struggling yet
With pangs of death, trust not his rolling eyes
And heaving gasps; for poison may be false,
The home thrust of a friendly sword is sure. [surpris'd;
 Mul.-Zeyd. Doubt not my conduct: they shall be
Mercy may wait without the gate one night,
At morn I'll take her in.
 Bend. Here lies your way,
You meet your brother there.
 Mul.-Zeyd. May we ne'er meet:
For, like the twins of Leyda, when I mount,
He gallops down the skies.   [*Exit* MUL.-ZEYD.
 Bend. He comes; now, heart,
Be ribbed with iron for this one attempt;
Set ope thy sluices, send the vigorous blood
Through every active limb for my relief:
Then take thy rest within thy quiet cell,
For thou shalt drum no more.

  Enter EMPEROR *and guards attending him.*

 Emp. What news of our affairs, and what of Dorax?
Is he no more! say that, and make me happy.
 Bend. May all your enemies be like that dog,
Whose parting soul is labouring at the lips.
 Emp. The people, are they raised?
 Bend. And marshall'd too;
Just ready for the march.
 Emp. Then I'm at ease.

Bend. The night is yours, the glittering host of heaven
Shines but for you; but most the star of love,
That twinkles you to fair Almeyda's bed.
Oh, there's a joy, to melt in her embrace,
Dissolve in pleasure;
And make the gods curse immortality,
That so they could not die.
But haste, and make them yours.
    Emp. I will; and yet
A kind of weight hangs heavy at my heart;
My flagging soul flies under her own pitch;
Like fowl in air too damp, and lugs along,
As if she were a body in a body,
And not a mounting substance made of fire.
My senses, too, are dull and stupefied,
Their edge rebated; sure some ill approaches,
And some kind sprite knocks softly at my soul,
To tell me fate's at hand.
    Bend. Mere fancies all.
Your soul has been before-hand with your body,
And drunk so deep a draught of promis'd bliss,
She slumbers o'er the cup; no danger's near,
But of a surfeit at too full a feast.
    Emp. It may be so; it looks so like the dream
That overtook me at my waking hour,
This morn; and dreams they say are then divine,
When all the balmy vapours are exhaled,
And some o'erpowering god continues sleep.
'Twas then methought Almeyda, smiling, came
Attended with a train of all her race,
Whom in the rage of empire I had murdered.
But now, no longer foes, they gave me joy
Of my new conquest, and with helping hands
Heaved me into our holy prophet's arms,
Who bore me in a purple cloud to Heaven.
    Bend. Good omen, sir, I wish you in that heaven
Your dreams portends you,
Which presages death——   [*Aside.*
    Emp. Thou too wert there;
And thou methought didst push me from below,
With thy full force to Paradise.
    Bend. Yet better.

Emp. Hah! what's that grizzly fellow that attends
Bend. Why ask you, sir?   [thee?
Emp. For he was in my dream,
And helped to heave me up.
Bend. With prayers and wishes,
For I dare swear him honest.
Emp. That may be;
But yet he looks damnation.
Bend. You forget,
The face would please you better.   Do you love,
And can you thus forbear?
Emp. I'll head my people;
Then think of dalliance when the danger's o'er.
My warlike spirits work now another way,
And my soul is tuned to trumpets.
Bend. You debase yourself,
To think of mixing with the ignoble herd.
Let such perform the servile work of war,
Such who have no Almeyda to enjoy.
What, shall the people know their god-like prince
Skulked in a nightly skirmish? stole a conquest,
Headed a rabble, and profaned his person,
Shouldered with filth, borne in a tide of ordure,
And stifled with their rank offensive sweat?
Emp. I am off again: I will not prostitute
The regal dignity so far, to head them.
Bend. There spoke a King.
Dismiss your guards, to be employed elsewhere
In ruder combats.   You will want no seconds
In those alarms you seek.
Emp. Go join the crowd;   [*To the Guards.*
Benducar, thou shalt lead them in my place. [*Ex. Guards.*
The God of love once more has shot his fires
Into my soul; and my whole heart receives him.
Almeyda now returns with all her charms;
I feel her as she glides along my veins,
And dances in my blood.   So when our prophet
Had long been hammering in his lonely cell,
Some dull, insipid, tedious paradise,
A brisk Arabian girl came tripping by;
Passing she cast at him a side-long glance,
And looked behind in hopes to be pursued.

He took the hint, embraced the flying fair;
And having found his heaven, he fixed it there.

[Exit Emp.

Bend. That paradise thou never shall possess.
His death is easy now, his guards are gone;
And I can sin but once to seize the throne.
All after-acts are sanctified by power.

   Orc. Command my sword and life.

   Bend. I thank thee Orchan,
And shall reward thy faith. This master-key
Frees every lock, and leads us to his person.
And should we miss our blow, as Heaven forbid,
Secure retreat. Leave open all behind us;
And first set wide the Mufti's garden gate,
Which is his private passage to the palace.
For there our mutineers appoint to meet,
And thence we may have aid. Now sleep ye stars,
That silently o'erwatch the fate of kings;
Be all propitious influences barred,
And none but murderous planets mount the guard.

[Exit with Orchan.

SCENE II.—A Night in the Mufti's Garden.

Enter the Mufti alone, in a slave's habit, like that of
Antonio.

Muf. This 'tis to have a sound head-piece; by this I have got to be chief of my religion; that is, honestly speaking, to teach others what I neither know nor believe myself. For what's Mahomet to me, but that I get by him? Now for my policy of this night: I have mewed up my suspected spouse in her own chamber. No more embassies to that lusty young gardener. Next, my habit of a slave; I have made myself as like him as I can, all but his youth and vigour; which, when I had, I passed my time as well as any of my holy predecessors. Now, walking under the windows of my seraglio: if Johayma look out, she will certainly take me for Antonio, and call to me; and by that I shall know what concupiscence is working in her; she cannot come down to commit iniquity, there's my safety; but if she

K ₂

peep, if she put her nose abroad, there's a demonstration of her pious will: and I'll not make the first precedent for a churchman to forgive injuries.

Enter MORAYMA *running to him with a casket in her hand, and embracing him.*

Mor. Now I can embrace you with a good conscience; here are the pearls and jewels, here's my father.

Muf. I am, indeed, thy father; but how the devil didst thou know me in this disguise? and what pearls dost thou mean?

Mor. [*Going back.*] What have I done, and what will now become of me!

Muf. Art thou mad, Morayma?

Mor. I think you'll make me so.

Muf. Why, what have I done to thee? Recollect thyself, and speak sense to me.

Mor. Then give me leave to tell you, you are the worst of fathers.

Muf. Did I think I had begotten such a monster? Proceed, my dutiful child, proceed, proceed.

Mor. You have been raking together a mass of wealth by indirect and wicked means: the spoils of orphans are in these jewels, and the tears of widows in these pearls.

Muf. Thou amazest me!

Mor. I would do so. This casket is loaded with your sins; 'tis the cargo of rapines, simony, and extortions; the iniquity of thirty years' muftiship converted into diamonds.

Muf. Would some rich railing rogue would say as much to me, that I might squeeze his purse for scandal.

Mor. No, sir; you get more by pious fools than railers, when you insinuate into their families, manage their fortunes while they live, and beggar their heirs by getting legacies, when they die. And do you think I'll be the receiver of your theft? I discharge my conscience of it. Here, take again your filthy mammon, and restore it, you had best, to the true owners.

Muf. I am finely documented by my own daughter.

Mor. And a great credit for me to be so. Do but think how decent a habit you have on, and how becoming your function to be disguised like a slave, and eves-dropping under the women's windows, to be saluted, as you deserve it rightly, with a chamber-pot. If I had not known you casually by your shambling gait, and a certain reverend awkwardness that is natural to all of your function, here you had been exposed to the laughter of your own servants; who have been in search of you through the whole seraglio, peeping under every petticoat to find you.

Muf. Prithee, child, reproach me no more of human failings; they are but a little of the pitch and spots of the world that are still sticking on me; but I hope to scour them out in time. I am better at bottom than thou thinkest: I am not the man thou takest me for.

Mor. No, to my sorrow, sir, you are not.

Muf. It was a very odd beginning though, methought, to see thee come running in upon me with such a warm embrace; prithee, what was the meaning of that?

Mor. I am sure I meant nothing by it, but the zeal and affection which I bear to the man of the world, whom I may love lawfully.

Muf. Why, this is as it should be now. Take the treasure again, it can never be put into better hands.

Mor. Yes, to my knowledge but it might. I have confessed my soul to you, if you understand me rightly; I never disobeyed you till this night; and now, since through the violence of my passion I have been so unfortunate, I humbly beg your pardon, your blessing, and your leave, that upon the first opportunity I may go for ever from your sight; for Heaven knows, I never desire to see you more.

Muf. [*Wiping his eyes.*] Thou makest me weep at thy unkindness—indeed, dear daughter, we will not part.

Mor. Indeed, dear daddy, but we will.

Muf. Why, if I have been a little pilfering, or so, I take it bitterly of thee to tell me of it; since it was to make thee rich; and I hope a man may make bold with his own soul, without offence to his own child. Here, take the jewels again; take them, I charge thee, upon thy obedience.

Mor. Well, then, in virtue of obedience I will take them; but on my soul, I had rather they were in a better hand.

Muf. Meaning mine, I know it.

Mor. Meaning his whom I love better than my life.

Muf. That's me again.

Mor. I would have you think so.

Muf. How thy good nature works upon me; well, I can do no less than venture damning for thee, and I may put fair for it, if the rabble be ordered to rise to-night.

Enter ANTONIO *in an African rich habit.*

Ant. What do you mean, my dear, to stand talking in this suspicious place, just underneath Johayma's window? [*To the* MUFTI.] You are well met comrade, I know you are the friend of our flight; are the horses ready at the postern gate?

Muf. Antonio, and in disguise? now I begin to smell a rat.

Ant. And I another, that outstinks it: false Morayma, hast thou thus betrayed me to thy father!

Mor. Alas, I was betrayed myself: he came disguised like you, and I, poor innocent, ran into his hands.

Muf. In good time you did so: I laid a trap for a bitch fox, and a worse vermin has caught himself in it. You would fain break loose now, though you left a limb behind you; but I am yet in my own territories and in call of company, that's my comfort.

Ant. [*Taking him by the throat.*] No; I have a trick left to put thee past thy squeaking: I will give thee the quinsey; that ungracious tongue shall preach no more false doctrine.

Mor. What do you mean? you will not throttle him? consider he's my father.

Ant. Prithee let us provide first for our own safety; if I do not consider him, he will consider us with a vengeance afterwards.

Mor. You may threaten him for crying out, but for my sake, give him back a little cranny of his windpipe, and some part of speech.

Ant. Not so much as one single interjection. Come away, father-in-law, this is no place for dialogues; when you are in the mosque you talk by hours, and there no man must interrupt you; this is but like for like, good father-in-law: now I am in the pulpit, 'tis your turn to hold your tongue. [*He struggles.*] Nay if you will be hanging back, I shall take care you shall hang forward.

[*Pulls him along the stage with his sword at his reins.*

Mor. T'other way, to the arbour with him; and make haste before we are discovered.

Ant. If I only bind and gag him there, he may commend me hereafter for civil usage; he deserves not so much favour by any action of his life.

Mor. Yes, pray bate him one, for begetting your mistress.

Ant. I would, if he had not thought more of thy mother than of thee; once more come along in silence, my Pythagorean father-in-law.

Joh. [*At the balcony.*] A bird in a cage may peep at least, tho' she must not fly; what bustle's there beneath my window? Antonio by all my hopes, I know him by his habit; but what makes that woman with him, and a friend, a sword drawn, and hasting hence? this is no time for silence: Who's within? call there, where are the servants? why, Omar, Abedin, Hassan, and the rest, make haste and run into the garden; there are thieves and villains; arm all the family and stop 'em.

Ant. [*Turning back.*] O that screech owl at the window! we shall be pursued immediately; which way shall we take?

Mor. [*Giving him the casket.*] 'Tis impossible to escape them, for the way to our horses lies back again by the house, and then we shall meet 'em full in the teeth: here, take these jewels; thou mayst leap the walls and get away.

Ant. And what will become of thee then, poor kind soul?

Mor. I must take my fortune: when you are got safe into your own country, I hope you will bestow a sigh on the memory of her who loved you.

Ant. It makes me mad to think how many a day will be lost betwixt us! take back thy jewels; 'tis an empty casket without thee; besides, I should never leap well with the weight of all thy father's sins about me; thou and they had been a bargain.

Mor. Prithee take 'em, 'twill help me to be revenged on him.

Ant. No; they'll serve to make thy peace with him.

Mor. I hear 'em coming: shift for yourself at least; remember I am yours for ever.

> [*Servants crying, " This way, this way,"
> behind the scenes.*

Ant. And I but the empty shadow of myself without thee! Farewell, father-in-law, that should have been, if I had not been curst in my mother's belly! Now, which way fortune?

> [*Runs amazedly backwards and forwards. Servants
> within, " Follow, follow, yonder are the villains."*

Ant. O here's a gate open; but it leads into the castle; yet I must venture it.   [*Going out.*

> [*A shout behind the scenes where* ANTONIO *is going out.*

Ant. There's the rabble in a mutiny; what, is the devil up at midnight! However, 'tis good herding in a crowd.   [*Runs out.*

> [MUFTI *runs to* MORAYMA, *and lays hold on her, then
> snatches away the casket.*

Muf. Now, to do things in order, first I seize upon the bag and then upon the baggage: for thou art but my flesh and blood, but these are my life and soul.

Mor. Then let me follow my flesh and blood, and keep to yourself your life and soul.

Muf. Both or none, come away to durance.

Mor. Well, if it must be so, agreed, for I have another trick to play you; and thank yourself for what shall follow.

Enter Servants.

Joh. [*From above.*] One of them took through the private way into the castle; follow him be sure, for these are yours already.

Mor. Help here quickly, Omar, Abedin; I have hold on the villain that stole my jewels; but 'tis a lusty rogue, and he will prove too strong for me; what! help I say; do you not know your master's daughter?

Muf. Now if I cry out, they will know my voice, and then I am disgraced for ever: O thou art a venomous cockatrice!

Mor. Of your own begetting. [*The servants seize him.*

1 Serv. What a glorious deliverance have you had, madam, from this bloody-minded Christian!

Mor. Give me back my jewels, and carry this notorious malefactor to be punished by my father. I'll hunt the other dry-foot.

[*Takes the jewels, and runs out after* ANTONIO *at the same passage.*

1 Serv. I long to be handfelling his hide, before we bring him to my master.

2 Serv. Hang him for an old covetous hypocrite: he deserves a worse punishment himself for keeping us so hardly.

1 Serv. Ay, would he were in this villain's place; thus I would lay him on, and thus. [*Beats him.*

2 Serv. And thus would I revenge myself of my last beating. [*He beats him too, and then the rest.*

Muf. Oh! ho, ho!

1 Serv. Now supposing you were the Mufti, sir.

[*Beats him again.*

Muf. The devil's in that supposing, rascal; I can bear no more; and I am the Mufti; now suppose yourselves my servants, and hold your hands: an anointed halter take you all.

1 Serv. My master! you will pardon the excess of our zeal for you, sir; indeed we all took you for a villain, and so we used you.

Muf. Ay, so I feel you did; my back and sides are abundant testimonies of your zeal. Run rogues, and bring me back my jewels, and my fugitive daughter: run, I say.

[*They run to the gate, and the first servant runs back again.*

1 Serv. Sir, the castle is in a most terrible combustion; you may hear 'em hither.

Muf. 'Tis a laudable commotion: the voice of the mobile is the voice of heaven. I must retire a little, to strip me of the slave, and to assume the Mufti; and then I will return; for the piety of the people must be encouraged, that they may help me to recover my jewels and my daughter. [*Exit* MUFTI *and Servants.*

The SCENE *changes to the Castle-Yard,*

And discovers ANTONIO, MUSTAPHA, *and the Rabble shouting: They come forward.*

Ant. And so at length, as I informed you, I 'scaped

out of his covetous clutches; and now fly to your illustrious feet for my protection.

Must. Thou shalt have it, and now defy the Mufti. 'Tis the first petition that has been made to me since my exaltation to tumult, in this second night of the month Ahib, and in the year of the Hegira—the Lord knows what year,—but 'tis no matter; for when I am settled, the learned are bound to find it out for me; for I am resolved to date my authority over the rabble like other monarchs.

Ant. I have always had a longing to be yours again, though I could not compass it before, and had designed you a casket of my master's jewels too; for I knew the custom, and would not have appeared before a great person, as you are, without a present; but he has defrauded my good intentions, and basely robbed you of them: 'tis a prize worthy a million of crowns, and you carry your letters of marque about you.

Must. I shall make bold with his treasure, for the support of my new government. [*The people gather about him.*] What do these vile raggamuffins so near our person? your savour is offensive to us; bear back there, and make room for honest men to approach us; these fools and knaves are always impudently crowding next to princes, and keeping off the more deserving; bear back, I say. [*They make a wider circle.*] That's dutifully done! now shout to show your loyalty. [*A great shout.*] Hear'st thou that, slave Antonio? these obstreperous villains shout, and know not for what they make a noise. You shall see me manage them, that you may judge what ignorant beasts they are. For whom do you shout now? Who's to live and reign? tell me that, the wisest of you.

1 Rabble. Even whom you please, captain.

Must. La you there; I told you so.

2 Rab. We are not bound to know who is to live and reign; our business is only to rise upon command, and plunder.

3 Rab. Ay, the richest of both parties; for they are our enemies.

Must. This last fellow is a little more sensible than the rest; he has entered somewhat into the merits of the cause.

1 Rab. If a poor man may speak his mind, I think,

Captain, that yourself are the fittest to live and reign. I mean not over, but next and immediately under the people; and thereupon I say, "A Mustapha, a Mustapha!"

[*All cry,* "*A Mustapha, a Mustapha!*"

Must. I must confess the sound is pleasing, and tickles the ears of my ambition; but alas, my good people, it must not be! I am contented to be a poor simple viceroy; but Prince Muley-Zeydan is to be the man: I shall take care to instruct him in the arts of government, and in his duty to us all; and therefore mark my cry, "A Muley-Zeydan, a Muley-Zeydan!"

[*All cry,* "*A Muley-Zeydan, a Muley-Zeydan!*"

Must. You see, slave Antonio, what I might have been.

Ant. I observe your modesty.

Must. But for a foolish promise I made once to my Lord Benducar, to set up any one he pleased.

Re-enter the MUFTI *with his Servants.*

Ant. Here's the old hypocrite again; now stand your ground, and bate him not an inch. Remember the jewels, the rich and glorious jewels; they are designed to be yours, by virtue of prerogative.

Must. Let me alone to pick a quarrel. I have an old grudge to him upon thy account.

Muf. [*Making up to the mobile.*] Good people, here you are met together.

1 Rab. Ay, we know that without your telling; but why are we met together, doctor? for that's it which nobody here can tell.

2 Rab. Why, to see one another in the dark; and to make holiday at midnight.

Muf. You are met as becomes good Mussulmen to settle the nation; for I must tell you, that though your tyrant is a lawful emperor, yet your lawful emperor is but a tyrant.

Ant. What stuff he talks!

Must. 'Tis excellent fine matter, indeed, slave Antonio; he has a rare tongue. Oh, he would move a rock or elephant!

Ant. [*Aside.*] What a block have I to work upon!— But still remember the jewels, sir, the jewels. [*To him.*

Must. Nay, that's true on the other side: the jewels must be mine; but he has a pure fine way of talking.

My conscience goes along with him, but the jewels have set my heart against him.

Muf. That your emperor is a tyrant is most manifest; for you were born to be Turks, but he has played the Turk with you, and is taking your religion away.

2 Rab. We find that in our decay of trade. I have seen for these hundred years that religion and trade always go together.

Muf. He is now upon the point of marrying himself without your sovereign consent; and what are the effects of marriage?

3 Rab. A scolding, domineering wife, if she prove honest; and if otherwise, a fine gaudy minx that robs our counters every night, and then goes out and spends it upon our cuckold-makers.

Muf. No, the natural effects of marriage are children. Now, on whom would he beget these children? Even upon a Christian! O, horrible; how can you believe me, though I am ready to swear it upon the Alcoran! Yes, true believers, you may believe that he is going to beget a race of misbelievers.

Must. That's fine in earnest. I cannot forbear hearkening to his enchanting tongue.

Ant. But yet remember——

Must. Ay, ay, the jewels! now again I hate him; but yet my conscience makes me listen to him.

Muf. Therefore, to conclude all, believers, pluck up your hearts, and pluck down the tyrant. Remember the courage of your ancestors; remember the majesty of the people; remember yourselves, your wives and children; and lastly, above all, remember your religion, and our holy Mahomet. All these require your timeous assistance; shall I say they beg it? No, they claim it of you, by all the nearest and dearest ties of these three P's—self-preservation, our property, and our prophet. Now answer me with a unanimous cheerful cry, and follow me, who am your leader, to a glorious deliverance.

[*All cry, " A Mufti, a Mufti !" and are following him off the stage.*

Ant. Now you see what comes of your foolish qualms of conscience. The jewels are lost, and they are all leaving you.

Must. What, am I forsaken of my subjects? Would the rogue purloin my liege people from me! I charge you in my own name, come back ye deserters, and hear me speak.

1 Rab. What, will he come with his balderdash, after the Mufti's eloquent oration?

2 Rab. He's our captain, lawfully picked up and elected upon a stall. We will hear him.

Omnes. Speak, captain, for we will hear you.

Must. Do you remember the glorious rapines and robberies you have committed? your breaking open and gutting of houses, your rummaging of cellars, your demolition of Christian temples, and bearing off in triumph the superstitious plate and pictures, the ornaments of their wicked altars, when all rich moveables were sentenced for idolatries, and all that was idolatrous was seized? Answer first for your remembrance of all these sweetnesses of mutiny; for upon those grounds I shall proceed.

Omnes. Yes, we do remember ; we do remember.

Must. Then make much of your retentive faculties. And who led you to those honeycombs? Your Mufti? No, believers, he only preached you up to it, but durst not lead you. He was but your counsellor, but I was your captain. He only loo'd you, but 'twas I that led you.

Omnes. That's true, that's true.

Ant. There you were with him for his figures.

Must. I think I was, slave Antonio. Alas! I was ignorant of my own talent. Say then, believers, will you have a captain for your Mufti, or a Mufti for your captain? And further to instruct you how to cry, Will you have a Mufti, or no Mufti?

Omnes. No Mufti, no Mufti.

Must. That I laid in for 'em, slave Antonio. Do I, then, spit upon your faces? Do I discourage rebellion, mutiny, rapine, and plundering? You may think I do, believers, but Heaven forbid! No, I encourage you to all these laudable undertakings. You shall plunder ; you shall pull down the Government ; but you shall do this upon my authority, and not by his wicked instigation.

3 Rab. Nay, when his turn is served he may preach up loyalty again and restitution that he might have another snack among us.

1 Rab. He may indeed ; for 'tis but his saying 'tis sin, and then we must restore ; and therefore I would have a new religion, where half the commandments should be taken away, the rest mollified, and there should be little or no sin remaining.

Omnes. Another religion—a new religion—another religion !

Must. And that may easily be done with the help of a little inspiration ; for I must tell you I have a pigeon at home of Mahomet's own breed ; and when I have learnt her to pick peas out of my ear rest satisfied till then, and you shall have another. But now I think on't, I am inspired already that 'tis no sin to depose the Mufti.

Ant. And good reason, for when kings and queens are to be discarded, what should knaves do any longer in the pack ?

Omnes. He is deposed—he is deposed—he is deposed !

Must. Nay, if he and his clergy will needs be preaching up rebellion, and giving us their blessing, 'tis but justice they should have the first fruits of it. Slave Antonio, take him into custody ; and dost thou hear boy, be sure to secure the little transitory box of jewels. If he be obstinate, put a civil question to him upon the rack, and he squeaks I warrant him.

Ant. [*Seizing the Mufti.*] Come, my quondam master, you and I must change qualities.

Muf. I hope you will not be so barbarous as to torture me. We may preach to others, but alas ! holy flesh is too well pampered to endure martyrdom.

Must. Now, late Mufti, not forgetting my first quarrel with you, we will enter ourselves to the plunder of your palace : 'tis good to sanctify a work, and begin in God's name.

1 Rab. Our prophet let the devil alone with the last mob.

Mob. But he takes care of this himself.

As they are going out, enter BENDUCAR *leading* AL- MEYDA : *he with a sword in one hand ;* BENDUCAR'S *slave follows, with* MULEY-MOLUCH'S *head upon a spear.*

Must. Not so much haste, masters ; come back again.

You are so bent upon mischief that you take a man upon
the first word of plunder. Here's a sight for you; the
Emperor is come upon his head to visit you. [*Bowing.*]
Most noble Emperor, now I hope you will not hit us in the
teeth that we have pulled you down, for we can tell you
to your face that we have exalted you. [*They all shout.*

    Bend. [*To* ALMEYDA, *apart.*] Think what I am, and
        what yourself may be,
In being mine: refuse not proffered love
That brings a crown.

    Alm. [*To him.*] I have resolved,
And these shall know my thoughts.

    Bend. [*To her.*] On that I build——
              [*He comes up to the rabble.*
Joy to the people for the tyrant's death!
Oppression, rapine, banishment, and blood
Are now no more, but speechless as that tongue
That lies for ever still.
How is my grief divided with my joy,
When I must own I killed him! Bid me speak,
For not to bid me is to disallow
What for your sakes is done.

    Must. In the name of the people we command you
speak; but that pretty lady shall speak first, for we have
taken somewhat of a liking to her person. Be not afraid,
lady, to speak to these rude ragganuffins. There's
nothing shall offend you, unless it be their stink, an't
please you.   [*Making a leg.*

    Alm. Why should I speak, who am your queen?
My peaceful father swayed the sceptre long;
And you enjoy'd the blessings of his reign,
While you deserved the name of Africans.
Then, not commanded, but commanding you,
Fearless I speak: know me for what I am.

    Bend. How she assumes! I like not this beginning.
                    [*Aside.*

    Alm. I was not born so base to flatter crowds,
And move your pity by a whining tale:
Your tyrant would have forced me to his bed;
But in the attempt of that foul brutal act
These loyal slaves secured me by his death.
                  [*Pointing to* BEND.

Bend. Makes she no more of me than of a slave! [*Aside.*
Madam, I thought I had instructed you   [*To* ALMEYDA.
To frame a speech more suiting to the times :
The circumstances of that dire design,
Your own despair, my unexpected aid,
My life endangered by his bold defence,
And after all, his death, and your deliverance,
Were themes that ought not to be slighted o'er.

Must. She might have passed over all your petty
businesses, and no great matter ; but the raising of my
rabble is an exploit of consequence, and not to be
mumbled up in silence, for all her pertness.

Alm. When force invades the gift of nature, life,
The eldest law of nature bids defend ;
And if in that defence a tyrant fall,
His death's his crime, not ours.
Suffice it that he's dead : all wrongs die with him :
When he can wrong no more, I pardon him :
Thus I absolve myself, and him excuse
Who saved my life and honour, but praise neither.

Bend. 'Tis cheap to pardon, whom you would not pay :
But what speak I of payment and reward !
Ungrateful woman, you are yet no Queen,
Nor more than a proud, haughty, Christian slave ;
As such I seize my right.
                              [*Going to lay hold of her.*

Alm. [*Drawing a dagger.*] Dare not to approach me ;
Now Africans,
He shows himself to you ; to me he stood
Confessed before, and owned his insolence
To espouse my person and assume the crown
Claimed in my right : for this he slew your tyrant ;
Oh, no, he only changed him for a worse ;
Embas'd your slavery by his own vileness,
And loaded you with more ignoble bonds.
Then think me not ungrateful, not to share
The imperial crown with a presuming traitor.
He says I am a Christian ; true, I am,
But yet no slave.   If Christians can be thought
Unfit to govern those of other faith,
'Tis left for you to judge.

Bend. I have not patience : she consumes the time

In idle talk, and owns her false belief;
Seize her by force, and bear her hence unheard.

Alm. [*To the people.*] No, rather let me die your sacri- [fice,
Than live his triumph.
I throw myself into my people's arms;
As you are men, compassionate my wrongs,
And as good men protect me.

Ant. Something must be done to save her. [*Aside to* Must.] This is all addressed to you, sir. She singled you out with her eye, as commander-in-chief of the mobility.

Must. Think'st thou so, slave Antonio?

Ant. Most certainly, sir, and you cannot in honour but protect her. Now, look to your hits, and make your fortune.

Must. Methought, indeed, she cast a kind leer towards me. Our prophet was but just such another scoundrel as I am, till he raised himself to power, and consequently to holiness, by marrying his master's widow. I am resolved I'll put forward for myself; for why should I be my Lord Benducar's fool and slave, when I may be my own fool and his master?

Bend. Take her into possession, Mustapha.

Must. That's better counsel than you meant it. Yes, I do take her into possession, and into protection, too. What say you, masters, will you stand by me?

Omnes. One and all; one and all.

Bend. Hast thou betrayed me, traitor? Mufti, speak, and mind them of religion! [MUFTI *shakes his head.*

Must. Alas, the poor gentleman has gotten a cold with a sermon of two hours long, and a prayer of four; and besides, if he durst speak, mankind is grown wiser at this time of day than to cut one another's throats about religion. Our Mufti's is a green coat, and the Christian's is a black coat; and we must go wisely together by the ears, whether green or black shall sweep our spoils.
[*Drums within and shouts.*

Bend. Now we shall see whose numbers will prevail;
The conquering troops of Muley-Zeydan come,
To crush rebellion, and espouse my cause.

Must. We will have a fair trial of skill for't, I can tell him that. When we have despatched with Muley-Zeydan, your lordship shall march in equal proportions of your body to the four gates of the city, and every tower shall have a quarter of you.

> [ANTONIO *draws them up, and takes* ALMEYDA *by the hand. Shouts again, and drums.*

Enter DORAX *and* SEBASTIAN *attended by African soldiers and Portuguese.* ALMEYDA *and* SEBASTIAN *run into each other's arms, and both speak together.*

Sebas. and Alm. My Sebastian! my Almeyda!

Alm. Do you then live?

Sebas. And live to love thee ever.

Bend. How! Dorax and Sebastian still alive!
The Moors and Christians joined! I thank thee, prophet.

Dor. The citadel is ours; and Muley-Zeydan
Safe under guard, but as becomes a prince.
Lay down your arms; such base plebeian blood
Would only stain the brightness of my sword,
And blunt it for some nobler work behind.

Must. I suppose you may put it up without offence to any man here present. For my own part, I have been loyal to my sovereign lady; though that villain, Bendu-car, and that hypocrite, the Mufti, would have corrupted me; but if those two escape public justice, then I and all my late honest subjects here deserve hanging.

Bend. [*To* DOR.] I'm sure I did my part to poison thee,
What saint soe'er has soldered thee again.
A dose less hot had burst through ribs of iron.

Muf. Not knowing that, I poisoned him once more,
And drenched him with a draught so deadly cold,
That, hadst not thou prevented, had congealed
The channel of his blood, and froze him dry.

Bend. Thou interposing fool, to mangle mischief,
And think to mend the perfect work of hell.

Dor. Thus, when Heaven pleases, double poisons cure.
I will not tax thee of ingratitude
To me thy friend, who hast betrayed thy prince.
Death he deserved, indeed, but not from thee.
But Fate, it seems, reserved the worst of men
To end the worst of tyrants.
Go bear him to his fate,
And send him to attend his master's ghost.

Let some secure my other poisoning friend,
Whose double diligence preserved my life.

Ant. You are fallen into good hands, father-in-law;
your sparkling jewels and Morayma's eyes may prove a
better bail than you deserve.

Muf. The best that can come of me, in this condition,
is to have my life begg'd first, and then to be begg'd for
a fool afterwards.

[*Exit* ANTONIO *with the* MUFTI, *and at the same time*
BENDUCAR *is carried off*.

Dor. [*To* MUST.] You and your hungry herd, depart un-
For justice cannot stoop so low, to reach   [touch'd;
The grovelling sin of crowds; but curs'd be they
Who trust revenge with such mad instruments,
Whose blindfold business is but to destroy;
And like the fire commissioned by the winds,
Begins on sheds, but rolling in a round,
On palaces return.   Away, ye scum,
That still rise upmost when the nation boils;
Ye mongrel work of Heaven with human shapes,
Not to be damned or saved, but breathe and perish,
That have but just enough of sense to know
The master's voice, when rated, to depart.

[*Exit* MUST. *and Rabble.*

Alm. With gratitude as low as knees can pay
[*Kneeling to him.*

To those blest holy fires, our guardian angels,
Receive these thanks, till altars can be raised.

Dor. Arise, fair excellence, and pay no thanks,
[*Raising her up.*

Till time discover what I have deserved.

Sebas. More than reward can answer.
If Portugal and Spain were joined to Africa,
And the main ocean crusted into land,
If universal monarchy were mine,
Here should the gift be placed.

Dor. And from some hands I should refuse that gift;
Be not too prodigal of promises;
But stint your bounty to one only grant,
Which I can ask with honour.

Sebas. What I am

M

Is but thy gift, make what thou canst of me,
Secure of no repulse.
    Dor. [*To* SEBAS.] Dismiss your train.
You, madam, please one moment to retire.   [*To* ALM.
        [SEBASTIAN *signs to the Portuguese to go off.* AL-
            MEYDA, *bowing to him, goes off also. The Africans
            follow her.*
    Dor. [*To. the Captain of the Guard.*] With you one
            word in private.   [*Goes out with the Captain.*
    Sebas. [*solus.*] Reserved behaviour, open nobleness,
A long mysterious track of stern bounty.
But now the hand of Fate is on the curtain,
And draws the scene to sight.

Re-enter DORAX, *having taken off his turban, and put on
            a peruke, hat, and cravat.*

    Dor. Now do you know me?
    Sebas. Thou shouldst be Alonzo.
    Dor. So you should be Sebastian ;
But when Sebastian ceased to be himself,
I ceased to be Alonzo.
    Sebas. As in a dream
I see thee here, and scarce believe mine eyes.
    Dor. Is it so strange to find me where my wrongs,
And your inhuman tyranny have sent me?
Think not you dream ; or, if you did, my injuries
Shall call so loud that lethargy should wake,
And death should give you back to answer me.
A thousand nights have brushed their balmy wings
Over these eyes, but ever when they closed
Your tyrant image forced them ope again,
And dried the dews they brought.
The long-expected hour is come at length,
By manly vengeance to redeem my fame ;
And that once cleared, eternal sleep is welcome.
    Sebas. I have not yet forgot I am a king,
Whose royal office is redress of wrongs ;
If I have wronged thee, charge me face to face;
I have not yet forgot I am a soldier.
    Dor. 'Tis the' first justice thou hast ever done me,
Then, though I loathe this woman's war of tongues,
Yet shall my cause of vengeance first be clear ;
And honour be thou judge.

Sebas. Honour befriend us both.
Beware, I warn thee yet, to tell thy griefs
In terms becoming majesty to hear.
I warn thee thus, because I know thy temper
Is insolent and haughty to superiors.
How often hast thou braved my peaceful Court,
Filled it with noisy brawls, and windy boasts;
And, with past service, nauseously repeated,
Reproached even me, thy prince?
Dor. And well I might, when you forgot reward,
The part of heaven in kings; for punishment
Is hangman's work, and drudgery for devils.
I must, and will reproach thee with my service,
Tyrant (it irks me so to call my prince),
But just resentment and hard usage coined
The unwilling word; and grating as it is,
Take it, for 'tis thy due.
Sebas. How, tyrant!
Dor. Tyrant.
Sebas. Traitor; that name thou canst not echo back.
That robe of infamy, that circumcision
Ill hid beneath that robe, proclaim the traitor;
And, if a name
More foul than traitor be, 'tis renegade.
Dor. If I'm a traitor, think, and blush thou tyrant,
Whose injustice betrayed me into treason,
Effaced my loyalty, unhinged my faith,
And hurried me from hopes of heaven to hell.
All these, and all my yet unfinished crimes,
When I shall rise to plead before the saints,
I charge on thee, to make thy damning sure.
Sebas. Thy old presumptuous arrogance again,
That bred my first dislike and then my loathing.
Once more be warned, and know me for thy King.
Dor. Too well I know thee, but for King no more;
This is not Lisbon, nor the circle this,
Where, like a statue, thou hast stood besieged
By sycophants and fools, the growth of Courts;
Where thy gulled eyes, in all the gaudy round,
Met nothing but a lie in every face;
And the gross flattery of a gaping crowd,
Envious who first should catch, and first applaud

The stuff or royal nonsense.　When I spoke,
My honest homely words were carped and censured,
For want of courtly style ; related actions,
Though modestly reported, passed for boasts ;
Secure of merit if I asked reward,
Thy hungry minions thought their rights invaded,
And the bread snatched from pimps and parasites.
Henriquez answered, with a ready lie,
To save his king's, the boon was begged before.

　　Sebas. What say'st thou of Henriquez ?　Now, by
Thou mov'st me more by barely naming him,　[heaven,
Than all thy foul, unmannered, scurril taunts.

　　Dor. And therefore 'twas to gall thee that I named him.
That thing, that nothing, but a cringe and smile,
That woman, but more daubed ; or if a man,
Corrupted to a woman : thy man mistress.

　　Sebas. All false as hell or thou.

　　Dor. Yes ; full as false
As that I served thee fifteen hard campaigns,
And pitched thy standard in these foreign fields ;
By me thy greatness grew, thy years grew with it,
But thy ingratitude outgrew them both.

　　Sebas. I see to what thou tendest, but tell me first,
If those great acts were done alone for me ;
If love produced not some, and pride the rest ?

　　Dor. Why, love does all that's noble here below ;
But all the advantage of that love was thine.
For, coming fraughted back, in either hand
With palm and olive, victory and peace,
I was indeed prepared to ask my own
(For Violante's vows were mine before).
Thy malice had prevention, ere I spoke ;
And asked me Violante for Henriquez.

　　Sebas. I meant thee a reward of greater worth.

　　Dor. Where justice wanted, could reward be hoped ?
Could the robbed passenger expect a bounty
From those rapacious hands who stripped him first ?

　　Sebas. He had my promise ere I knew thy love.

　　Dor. My services deserved thou shouldst revoke it.

　　Sebas. Thy insolence had cancelled all thy service ;
To violate my laws, even in my Court,
Sacred to peace, and safe from all affronts :

Even to my face, and done in my despite,
Under the wing of awful majesty
To strike the man I loved !

Dor. Even in the face of Heaven, a place more sacred,
Would I have struck the man who, prompt by power,
Would seize my right, and rob me of my love ;
But, for a blow provoked by thy injustice,
The hasty product of a just despair,
When he refused to meet me in the field,
That thou shouldst make a coward's cause thy own ?

Sebas. He durst ; nay, more, desired and begged with
To meet thy challenge fairly ; 'twas thy fault   [tears,
To make it public ; but my duty then
To interpose, on pain of my displeasure,
Betwixt your swords.

Dor. On pain of infamy
He should have disobeyed.

Sebas. The indignity thou didst was meant to me ;
Thy gloomy eyes were cast on me with scorn,
As who should say, the blow was there intended ;
But that thou didst not dare to lift thy hands
Against anointed power. So I was forced
To do a sovereign justice to myself,
And spurn thee from my presence.

Dor. Thou hast dared
To tell me what I durst not tell myself ;
I durst not think that I was spurned, and live ;
And live to hear it boasted to my face.
All my long avarice of honour lost,
Heaped up in youth, and hoarded up for age ;
Has honour's fountain then sucked back the stream ?
He has ; and hooting boys may dry-shod pass,
And gather pebbles from the naked ford.
Give me my love, my honour ; give them back.
Give me revenge, while I have breath to ask it.

Sebas. Now by this honoured Order which I wear,
More gladly would I give than thou dar'st ask it ;
Nor shall the sacred character of king
Be urged to shield me from thy bold appeal.
If I have injured thee, that makes us equal :
The wrong, if done, debased me down to thee.
But thou hast charged me with ingratitude ;
Hast thou not charged me ? speak.

Dor. Thou know'st I have;
If thou disown'st that imputation, draw,
And prove my charge a lie.
    Sebas. No; to disprove that lie I must not draw.
Be conscious of thy worth, and tell thy soul
What thou hast done this day in my defence;
To fight thee, after this, what were it else
Than owning that ingratitude thou urgest?
That isthmus stands between two rushing seas,
Which, mounting, view each other from afar,
And strive in vain to meet.
    Dor. I'll cut that isthmus.
Thou knowest I meant not to preserve thy life,
But to reprieve it, for my own revenge.
I saved thee out of honourable malice.
Now draw; I should be loath to think thou darest not.
Beware of such another vile excuse.
    Sebas. O, patience, Heaven!
    Dor. Beware of patience too;
That's a suspicious word.   It had been proper,
Before thy foot had spurned me; now 'tis base.
Yet, to disarm thee of thy last defence,
I have thy oath for my security.
The only boon I begged was this fair combat.
Fight or be perjured now; that's all thy choice.
    Sebas. Now can I thank thee as thou wouldst be thanked.
Never was vow of honour better paid,   [*Drawing.*
If my true sword but hold, than this shall be.
The sprightly bridegroom, on his wedding-night,
More gladly enters not the lists of love.
Why 'tis enjoyment to be summoned thus.
Go; bear my message to Henriquez' ghost,
And say his master and his friend revenged him.
    Dor. His ghost! then is my hated rival dead?
    Sebas. The question is beside our present purpose;
Thou seest me ready; we delay too long.
    Dor. A minute is not much in either's life,
When there's but one betwixt us; throw it in,
And give it him of us who is to fall.   [*o'ertake him.*
    Sebas. He's dead.   Make haste, and thou may'st yet
    Dor. When I was hasty, thou delayed'st me longer.
I prithee let me hedge one moment more

Into thy promise.   For thy life preserved,
Be kind; and tell me how that rival died,
Whose death next thine I wished.
    Sebas. If it would please thee, thou shouldst never know.
But thou, like jealousy, enquirest a truth,
Which found will torture thee.   He died in fight;
Fought next my person, as in consort fought.
Kept pace for pace, and blow for every blow,
Save when he heaved his shield in my defence,
And on his naked side received my wound.
Then when he could no more, he fell at once;
But rolled his falling body cross their way,
And made a bulwark of it for his Prince.
    Dor. I never can forgive him such a death!
    Sebas. I prophesied thy proud soul could not bear it.
Now judge thyself, who best deserved my love.
I knew you both; and (durst I say) as Heaven
Foreknew among the shining angel host
Who would stand firm, who fall.
    Dor. Had he been tempted so, so had he fallen;
And so, had I been favoured, had I stood.
    Sebas. What had been, is unknown; what is, appears;
Confess he justly was preferred to thee.
    Dor. Had I been born with his indulgent stars,
My fortune had been his, and his been mine.
O worse than hell! what glory have I lost,
And what has he acquired by such a death?
I should have fallen by Sebastian's side,
My corpse had been the bulwark of my King.
His glorious end was a patched work of fate,
Ill sorted with a soft effeminate life;
It suited better with my life than his
So to have died.   Mine had been of a piece,
Spent in your service, dying at your feet.
    Sebas. The more effeminate and soft his life,
The more his fame to struggle to the field,
And meet his glorious fate.   Confess, proud spirit
(For I will have it from thy very mouth),
That better he deserved my love than thou.
    Dor. O, whither would you drive me!   I must grant,
Yes I must grant, but with a swelling soul,
Henriquez had your love with more desert.

For you he fought, and died; I fought against you;
Through all the mazes of the bloody field,
Hunted your sacred life; which that I missed
Was the propitious error of my fate,
Not of my soul; my soul's a regicide.
    Sebas. Thou might'st have given it a more gentle name.
Thou mean'st to kill a tyrant, not a King. [*More calmly.*
Speak, did'st thou not, Alonzo?
    Dor. Can I speak!
Alas, I cannot answer to Alonzo.
No, Dorax cannot answer to Alonzo.
Alonzo was too kind a name for me.
Then, when I fought and conquered with your arms,
In that blest age I was the man you named;
Till rage and pride debased me into Dorax,
And lost, like Lucifer, my name above.
    Sebas. Yet twice this day I owed my life to Dorax.
    Dor. I saved you but to kill you; there's my grief.
    Sebas. Nay, if thou canst be grieved, thou canst repent.
Thou couldst not be a villain, though thou wouldst.
Thou own'st too much in owning thou hast erred,
And I too little, who provoked thy crime.
    Dor. O stop this headlong torrent of your goodness.
It comes too fast upon a feeble soul
Half drowned in tears before; spare my confusion;
For pity spare, and say not, first, you erred.
For yet I have not dared, through guilt and shame,
To throw myself beneath your royal feet.
                          [*Falls at his feet.*
Now spurn this rebel, this proud renegade;
'Tis just you should, nor will I more complain.
    Sebas. Indeed, thou shouldst not ask forgiveness first,
But thou prevent'st me still in all that's noble.
                          [*Taking him up.*
Yes, I will raise thee up with better news.
Thy Violante's heart was ever thine;
Compelled to wed, because she was my ward,
Her soul was absent when she gave her hand.
Nor could my threats, or his pursuing courtship,
Effect the consummation of his love.
So, still indulging tears, she pines for thee,
A widow and a maid.

Dor. Have I been cursing Heaven, while Heaven blest
I shall run mad with ecstasy of joy.   [me!
What, in one moment, to be reconciled
To Heaven, and to my King, and to my love!
But pity is my friend, and stops me short,
For my unhappy rival: poor Henriquez!
   Sebas. Art thou so generous, too, to pity him?
Nay, then I was unjust to love him better.
Here let me ever hold thee in my arms. [*Embracing him.*
And all our quarrels be but such as these,
Who shall love best and closest shall embrace.
Be what Henriquez was; be my Alonzo.
   Dor. What, my Alonzo, said you? my Alonzo!
Let my tears thank you, for I cannot speak;
And if I could,
Words were not made to vent such thoughts as mine.
   Sebas. Some strange reverse of fate must sure attend
This vast profusion, this extravagance
Of Heaven, to bless me thus.   'Tis gold so pure,
It cannot bear the stamp without alloy.
Be kind, ye powers, and take but half away;
    With ease the gifts of fortune I resign,
    But let my love and friend be ever mine.   [*Exeunt.*

ACT V. SCENE I.

The Scene is a Room of State.

Enter DORAX *and* ANTONIO.

   Dor. Joy is on every face, without a cloud,
As in the scene of opening Paradise;
The whole creation danced at their new being,
Pleased to be what they were, pleased with each other.
Such joy have I, both in myself and friends,
And double joy that I have made them happy.
   Ant. Pleasure has been the business of my life;
And every change of fortune easy to me,
Because I still was easy to myself.
The loss of her I loved would touch me nearest;
Yet, if I found her, I might love too much,
And that's uneasy pleasure.
   Dor. If she be fated

To be your wife, your fate will find her for you ;
Predestinated ills are never lost.
 Ant. I had forgot
To inquire before, but long to be informed,
How, poisoned and betrayed, and round beset,
You could unwind yourself from all these dangers,
And move so speedily to our relief?
 Dor. The double poisons, after a short combat,
Expelled each other in their civil war,
By Nature's benefit, and roused my thoughts
To guard that life which now I found attacked.
I summoned all my officers in haste,
On whose experienced faith I might rely ;
All came resolved to die in my defence,
Save that one villain who betrayed the gate.
Our diligence prevented the surprise
We justly feared ; so Muley-Zeydan found us
Drawn up in battle, to receive the charge.
 Ant. But how the Moors and Christian slaves were
You have not yet unfolded.   [joined,
 Dor. That remains.
We knew their interest was the same with ours ;
And though I hated more than death Sebastian,
I could not see him die by vulgar hands ;
But prompted by my angel, or by his,
Freed all the slaves, and placed him next myself.
Because I would not have his person known.
I need not tell the rest, the event declares it.
 Ant. Your conquests came, of course; their men were
And yours were disciplined. One doubt remains, [raw,
Why you industriously concealed the king,
Who, known, had added courage to his men?
 Dor. I would not hazard civil broils betwixt
His friends and mine, which might prevent our combat ;
Yet, had he fallen, I had dismissed his troops ;
Or if victorious, ordered his escape.
But I forgot a new increase of joy,
To feast him with surprise ; I must about it :
Expect my swift return.   [*Exit* DORAX.

Enter a Servant to ANTONIO.

 Serv. Here's a lady at the door, that bids me tell you

she is come to make an end of the game that was broken off betwixt you.

Ant. What manner of woman is she? Does she not want two of the four elements? Has she anything about her but air and fire?

Serv. Truly, she flies about the room as if she had wings instead of legs; I believe she's just turning into a bird; a house-bird, I warrant her. And so hasty to fly to you that rather than fail of entrance, she would come tumbling down the chimney like a swallow.

Enter MORAYMA.

Ant. [*Running to her and embracing her.*] Look, if she be not here already! Thou little dun, is thy debt so pressing?

Mor. Little devil, if you please. Your lease is out, good Mr. Conjurer; and I am come to fetch your soul and body.

Ant. Where the devil hast thou been? and how the devil did'st thou find me here?

Mor. I followed you into the castle-yard, but there was nothing but tumult and confusion; and I was bodily afraid of being picked up by some of the rabble, considering I had a charge about me—my jewels.

Ant. Intended for my worship's sole use and property.

Mor. And what was poor little I among them all?

Ant. Not a mouthful a-piece. 'Twas too much odds, in conscience.

Mor. So, seeking for shelter, I naturally ran to the old place of assignation, the garden-house; where for want of instinct, you did not follow me.

Ant. Well, for thy comfort, I have secured thy father; and I hope thou hast secured his effects for us.

Mor. Yes, truly, I had the prudent foresight to consider that when we grow old and weary of one another, we might have, at least, wherewithal to make merry with the world: and take up with a worse pleasure of eating and drinking.

Ant. Thy fortune will be e'en too good for thee; for thou art going into the country of serenades and gallantries; where thy street will be haunted every night with thy foolish lovers, and my rivals; who will be sighing and singing, under thy inexorable windows, lamentable ditties, and call thee cruel, and goddess, and moon, and stars, and all the poetical names of wicked rhyme, while thou and I are minding our business, and jogging on, and laughing at them.

Mor. I am afraid you are not very valiant, that you huff so much. But they say your churches are fine places for love-devotion. Many a she saint is there worshipped.

Ant. Temples are there as they are in all other countries, good conveniencies for dumb interviews. I hear the Protestants are not much reformed in that point, neither, for their sectaries call their churches by the natural name of meeting-houses. Therefore, I warn thee in good time, not more of devotion than needs must, good future spouse; and always in a veil, for those eyes of thine are enemies to mortification.

Mor. The best thing I have heard of Christendom is, that we women are allowed the privilege of having souls, and I assure you I shall make bold to bestow mine upon some lover whenever you begin to go astray.

Ant. When that day comes, I must take my revenge, and turn gardener again.

Mor. But take heed, in the meantime, that some young Antonio does not spring up in your own family, as false as his father.

Re-enter DORAX *with* SEBASTIAN *and* ALMEYDA. SEBASTIAN *enters speaking to* DORAX, *while in the meantime* ANTONIO *presents* MORAYMA *to* ALMEYDA.

Sebas. How fares our royal prisoner, Muley-Zeydan?

Dor. Disposed to grant whatever I desire,
To gain a crown and freedom. Well I know him,
Of easy temper, naturally good,
And faithful to his word.

Sebas. Yet one thing wants,
To fill the measure of my happiness;
I'm still in pain for poor Alvarez' life.

Dor. Release that fear, the good old man is safe;
I paid his ransom,
And have already ordered his attendance.

Sebas. O, bid him enter, for I long to see him.

Enter ALVAREZ *with a Servant, who departs when* ALVAREZ
is entered.

Alv. Now by my soul, and by these hoary hairs,

[*Falling down and embracing the King's knees.*

I'm so o'erwhelmed with pleasure, that I feel
A latter spring within my withering limbs,
That shoots me out again.

    Sebas. Thou good old man!   [*Raising him.*
Thou hast deceived me into more, more joys,
Who stood brim full before.

    Alv. O, my dear child!
I love thee so, I cannot call thee king,
Whom I so oft have dandled in these arms!
What, when I gave thee lost, to find thee living!
'Tis like a father who himself had 'scaped
A falling house, and after anxious search,
Hears from afar his only son within,
And digs through rubbish, till he drags him out
To see the friendly light.
Such is my haste, so trembling is my joy,
To draw thee forth from underneath thy fate.

    Sebas. The tempest is o'erblown, the skies are clear,
And the sea charmed into a calm so still,
That not a wrinkle ruffles her smooth face.

    Alv. Just such she shows before a rising storm;
And therefore am I come with timely speed,
To warn you into port.

    Alm. My soul forebodes   [*Aside.*
Some dire event involved in those dark words,
And just disclosing in a birth of fate.

    Alv. Is there not yet an heir of this vast empire,
Who still survives of Muley-Moluch's branch?

    Dor. Yes, such an one there is a captive here,
And brother to the dead.

    Alv. The powers above
Be praised for that: my prayers for my good master
I hope are heard.

    Sebas. Thou hast a right in Heaven;
But why these prayers for me?

    Alv. A door is open yet for your deliverance.
Now you, my countrymen, and you Almeyda,

Now all of us, and you (my all in one)
May yet be happy in that captive's life.
   Sebas. We have him here, an honourable hostage,
For terms of peace.   What more he can contribute
To make me blest, I know not.
   Alv. Vastly more.
Almeyda may be settled in the throne,
And you review your native clime with fame;
A firm alliance, and eternal peace
(The glorious crown of honourable war),
Are all included in that prince's life.
Let this fair queen be given to Muley-Zeydan,
And make her love the sanction of your league.
   Sebas. No more of that.   His life's in my dispose;
And prisoners are not to insist on terms,
Or if they were, yet he demands not these.
   Alv. You should exact them.
   Alm. Better may be made;
These cannot; I abhor the tyrant's race;
My parents' murderers, my throne's usurpers.
But, at one blow, to cut off all dispute,
Know this, thou busy, old, officious man,
I am a Christian; now be wise no more;
Or if thou wouldst be still thought wise, be silent.
   Alv. O, I perceive you think your interest touched;
'Tis what before the battle I observed;
But I must speak, and will.
   Sebas. I prithee peace;
Perhaps she thinks they are too near of blood.
   Alv. I wish she may not wed to blood more near.
   Sebas. What if I make her mine?
   Alv. Now, Heaven forbid!
   Sebas. Wish rather Heaven may grant,
For, if I could deserve, I have deserved her.
My toils, my hazards, and my subjects' lives
(Provided she consent), may claim her love;
And that, once granted, I appeal to these,
If better I could choose a beauteous bride.
   Ant. The fairest of her sex.
   Mor. The pride of nature.
   Dor. He only merits her; she only him.
So paired, so suited in their minds and persons,

That they were framed the tallies for each other.
If any alien love had interposed,
It must have been an eyesore to beholders,
And to themselves a curse.

Alv. And to themselves
The greatest curse that can be were to join.

Sebas. Did not I love thee, past a change to hate,
That word had been thy ruin; but no more,
I charge thee on thy life, perverse old man.

Alv. Know, sir, I would be silent if I durst.
But, if on shipboard, I should see my friend
Grown frantic in a raging calenture,
And he, imagining vain flowery fields,
Would headlong plunge himself into the deep;
Should I not hold him from that mad attempt,
Till his sick fancy were by reason cured?

Sebas. I pardon thee the effects of doting age,
Vain doubts, and idle cares, and over-caution;
The second nonage of a soul, more wise,
But now decayed, and sunk into the socket,
Peeping by fits, and giving feeble light.

Alv. Have you forgot?

Sebas. Thou mean'st my father's will,
In bar of marriage to Almeyda's bed.
Thou seest my faculties are still entire,
Though thine are much impaired. I weighed that will,
And found 'twas grounded on our different faiths;
But, had he lived to see her happy change,
He would have cancelled that harsh interdict,
And joined our hands himself.

Alv. Still had he lived and seen this change,
He still had been the same.

Sebas. I have a dark remembrance of my father;
His reasonings and his actions both were just;
And, granting that, he must have changed his measures.

Alv. Yes, he was just, and therefore could not change.

Sebas. 'Tis a base wrong thou offerest to the dead.

Alv. Now, Heaven forbid,
That I should blast his pious memory;
No, I am tender of his holy fame;
For, dying, he bequeathed it to my charge.
Believe, I am; and seek to know no more,

But pay a blind obedience to his will.
For to preserve his fame I would be silent.

Sebas. Crazed fool, who wouldst be thought an oracle,
Come down from off the tripos and speak plain.
My father shall be justified, he shall;
'Tis a son's part to rise in his defence,
And to confound thy malice, or thy dotage.

Alv. It does not grieve me that you hold me crazed;
But to be cleared at my dead master's cost,
O there's the wound! but let me first adjure you,
By all you owe that dear departed soul,
No more to think of marriage with Almeyda.

Sebas. Not Heaven and earth combined can hinder it.

Alv. Then witness Heaven and earth; how loath I am
To say, you must not, nay, you cannot wed.
And since not only a dead father's fame,
But more, a lady's honour, must be touched,
Which nice as ermines will not bear a soil,
Let all retire: that you alone may hear
What even in whispers I would tell your ear.

[*All are going out.*

Alm. Not one of you depart; I charge you stay.
And were my voice a trumpet loud as fame,
To reach the round of Heaven, and earth, and sea,
All nations should be summoned to this place.
So little do I fear that fellow's charge.
So should my honour, like a rising swan,
Brush with her wings the falling drops away,
And proudly plough the waves.

Sebas. This noble pride becomes thy innocence:
And I dare trust my father's memory
To stand the charge of that foul forging tongue.

Alv. It will be soon discovered if I forge.
Have you not heard your father in his youth,
When newly married, travelled into Spain,
And made a long abode in Philip's court?

Sebas. Why so remote a question? which thyself
Can answer to thyself, for thou wert with him,
His favourite, as I oft have heard thee boast,
And nearest to his soul.

Alv. Too near, indeed, forgive me, gracious Heaven,
That ever I should boast I was so near:

The confident of all his young amours.
And have not you, unhappy beauty, heard,   [*To* ALM.
Have you not often heard your exiled parents
Were refuged in that court, and at that time?

Alm. 'Tis true.   And often since, my mother owned
How kind that prince was to espouse her cause;
She counselled, nay, enjoined me on her blessing, ·
To seek the sanctuary of your court,
Which gave me first encouragement to come,
And, with my brother, beg Sebastian's aid.

Sebas. Thou help'st me well, to justify my war.
My dying father swore me, then a boy,   [*To* ALM.
And made me kiss the cross upon his sword,
Never to sheathe it, till that exiled queen
Were by my arms restored.

Alv. And can you find
No mystery couched in this excess of kindness?
Were kings e'er known, in this degenerate age,
So passionately fond of noble acts,
Where interest shared not more than half with honour?

Sebas. Base grovelling soul, who knowest not honour's
But weighest it out in mercenary scales;   [worth,
The secret pleasure of a generous act
Is the great mind's great bribe.

Alv. Show me that king, and I'll believe the phœnix;
But knock at your own breast, and ask your soul
If those fair fatal eyes edged not your sword
More than your father's charge, and all your vows?
If so, and so your silence grants it is,
Know, king, your father had, like you, a soul;
And love is your inheritance from him.
Almeyda's mother, too, had eyes like her,
And not less charming; and were charmed no less
Than yours are now with her, and hers with you.

Alm. Thou liest, impostor; perjured fiend, thou liest.

Sebas. Was't not enough to brand my father's fame,
But thou must load a lady's memory?
O infamous, O base, beyond repair!
And to what end this ill-concerted lie,
Which palpable and gross, yet granted true,
It bars not my inviolable vows?

Alv. Take heed, and double not your father's crimes,

N

To his adultery do not add your incest.
Know, she's the product of unlawful love,
And 'tis your carnal sister you would wed.

 Sebas. Thou shalt not say thou wert condemned unheard,
Else, by my soul, this moment were thy last.

 Alm. But think not oaths shall justify thy charge,
Nor imprecations on thy cursed head;
For who dares lie to Heaven, thinks Heaven a jest.
Thou hast confessed thyself the conscious pander
Of that pretended passion;
A single witness, infamously known,
Against two persons of unquestioned fame.

 Alv. What interest can I have, or what delight,
To blaze their shame, or to divulge my own?
If proved, you hate me; if unproved, condemn.
Not racks or tortures could have forced this secret,
But too much care to save you from a crime,
Which would have sunk you both. For let me say,
Almeyda's beauty well deserves your love.

 Alm. Out base impostor, I abhor thy praise.

 Dor. It looks not like imposture, but a truth,
On utmost need revealed.

 Sebas. Did I expect from Dorax this return?
Is this the love renewed?

 Dor. Sir, I am silent;
Pray, Heaven, my fears prove false.

 Sebas. Away; you all combine to make me wretched.

 Alv. But hear the story of that fatal love,
Where every circumstance shall prove another,
And truth so shine by her own native light,
That if a lie were mixed, it must be seen.

 Sebas. No; all may still be forged and of a piece.
No; I can credit nothing thou canst say.

 Alv. One proof remains, and that's your father's hand,
Firmed with his signet, both so fully known
That plainer evidence can hardly be,
Unless his soul would want her Heaven awhile,
And come on earth to swear.

 Sebas. Produce that writing.

 Alv. [*To* Dorax.] Alonzo has it in his custody.
The same, which when his nobleness redeemed me,
And in a friendly visit owned himself

For what he is, I then deposited,
And had his faith to give it to the King.
 Dor. Untouched, and sealed, as when intrusted with
   me,   [*Giving a sealed paper to the King.*
Such I restore it with a trembling hand,
Lest ought within disturb your peace of soul.
 Sebas. Draw near, Almeyda: thou art most concerned:
         [*Tearing open the seals.*
For I am most in thee.
Alonzo, mark the characters:
Thou know'st my father's hand, observe it well:
And if the impostor's pen has made one slip,
That shows it counterfeit, mark that and save me.
 Dor. It looks, indeed, too like my master's hand:
So does the signet: more I cannot say;
But wish 'twere not so like.
 Sebas. Methinks it owns
The black adultery, and Almeyda's birth;
But such a mist comes o'er my eyes,
I cannot, or I would not read it plain.
 Alm. Heaven cannot be more true than this is false.
 Sebas. O couldst thou prove it with the same assurance!
Speak, hast thou seen my father's hand?
 Alm. No; but my mother's honour has been read
By me, and by the world, in all her acts;
In characters more plain and legible
Than this dumb evidence, this blotted lie;
Oh that I were a man, as my soul's one,
To prove thee traitor and assassinate
Of her fame: thus moved I'd tear thee thus—
         [*Tearing the paper.*
And scatter o'er the field thy coward limbs,
Like this foul offspring of thy forging brain.
         [*Scattering the paper.*
 Alv. Just so shalt thou be torn from all thy hopes.
For know, proud woman, know in thy despite,
The most authentic proof is still behind.
Thou wear'st it on thy finger; 'tis that ring,
Which matched to that on his, shall clear the doubt.
'Tis no dumb forgery: for that shall speak;
And sound a rattling peal to either's conscience.
 Sebas. This ring indeed, my father, with a cold

And shaking hand, just in the pangs of death,
Put on my finger; with a parting sigh,
And would have spoke; but faltered in his speech
With undistinguished sound.

Alv. I know it well:
For I was present: now, Almeyda, speak,
And truly tell us how you came by yours.

Alm. My mother, when I parted from her sight
To go to Portugal, bequeathed it to me,
Presaging she should never see me more:
She pulled it from her finger, shed some tears,
Kissed it, and told me 'twas a pledge of love,
And hid a mystery of great importance
Relating to my fortunes.

Alv. Mark me now,
While I disclose that fatal mystery.
Those rings, when you were born and thought another's,
Your parents, glowing yet in sinful love,
Bid me bespeak: a curious artist wrought them,
With joints so close, as not to be perceived;
Yet are they both each other's counterpart,
Her part had *Juan* inscribed, and his had *Zayda*,
(You know these names are theirs:) and in the midst,
A heart divided in two halves was placed.
Now if the rivets of those rings enclosed,
Fit not each other, I have forged this lie:
But if they join, you must for ever part.

[Sebastian *pulling off his ring*, Almeyda *does the same, and gives it to* Alvarez *who unscrews both the rings, and fits one half to the other.*

Sebas. Now life or death.
Alm. And either thine or ours.
I'm lost for ever.——   [*Swoons.*

[*The women and* Morayma *take her up and carry her off.* Sebastian *here stands amazed, without motion, his eyes fixed upwards.*

Sebas. Look to the Queen, my wife; for I am past
All power of aid to her or to myself.

Alv. His wife, said he, his wife! O fatal sound!
For, had I known it, this unwelcome news
Had never reached their ears.

So they had still been blest in ignorance,
And I alone unhappy.
    Dor. I knew it, but too late, and durst not speak.
    Sebas. [*Starting out of his amazement.*] I will not live,
        no, not a moment more ;
I will not add one moment more to incest ;
I'll cut it off, and end a wretched being,
For, should I live, my soul's so little mine,
And so much hers, that i should still enjoy.
Ye cruel powers,
Take me as you have made me, miserable ;
You cannot make me guilty ; 'twas my fate,
And you made that, not I.   [*Draws his sword.*
    [ANTONIO *and* ALVAREZ *lay hold on him, and* DORAX
      wrests the sword out of his hands.
    Ant. For Heaven's sake hold, and recollect your mind.
    Alv. Consider whom you punish, and for what ;
Yourself unjustly. You have charged the fault
On Heaven, that best may bear it.
Though incest is indeed a deadly crime,
You are not guilty, since unknown 'twas done,
And known, had been abhorred.
    Sebas. By heaven, you're traitors all that hold my hands.
If death be but cessation of our thought,
Then let me die, for 1 would think no more.
I'll boast my innocence above,
And let them see a soul they could not sully.
I shall be there before my father's ghost ;
That yet must languish long in frosts and fires,
For making me unhappy by his crime. [*Struggling again.*
Stand off, and let me take my fill of death ;
For I can hold my breath in your despite,
And swell my heaving soul out, when I please.
    Alv. Heaven comfort you !
    Sebas. What, art thou giving comfort !
Would'st thou give comfort who hast given despair ?
Thou seest Alonzo silent ; he's a man.
He knows that men abandoned of their hopes
Should ask no leave, nor stay for suing out
A tedious writ of ease from lingering heaven,
But help themselves, as timely as they could,
And teach the fates their duty.

Dor. [*To* ALV. *and* ANT.] Let him go.
He is our King, and he shall be obeyed.

    Alv. What, to destroy himself? O parricide!

    Dor. Be not injurious in your foolish zeal,
But leave him free, or by my sword I swear
To hew that arm away that stops the passage
To his eternal rest.

    Ant. [*Letting go his hold.*] Let him be guilty of his
own death if he pleases: for I'll not be guilty of mine by
holding him.   [*The King shakes off* ALV.

    Alv. [*To* DORAX.] Infernal fiend,
Is this a subject's part?

    Dor. 'Tis a friend's office.
He has convinced me that he ought to die,
And rather than he should not, here's my sword
To help him on his journey.

    Sebas. My last, my only friend, how kind art thou,
And how inhuman these!

    Dor. To make the trifle death a thing of moment!

    Sebas. And not to weigh the important cause I had
To rid myself of life!

    Dor. True; for a crime
So horrid in the face of men and angels,
As wilful incest is!

    Sebas. Not wilful neither.

    Dor. Yes, if you lived, and with repeated acts
Refreshed your sin, and loaded crimes with crimes,
To swell your scores of guilt.

    Sebas. True; if I lived.

    Dor. I said so, if you lived.

    Sebas. For hitherto was fatal ignorance,
And no intended crime.

    Dor. That you best know:
But the malicious world will judge the worst.

    Alv. O what a sophister has hell procured,
To argue for damnation!

    Dor. Peace, old dotard.
Mankind that always judge of kings with malice,
Will think he knew this incest, and pursued it.
His only way to rectify mistakes,
And to redeem her honour, is to die.

    Sebas. Thou hast it right, my dear, my best Alonzo!

And that but petty reparation too;
But all I have to give.
   Dor. Your pardon, sir;
You may do more, and ought.
   Sebas. What! more than death?
   Dor. Death? why, that's children's sport; a stage-
       play, death.
We act it every night we go to bed.
Death to a man in misery is sleep.
Would you, who perpetrated such a crime
As frightened Nature, made the saints above
Shake Heaven's eternal pavement with their trembling
To view that act, would you but barely die?
But stretch your limbs, and turn on t'other side,
To lengthen out a black voluptuous slumber,
And dream you had your sister in your arms?
   Sebas. To expiate this, can I do more than die?
   Dor. O yes; you must do more; you must be damned;
You must be damned to all eternity;
And sure self-murder is the readiest way.
   Sebas. How, damned?
   Dor. Why, is that news?
   Alv. O, horror! horror!
   Dor. What, thou a statesman,
And make a business of damnation
In such a world as this! Why, 'tis a trade:
The scrivener, usurer, lawyer, shop-keeper,
And soldier, cannot live but by damnation.
The politician does it by advance,
And gives all gone beforehand.
   Sebas. O thou hast given me such a glimpse of hell,
So pushed me forward, even to the brink
Of that irremediable burning gulf,
That looking in the abyss, I dare not leap.
And now I see what good thou mean'st my soul,
And thank thy pious fraud: thou hast indeed
Appeared a devil, but didst an angel's work.
   Dor. 'Twas the last remedy to give you leisure;
For if you could but think, I knew you safe.
   Sebas. I thank thee, my Alonzo. I will live,
But never more to Portugal return;
For, to go back and reign, that were to show

Triumphant incest, and pollute the throne.

 Alv. Since ignorance——

 Sebas. O, palliate not my wound ;

When you have argued all you can, 'tis incest.

No, 'tis resolved, I charge you plead no more ;

I cannot live without Almeyda's sight,

Nor can I see Almeyda but I sin.

Heaven has inspired me with a sacred thought,

To live alone to Heaven, and die to her.

 Dor. Mean you to turn an anchorite ?

 Sebas. What else ?

The world was once too narrow for my mind,

But one poor little nook will serve me now,

To hide me from the rest of human kind.

Afric has deserts wide enough to hold

Millions of monsters, and I am, sure, the greatest.

 Alv. You may repent, and wish your crown too late.

 Sebas. O never, never ; I am past a boy.

A sceptre's but a plaything, and a globe

A bigger bounding stone.   He who can leave

Almeyda, may renounce the rest with ease.

 Dor. O truly great !

A soul fixed high, and capable of Heaven.

Old as he is, your uncle cardinal

Is not so far enamoured of a cloister

But he will thank you for the crown you leave him.

 Sebas. To please him more, let him believe me dead ;

That he may never dream I may return.

Alonzo, I am now no more thy king,

But still thy friend, and by that holy name

Adjure thee to perform my last request.

Make our conditions with yon captive king.

Secure me but my solitary cell ;

'Tis all I ask him for a crown restored.

 Dor. I will do more:

But fear not Muley-Zeydan; his soft metal

Melts down with easy warmth; runs in the mould,

And needs no further forge.   *Exit* DORAX.

  Re-enter ALMEYDA *led by* MORAYMA, *and followed*
    by her attendants.

 Sebas. See where she comes again.

By Heaven, when I behold those beauteous eyes,
'Repentance lags, and sin comes hurrying on.
    Alm. This is too cruel!
    Sebas. Speak'st thou of love, of fortune, or of death,
Or double death? for we must part, Almeyda.
    Alm. I speak of all ;
For all things that belong to us are cruel.
But what's most cruel, we must love no more.
O 'tis too much that I must never see you,
But not to love you is impossible:
No, I must love you: Heaven may hate me that,
And charge that sinful sympathy of souls
Upon our parents, when they loved too well.
    Sebas. Good Heaven, thou speakest my thoughts, and I
Nay, then there's incest in our very souls; [speak thine.
For we were formed too like.
    Alm. Too like indeed,
And yet not for each other.
Sure when we part (for I resolved it too,
Though you proposed it first), however distant,
We shall be ever thinking of each other;
And, the same moment, for each other pray.
    Sebas. But if a wish should come athwart our prayers.
    Alm. It would do well to curb it, if we could.
    Sebas. We cannot look upon each other's face,
But, when we read our love, we read our guilt:
And yet, methinks, I cannot choose but love.
    Alm. I would have asked you, if I durst for shame,
If still you loved? you gave it air before me.
Ah, why were we not born both of a sex?
For then we might have loved without a crime.
Why was not I your brother? though that wish
Involved our parents' guilt, we had not parted;
We had been friends, and friendship is no incest.
    Sebas. Alas, I know not by what name to call thee!
Sister and wife are the two dearest names;
And I would call thee both; and both are sin.
Unhappy we! that still we must confound
The dearest names into a common curse.
    Alm. To love, and be beloved, and yet be wretched!
    Sebas. To be together but so short a period;
So happy, that, forgive me, Heaven, I wish

With all its guilt, it were to come again.
Why did we know so soon, or why at all,
That sin could be concealed in such a bliss?
Alm. Men have a larger privilege of words,
Else I should speak: but we must part, Sebastian,
That's all the name that I have left to call thee.
I must not call thee by the name I would;
But when I say Sebastian, dear Sebastian,
I kiss the name I speak.
Sebas. We must make haste, or we shall never part.
I would say something that's as dear as this;
Nay, would do more than say: one moment longer,
And I should break through laws divine and human;
And think them cobwebs, spread for little man,
Which all the bulky herd of nature breaks.
The vigorous young world was ignorant
Of these restrictions, 'tis decrepit now;
Not more devout, but more decayed, and cold.
All this is impious; therefore we must part:
For gazing thus, I kindle at thy sight,
And once burnt down to tinder, light again
Much sooner than before.

Re-enter DORAX.

Alm. Here comes the sad denouncer of my fate,
To toll the mournful knell of separation:
While I, as on my death-bed, hear the sound,
That warns me hence for ever.
Sebas. [*To* DORAX.] Now be brief,
And I will try to listen,
And share the minute that remains betwixt
The care I owe my subjects, and my love.
Dor. Your fate has gratified you all she can;
Gives easy misery, and makes exile pleasing.
I trusted Muley-Zeydan as a friend,
But swore him first to secrecy; he wept
Your fortune, and with tears, not squeezed by art,
But shed from nature, like a kindly shower;
In short, he proffered more than I demanded:
A safe retreat, a gentle solitude,
Unvexed with noise, and undisturbed with fears.
I chose you one——

Alm. O do not tell me where :
For if I knew the place of his abode
I should be tempted to pursue his steps,
And then we both were lost—
    Sebas. Even past redemption.
For, if I knew thou wert on that design
(As I must know, because our souls are one),
I should not wander, but by sure instinct,
Should meet thee just half-way in pilgrimage,
And close for ever ; for I know my love
More strong than thine, and I more frail than thou.
    Alm. Tell me not that, for I must boast my crime,
And cannot bear that thou should'st better love.
    Dor. I may inform you both ; for you must go
Where seas, and winds, and deserts will divide you.
Under the ledge of Atlas lies a cave,
Cut in the living rock by Nature's hands—
The venerable seat of holy hermits,
Who there, secure in separated cells,
Sacred e'en to the Moors, enjoy devotion ;
And from the purling streams, and savage fruits,
Have wholesome beverage, and unbloody feasts.
    Sebas. 'Tis penance too voluptuous for my crime.
    Dor. Your subjects, conscious of your life, are few ;
But all desirous to partake your exile,
And to do office to your sacred person.
The rest, who think you dead, shall be dismissed
Under safe convoy, till they reach your fleet.
    Alm. But how am wretched I to be disposed ?
A vain enquiry, since I leave my lord ;
For all the world beside is banishment !
    Dor. I have a sister, abbess in Terceras,
Who lost her lover on her bridal day.
    Alm. There fate provided me a fellow-turtle,
To mingle sighs with sighs, and tears with tears.
    Dor. Last, for myself, if I have well fulfilled
My sad commission, let me beg the boon,
To share the sorrows of your last recess,
And mourn the common losses of our loves.
    Alv. And what becomes of me ? must I be left,
As age and time had worn me out of use ?
These sinews are not yet so much unstrung,

To fail me when my master should be served;
And when they are, then will I steal to death
Silent and unobserved, to save his tears.

Sebas. I've heard you both; Alvarez have thy wish.
But thine, Alonzo, thine is too unjust.
I charge thee with my last commands return,
And bless thy Violante with thy vows.
Antonio, be thou happy too in thine.
Last, let me swear you all to secrecy;
And to conceal my shame conceal my life.

Dor. Ant. Mor. We swear to keep it secret.

Alm. Now I would speak the last farewell, I cannot.
It would be still farewell a thousand times,
And multiplied in echoes, still farewell.
I will not speak, but think a thousand, thousand;
And be thou silent too, my last Sebastian:
So let us part in the dumb pomp of grief.
My heart's too great, or I would die this moment;
But Death, I thank him, in an hour has made
A mighty journey, and I haste to meet him.

　　　　　　[*She staggers, and her women hold her up.*

Sebas. Help to support this feeble drooping flower,
This tender sweet, so shaken by the storm.
For these fond arms must thus be stretched in vain,
And never, never must embrace her more.
'Tis past—my soul goes in that word—farewell.

　　[ALVAREZ *goes with* SEBASTIAN *to one end of the
　　　　stage; women with* ALMEYDA *to the other.*

Dor. [*Coming up to* ANTONIO *and* MORAYMA, *who stand
　　　　on the middle of the stage.*

Haste to attend Almeyda; for your sake
Your father is forgiven; but to Antonio
He forfeits half his wealth; be happy both.
　And let Sebastian and Almeyda's fate
This dreadful sentence to the world relate:
That unrepented crimes of parents dead,
Are justly punished on their children's head.

Just Published, Octavo, 12s. 6d.,

THE WHOLE
FAMILIAR COLLOQUIES

OF

DESIDERIUS ERASMUS.

TRANSLATED BY N. BAILEY.

CONTENTS.

Octavo, Price 21s.

THE
SCOTTISH GALLOVIDIAN ENCYCLOPÆDIA;

OR,

THE ORIGINAL, ANTIQUATED, AND NATURAL CURIOSITIES OF THE SOUTH OF SCOTLAND.

BY

JOHN MACTAGGART.